RICH *Losers*

RICH Losers

GURSIMRAN BINDRA

PARTRIDGE

A Penguin Random House Company

To order additional copies of this book, contact
Partridge India
000 800 10062 62
orders.india@partridgepublishing.com

www.partridgepublishing.com/india

CONTENTS

LIVE LONG LIFE

DEDICATION

To the immovable yet a very special part of my life that wouldn't leave me, and I appreciate its loyalty towards me—the unshared, unspoken yet understood and heard. It's the seedbed of love and need.

I carry you inside me with surprise and embrace the chilly wind, with open arms, which throws my hair backwards as if you have touched them.

You set me free, and I fly high, leaving the unwanted behind as it produces joy. It feels as if I am wearing you, and something inside me is appreciating and saying, 'Go places!'

With you now and always, Laughter, Sunshine, and Cheer.

NOTES AND ACKNOWLEDGEMENTS

I am a dreamer by nature. During my childhood, when I felt a touch of emptiness, I used to imagine various things, observing the sky for God knows how long. This brought me joy and fulfilment. The wind that blew through my hair, leaving my cheeks pink, made me feel loved and needed, bringing me laughter and cheer.

I used to write in a diary daily before sleeping during those days of innocence, mentioning the bits of life lived with my cousins and buddies, laughing, arguing, and cheating while playing games. It also included a square box, in which I mentioned my opponents who dumped me. Later when I grew older, I enjoyed reading my diary and started writing more. This is the first work that I will be sharing with you all, and I am sure you will like it.

I would like to thank my family for tolerating me each time when I tried to change my world by doing things my way. I know sometimes they find it hard to understand, but they are still there to show their support, love and patience. I would like to speak the truth, which is that I took a bite of this because it tasted nice. Thank you for bearing an eccentric person like me. I love you people.

To my father: The truth I know! You have always accepted my behaviour, no matter what. Even if I asked you to stay away when I got irritated by your pampering of me all the time, you still managed to kiss me cheer. And did I tell you that you looked great, wearing your sports dress when you played football in the stadium like a handsome young Daddy?

I am sorry I couldn't be a doctor. I don't know what my future will be like. All I know is that I am cultivating true seeds to live a happy, independent life. Eagerness and curiosity keep me alive. I'll love you till eternity, Dad, and more than every other living being. You are that part of my life which is very kind and humble, my kind heart. And please don't get emotional after reading this. I am laughing while writing this.

I must also thank my cousins as they have all loved me very much and brought me many things to eat and play with. I love all my *bindas* friends.

You all constitute sweet memories and my amazing life.

ONE

It's time to get up; the time is 6 a.m.
It's time to get up; the time is 6 a.m.
It's time to get up; the time is 6 a.m.

The maddening sound of my alarm clock in the shape of a skull interrupted my pleasurable sleep. Now for the fourth time as it began with 'It's time to . . .', I pressed the button hard and interrupted it. No revenge left—all settled! Given no other choice, I decided to get up from my bed and get ready for school.

Walking with my eyes half shut, I finally managed to find the way to the bathroom after bumping into walls and furniture. I brushed my teeth for five minutes, appreciating my eyes in the washbasin mirror. I didn't wash my face; people say, 'The king of the jungle never washes his face.' I was the female version, though.

I opened my cupboard to put on my school dress. I checked all the drawers of the cupboard but could find only my tie, not the rest of it.

After inspecting all the possible places in my room, I sat on my bed, thinking if I had ever bought one.

'Did I?' I questioned myself. I scanned my past days in school when I had worn it. 'Of course I did.'

'What the hell is wrong with me? Am I blind?' I went to wash my eyes, looked myself in the mirror, and saw that I was actually wearing my school dress. 'No way! No, I am not drunk.'

I went back to my room and saw that the time was 6.50 a.m. I quickly wore my shoes, did my hair, and rushed to the main road for an auto as I didn't go in my school bus. I had grown up, after all.

I waited for fifteen minutes and started walking towards my school in search of a vehicle. I found a woman riding her scooter, going in the same direction as I was going. 'Excuse me, madam,' I shouted. She stopped and looked behind. I went running to her and asked if she could drop me on the way. I sat behind her without permission. She didn't mind, and I asked, 'Where are you going?'

'I am going to get married,' she said.

What a weird answer! Anyways, 'Good luck,' I said. She was wearing a white gown and had covered her face with a scarf. She stopped outside my school entrance; before I could thank her, she went away. It was 7.15 a.m., but the sky was dark like night, and there came a heavy storm with dust and dry leaves.

I went inside through the school gate, smiling as if I was to be given an award. I couldn't wait to meet my classmates; therefore, I started walking fast with eagerness. As I kept walking, I could hear students shouting. This increased the excitement burning inside me, and I started walking quickly.

I then heard my classmates repeat, 'We don't want to die,' and another voice echoed, '*Ha! Ha! Ha*! I've come to take your soul.' This was the voice of the cruellest teacher in the school, who was, unfortunately, our science teacher. Her name was Shanta, and she didn't like the word *ma'am*. Therefore, we called her Madam Shanta.

I was scared of misfortune, and before she could catch hold of me, timidly I started walking faster towards the school gate. Regrettably, I have always been on top of the list of students whom she never liked, though the list included every student, for she didn't like anyone.

I heard her shout, 'Mahi Arora, where are you going?'

I looked behind, smiled, and said hesitatingly, 'Nowhere, madam. I was coming to you to apologise.'

'I am not here to take apologies,' she said in her heavy voice.

'Anyways, how have you been, madam?' I asked courteously. I couldn't dare to speak casually.

'Shut up and get inside the classroom, you dumb fellow,' she yelled.

'Yes, OK, sorry, madam,' I murmured and went towards the veranda that had the entry gate.

I could hear students screaming, crying, and seeking help. I looked everywhere and could sense that the situation was next to hell. While walking towards my classroom, I saw someone crying in the library. I went inside to see if it was who I thought it could be, and I was right.

It was none other than my best friend, Rasheen. She hugged me and said, 'She would kill each one of us who couldn't score in nineties.'

I was scared myself but consoled her, saying, 'She can't. It's not that easy to kill a rich brat. My father would drag the hell out of her in court. Come with me. Let's get out of here.'

We went behind the school building, where there was a graveyard. On the trees, we could see our classmates hanged with their ties. I was lucky enough to have forgotten my tie on the bed. 'Remove your tie,' I said to Rasheen. She removed it, and I threw it behind a tree.

We made our way towards the back gate. What we saw horrified us to the extent that our legs started trembling with fear, and we fell on the ground. Madam Shanta was kissing a student, biting his lips, and putting his blood on her own lips. Now we knew that what she put on her lips was not red lipgloss. I started crying and still kept on comforting my best friend by saying, 'Things will be fine.'

We went behind a tree to hide ourselves and saw Madam Shanta dragging another dead body. It was the dead body of our school principal, Father Edward. We couldn't bear the loss of someone so lovable, so we started crying loudly. We were caught, and she started coming towards us. I quickly broke a stick from the tree, which left me with cuts in my fingers, and shouted, fumbling, 'Don't you dare come to kill us.' As she came closer, I changed my tone to a polite one. 'Please don't, madam.' She laughed and walked faster.

'I will hit you with this in your eyes, and you will no longer be able to stare at us,' I shouted and ran away.

The area seemed a tangled web; we were stuck and couldn't manage to find a way to come out. We kept on running for our lives, and wherever we went, she came closer to kill us. I had lost my friend Rasheen somewhere in this jungle-like place. I shouted her name and could feel somebody hug me from behind.

I thanked God that Rasheen had come back, but as I looked behind, I was shocked to see Madam Shanta. I was scared to death because it wasn't my friend who was hugging me; it was Madam Shanta. She started pinching me hard on my waist and scratching my cheeks with her nails. I cried, 'You are a rich loser who kills innocent people.' She then started squeezing life out of me.

I was half dead with closed eyes but still kept on murmuring, 'Please don't kill me' and 'Don't kill me, please.'

'Who is killing you?' asked a known voice.

I replied, 'Please don't kill me.' I could feel soft hands caress my hair.

'What happened?' asked the same voice again, and I replied, 'Don't kill me, please.'

'You are my brave girl,' said she, and I replied, 'You are a rich loser.'

I felt a smack on my face. I slightly opened my eyes and saw my grandmother looking at me with a glint in her eyes. 'If you don't visit the temple, you will experience such bad dreams. Get up now,' she ordered.

I got off my bed, recalling the episode that almost ended my life. I was looking for my slippers under the bed when Granny brought them to me as neat as a new pin. I thanked her. She kept on smiling for the next five minutes. 'Get ready,' she said and started smiling again, looking at me in a motherly manner. I took a shower and saw Granny waiting in my room, smiling broadly this time.

There was a small temple in our house, which every member of the family had to visit after taking bath and before having breakfast. It was a strict rule set by my great-grandmother. I saw Granny waiting outside the temple with a mug of strawberry shake for me; the smile had widened.

My mom came from her room, asking if I was ready for school. I glanced at her like a confused newborn. 'It's report card day today,' she exclaimed. I wasn't drunk; I had just forgotten the day.

It was *30 March 2005!*

1. The big day of the year for teachers—the day they could explode their anger on students they never liked.
2. The worst day of the year for not-so-sharp bookworms like me. This was why I had experienced such a dream.
3. An outing day for my family because it was my grandmother's birthday.

That was when I realised the reason behind her smiles. I went to her with the mug of milkshake in my hand, kissed her and wished her happy birthday, and made her take a sip from the shake she always prepared for me.

Mom shouted again, asking me if I was ready. 'The meeting is till 11.30 a.m.' I replied.

'I have got to meet all your subject teachers. Be quick, we will leave within the next twenty minutes,' she said. I always hated Mom when she kept an eye on me to know if I studied or not. 'Why does she want to meet all my teachers? It's a waste of time as they would all say the same thing that I need to improve.' I gave her an irritated look.

I was ready and could hear my grandfather tease me by saying 'report card' again and again. 'It's not a card. It's an eight-page booklet with feedback by every teacher,' I replied irately.

'Grow up,' said my granny to him. She was my staunchest support, and so was I to her. Mom and I were about to leave the house when Granny's whistle broke my chain of steps.

According to my great-grandmother, it was considered inauspicious to call a person by his name when he was on his way to work, which was why she whistled. She came running to me, kissed my forehead, and said, 'God is with you.'

'The report card is made already. God can't do anything now,' I replied.

'You will have a good day,' she said patiently.

Mom had almost reached the main road. I ran after her. A vacant auto rickshaw stopped, and we got inside it. I sat on the outside and Mom in between me and a vacant seat. The auto had a music system, which was playing *Aashiq banaya aapne*, meaning 'you made me your lover' by an Indian singer Himesh Reshamiya. Each time the main stanza came, I could see the auto driver staring at my beautiful mother through the front mirror. 'Change the song,' I said abruptly. He knew that he was caught.

Without stopping for any other passenger and by taking a wrong turn, impressing Mom, as he thought so, he dropped us outside the big board that read 'Bartha Convent'. I pulled my mom behind, gave him the money, and asked him to get lost.

There were many cars parked outside the school. It was the best school in the city where mostly rich children studied. I admired the other mothers who drove cars, wearing sunglasses. My mother was very beautiful but would not learn to drive a car; she was not confident.

While walking towards the entry gate, I looked behind and saw him staring at Mom. I started walking towards him to confront him for his cheapness, but he disappeared. 'Irritating loser!'

I was very irritated at him and also at Mom for not learning to drive a car. Also, we didn't have drivers. She refused to have one for herself each time when Dad asked her. She said that she didn't like wasting money. Mom always taught me to forget and forgive as she never wanted me to fight with anyone, but I was no obedient daughter.

With an incensed look, I walked up to Mom and said, 'Can't you learn driving a car? I feel stupid coming to school in an auto with a hot rich mom. It hits my ego.'

'Who would take care of my kids if I am sent to jail after I kill someone while driving?' she said.

'Think positive, Mom! You might drive us safe to Delhi in just four hours,' I said.

'Get your daddy with you next time. He will drive you to school,' she added. I was all set mentally and, therefore, couldn't dare to get Dad to school.

While entering the gate, I saw my classmate exit from the right side. 'Hey, Amaar! How was the result, bro?' I asked.

'Not bad,' he said, showing his brown teeth, and added, 'Just three retests.'

'Three out of six subjects. That's an achievement,' I said, praising him. 'What subjects?' I asked.

'Maths, science, and English,' he replied.

'All the best!' I said.

'I'll make it,' he said boldly.

'I am sure you will,' I replied and continued walking towards my class.

'Nice circle of friends,' said Mom sarcastically.

'He is just a mate by chance,' I said, though we were mates of indiscipline.

'Hello, sweetheart, how was the result?' asked Mom to Rasheen.

'Good! 72 per cent,' she replied.

'You've done well too,' she said to me as she had peeped inside the register where our class teacher had mentioned marks. I felt easy, regaining confidence.

I said hurriedly, 'Let's go, Mom. We have got to leave for farmhouse.'

'Would you like to join us?' asked Mom to Rasheen.

'Of course,' she said. She lived in a hostel which was quite near to our school.

'Go tell your warden that you are coming with us,' I said, and she went running. Her hostel warden was a very kind lady, who would never refuse trustworthy students for such things, and she also knew me well.

We walked up the stairs and waited outside my classroom. There were two students sitting inside with their parents, viewing the result booklet. One of those was the topper of our class, and the other was a junior. There were two teachers sitting inside: our English teacher, Anusha Ma'am, who was luckily our class teacher, and our science teacher, Madam Shanta, the protagonist of the horrifying dream I had this morning.

I saw her looking at me, she stared at me with such hunger as if she was going to eat me alive. 'Mahi Arora,' she said, smiling scornfully, flaunting her red lipstick and scary teeth that could have led a fourteen-year-old die of a heart attack.

'Good morning, madam,' I said kindly.

'Please come in,' said the kind lady, my class teacher. My mom was asked to sit by that wicked creature with biggest eyes and smallest forehead, Madam Shanta.

I neglected her and started talking with my class teacher about a novel that I had lately bought her. Madam Shanta handed my report card to Mom and read the marks I had scored in her subjects.

'Seventy-one,' she said, and, later dividing into three sections, she started, 'Physics—20/35, chemistry—24/35, and biology—27/30.' I smiled when I heard her say seventy-one. 'Not so bad,' I said to myself.

'You seem to be happy with your performance,' she said rudely.

'No, ma'am,' I said with the most innocent face to agree with her.

I was happy with it, though, and murmured inside, 'I never asked to expect much from me.' I wasn't so brave to talk boldly with her and tell her that I was happy with it. She was the cruellest teacher, not my schoolmate.

She looked at me as if I had scored seventeen and asked, 'Why so less in physics?'

'I don't understand it too well,' I said and was interrupted by the topper of my class named Aaron Dsilva.

'It's the simplest of all subjects,' he laughed.

'See, that's how intelligent students are. Leave idiocy and start focussing on your studies,' said Madam Shanta. I couldn't give him a punch for his unwanted avowal in the presence of my mom and teachers and, therefore, I thought of simply ignoring him.

My class teacher's feedback for me was 'Increase you writing speed so that you complete your exam on time', 'Read the unseen passage properly', and 'You are going well'. I had scored eighty-nine in English, which wasn't bad at all. She then asked my mom to sign the register, opposite my name.

'What have you thought of physics?' asked Madam Shanta.

'I would probably take tuitions,' I said.

'You need to work hard this time,' said she.

'Of course,' said Mom.

'Certainly,' said I.

Admiring her own pout and her red lips, 'Thank you, Mrs Arora,' she said. I quite ignored her, bid goodbye to my class teacher, and went away.

Mom and I walked out of the class, and she said that I was not listening much to Madam Shanta.

'Of course I did,' I said.

'We are now to meet your maths teacher,' she said.

'Mom, it's 11 a.m. Let's go home,' I said.

And I heard somebody shout, 'Clever Arora, get inside.' I peeped inside the staffroom and saw a man with French beard sitting with a parent. I was amazed to have been caught by my maths teacher, Mr Rana.

'I was waiting for you. What did you think? You wouldn't let me discuss your performance with your parents?' he asked.

'No, I was looking for you,' I said, ashamed.

'And I caught you. What a coincidence!' he said mockingly. 'Please take a seat, Mrs Arora. 68/100,' he said without looking into the register.

'There are forty children in one section. Therefore, I remember every name with score. Even if there were 400, I would have remembered "the very famous". Every subject teacher would have. Some people are born with fame in their destinies,' he said, making fun of me.

Though he enjoyed making fun of students, he was a good man at heart—like a friend; therefore, we never hated him. 'Your performance is getting deteriorated day by day. No more a back-bencher. I'll make sure you sit in the front row and be friends with toppers Maria, Shyna, and Aaron,' he said. I was on good terms with Maria and also Shyna, but Aaron was an ass-wipe, so no way.

He looked at my mom and said, 'She enjoys the company of mutts like Amaar,—whose future lies in his dad's meat shop, Rishabh—who wants to be an engineer without studying, and Kokila—whose aim is to get married to her family friend after class XII. You aren't one of them, are you?' he asked.

'Of course not, Sir. My dad doesn't own a meat shop. He has an industry that manufactures auto parts. I don't like science so can't be an engineer, and I believe in open relationships more,' I said to myself. Mom looked at me as if she was irritated.

'You like the Indian cricketer Yuvraj Singh, right?' he asked.

'I love him, Sir,' I said.

'Go, study hard. Be an entrepreneur. Make him the brand ambassador,' he suggested laughingly. I gave a million-dollar smile and shook hands with him.

'Thank you, Sir,' I said, flaunting my right dimple. I looked at him to hear more of such stuff when he asked us to leave.

Rasheen was waiting for us at the exit with her bag. 'How was the feedback?' she asked.

'It was good,' I said.

'By Madam Shanta?' she questioned.

'Don't take her name so often. I see her in my dreams, making them horrendous.'

'She is really fond of us,' she said.

'Remember that some people don't need a reason to hate,' I replied and changed the topic.

We took an auto from the main road and continued discussing. 'Did you meet Mr Rana?' she asked.

'I wasn't in a mood, but he caught me, and I don't regret,' I said.

'Why?' she asked.

'He doesn't suggest bad,' I replied.

'He is one man who expects the most,' she said.

'Not more than my dad,' I replied.

We reached home and saw Granny waiting outside the house. The look on her face was like that of a soldier's mother, waiting to see him come home proudly.

'Granny, we made it to the next year,' shouted Rasheen. Granny smiled after hearing the positive news. The minute I entered the house, Dad came up to me, asking how much was my percentage.

'It's 77.6 per cent,' I said proudly.

'Seventy-seven per cent? That's it?' Dad confirmed.

'It's 77.6, which makes 78 per cent, not 77 per cent,' I said proudly.

'Compete with the toppers,' he said and went away. Like I just told you, he expects a lot. If he didn't, he wouldn't get disappointed.

My brother Arhaan, who was nine years younger to me, was Rasheen's lover and asked her to marry him each time she came to my place.

My grandfather was cheerful; ignoring his smile, I asked, 'Who was teasing me early morning that it is report card day?'

'I knew that you would make the family proud,' he replied.

'Lock your mouth,' said Granny to him and took me to her room. My grandfather stood rigidly, looking at her.

My grandfather had an extramarital affair, and, therefore, she never liked him much. Granny also told me that he had a son from that lady and he often visited them in Punjab. I've seen Granny cry after arguing on this topic with him; that was long time back. Now she stays away from him.

He was always rude to her, which I didn't like, and, therefore, I promised my granny that I would stand by her all my life. She was the one I loved the most and vice versa. His rough behaviour had made her this way. 'Otherwise, she was very soft-spoken,' said my great-grandmother, whose favourite she was. It was just me left with Granny after my great-grandmother's death.

We left at midday and reached the farmhouse, which was two hours' drive from our house. It was a beautiful place with a villa surrounded by greenery. The gardener lived there with his family, and the caretaker also lived there with our dog named Jwala and a bitch named Mukhi for security purposes. His wife took care of cleanliness and all. Granny had grown plants of tomatoes everywhere.

We went inside the villa to freshen up and settled at the dining table for lunch. Our family cook named Moti was best at cooking almost everything. The food was appetising. We sat there, discussing the party. Dad had invited five families for dinner. I was reading the menu for the evening, which Dad had scribbled on a piece of paper. My eyes widened when I saw that the menu also included drinks.

'We will drink tonight,' I murmured into Granny's ear. She nodded, and I smiled. Luckily, Granny's room was on the ground floor, and behind it, we had a swimming pool. Rasheen and I decided to drink that night with Granny. By that time, it was evening, and we had to get ready for dinner.

The guests had come; they were five couples with their children. I knew one of them, for they had visited us twice before that in my presence. We sat after greeting them. Dad introduced me to the ones I had never met before. They said that I looked like my father. Also, I shook hands with their kids, some of whom were of my age and some younger than me.

Mom confirmed from Rasheen what she would like to have for dinner. She read the entire menu, and I reminded her that we had to leave some space in stomach for drinks also, and she nodded. Rasheen ate the most amongst all my friends and still looked so thin.

The dinner was delicious, and I really wanted to empty all the bowls. I could see Arhaan play and hit other children, but because he was not getting beaten up, I didn't bother. After the cake was cut, we sat there, talking to the guests who had come.

What kind of conversations do teenagers have with their aunts and uncles? We answered questions like 'Which grade?' 'What subjects?' 'Future plans?' and so on. Before Dad could say that he wanted me to be a doctor, I interrupted and said that I wanted to be the biggest earner. 'Well, that's a smart, diplomatic answer,' I praised myself. I could see some kids of my age staring at me as if I looked like the topper of the school.

They seemed to me bookworms, and I never enjoyed their company so much. They were all very uninteresting, had weird attitudes, sat together in a group, and discussed things like their syllabus and their school rules. I was living life in the best way—school life at its best—and life outside was amazing too.

A girl seemed to be holding her mother's hand all the time. I had never been fond of my mother. Since childhood, I had thought my mother as someone who would always scold me for my negatives yet rarely appreciated my positives. Granny was my real mother, and I knew it too well. She was the only one who knew my ins and outs, no matter what.

At dinner, my mom introduced me to a girl who was the daughter of another family friend and said, 'She has been the topper of her school since the last five years. Be friends with people like her.' I could see that girl smile wickedly on hearing this.

'What am I supposed to do if she is a topper? I don't appreciate crap like this, praising others by saying they are school toppers, the richest, and the like. I am smart as I try many things without fearing.' I feared being the subject of comparison, though.

I showed no interest when Mom said to her, 'Teach her something good and make her like you.'

That girl half smiled at me, thinking that I was a loser. I got irritated and left the place. I was not emotional but just irritated. The girl looked extremely stupid. I didn't know what Mom liked in her. My happy life was shattered by comparing it with the dull life; my life had class.

Mom came after me and asked me to behave myself. I was proud of my misbehaviour because I didn't take nonsense like that. I was the best amongst those teenagers—smart and talented—as I didn't live a scripted life. I did what I liked to do—like I read books, had dreams, and liked doing creative things like writing and drawing. I was not a good painter, but something that I made really well was the logo of Real Madrid football club. My best friend Karan loved it. I had the courage to follow my talent.

Apart from this, I knew how to live life much better than them. I believed in celebrating every moment in my own way, unlike the four of them who looked foolish. My best family friend was Jay, who was much better than them but was absent as his schooling was in a different city. Jay and I went together for tours with our families. We were very good friends, though we were not in touch with each other on a regular basis.

We shared the same table with the fools of our age, but we weren't sad at all as we knew how to keep ourselves happy and involved in activities. I have always appreciated life without being dependent on someone for happiness. I was taught this by Granny—how to stay happy with myself. Sometimes I was confused with my life, but I knew I would overcome it by giving it a thought, though I rarely did. My mind always had something to do. I would read a topic on Internet to be aware of things and also out of curiosity.

Amongst the fools, there was a girl named Bhuvi, who was a fan of Mohammad Kaif, another Indian cricketer. She spoke negatively about Yuvraj Singh, who was my all-time favourite cricket player, and also about me when we were in class VIII. I had gone to her place with my parents. I remembered hitting her hard on her mouth with her own maths book; her lips started bleeding. I gave no fuck ever. She looked at me thrice today, but I didn't bother to look at her. Nobody has a right to talk against anybody or anyone's decision to choose whoever. For me, it was Yuvraj Singh, the only celebrity I loved very much.

Granny called me to a corner and asked me to get Rasheen to her room. I told her that the guests hadn't left, and she replied they wouldn't get out so early. We had our plan, so after thanking them all, Granny went to her room, accompanied by us. My mom called me and asked me not to drink as she didn't like it much. 'It's red wine, Mom, not drugs, please,' I said.

'You are not drinking, Mahi. It's not the right age,' she exclaimed.

'I know how to take care of myself, and you know that,' I said and left.

I have always lived with Granny; my mom was mostly with my dad. They had their own life. I did complain a lot many times but did not hate them much as they were my parents, but I knew that Granny was my real carer, and I loved her the most. I didn't give as much importance to my parents as I gave to Granny. A personal matter indeed! Otherwise, I would thrash anyone who tried to talk negative about them. Ours wasn't a stupid emotional family; we also had fun when we were together.

We sat in Granny's room, and she brought a bottle of red wine with chocolate cake she had made herself for us to celebrate our result. She poured wine in three glasses and put cake slices on our plates. Chocolate cake with red wine was the best combination, which I loved so much.

Later, she asked us if we had boyfriends. We refused to answer and told her about our friends, whom she already knew.

We were six friends in total; we had been batchmates of maths tuition for the last three years. Rasheen, Rishabh, and I were from one school, and Karan, Adhiraaj, and Nayan were from another. Rasheen had a crush on Adhiraaj; however, Adhiraaj had a girlfriend in a different school. Nayan and Rishabh were neighbours. Rishabh didn't know how to react to situations and, therefore, was always affronted by Nayan. Karan was a Casanova, who had a girlfriend in almost every school in the city.

Granny told me that she thought I was dating Karan, and I laughed, telling her it was nothing new as everybody thought the same. I confirmed that the world seemed the best when we were together, but we never thought of dating each other. She seemed to get confused and asked why we spent so much time together. I had nothing to explain.

She told us that it was the beginning of the new part of our life—the real teens. Before she could teach us what adolescence was all about as per her own experience, I refused to accept her views as I wanted life to surprise me with the unexpected because that was how I always understood situations well when I did things on my own, no matter what it led to. She was happy to see me get promoted to class X as she finally accepted that I had grown up.

She asked if we wanted to have boyfriends. Rasheen refused to have a boyfriend as she loved Adhiraaj and went to bed, but I gave the nod to Granny.

'After all, who doesn't need romance? I do. I have imagined what it would feel like if a boy kisses me.'

Before going to sleep, Granny murmured in my ears, teasing me that she knew I already had a boyfriend, though I was single.

It was time to do something I wanted to do for a long time. Impatiently, I took the laptop to another room and started reading about sex. I desperately wanted to know about it. My friends knew it well and I was the only stupid creature who didn't. So I thought it's about time I should learn about it. But I did not learn much though, besides, I also had to sleep.

The next morning, I was sitting with my family and thinking about the previous night—the topic I had read on the Internet. Before this, I wasn't much aware about it but now I was. I had always thought that when a boy and a girl kiss each other, some hormones are secreted which make a girl pregnant. How could I believe this? I laughed at myself. I never showed interest in this, though I loved the kissing part very much and wanted to experience it in my life.

After some time, Rasheen's phone rang, and who were the callers? Our dearest buddies!

When it comes to conversations, Adhiraaj and I was a match. We got along so well and we always had interesting conversations together. I discussed such topics with Adhiraaj as Karan said he liked to talk about such things to girls who were of different type. Which type, I didn't know. Nayan and Rasheen shared immature-cum-funny behaviour. Karan had an intimate relationship with his shoes that Rishabh admired the most. Otherwise, Karan and I were so close that everybody thought that we were dating. We neither accepted it nor denied it. Rasheen had only two things to do when she was with Adhiraaj: hate his girlfriend, Pearl, and smile at him unnecessarily. Rishabh was born to get beaten up by Nayan, no matter what reason.

'It's him. Hello, Karan,' said Rasheen in a cheerful tenor.
'Where is Mahi?' he asked.

'I said hello to you, mate. At least reply.'

'Oh, yeah! Adhiraaj said hi.'

'What do you get by ignoring me?'

'Mahi,' he said nonchalantly.

'You have dialled a wrong number,' said Rasheen and hung up on him.

Karan always loved getting the hell out of Rasheen, who was bad-tempered; otherwise, there were no issues really. He dialled again.

'Hello, Rasheen, how are you?' he said.

'I am good. Who are you?'

'Excuse me?'

'What do you need?'

'Not you. Dumbo, we all are planning to meet this evening. Are you in?' he asked and continued, 'Adhiraaj is also coming along.'

This brought a smile on Rasheen's face. 'We are at the farmhouse and shall leave within the next thirty minutes,' she said.

'Sorted! See you at 6 p.m.,' he said and disconnected the call. Everyone knew that it was Granny's birthday as that was the only day the entire family visited the farmhouse together.

We were both very excited to go for a ride.

6 p.m.

We heard the honk of scooters and rushed towards the main door. It was Rishabh and Nayan on their respective scooters. Rasheen sat behind Rishabh, and I behind Nayan. Nayan interrupted Rishabh's way, and we reached before them to the main road where Karan was waiting with Adhiraaj on his bike, which was my favourite. Rasheen yelled, 'Red is my favourite colour! Adhiraaj, you look so handsome today.'

'Thanks,' he said, smiling. Whatever colour Adhiraaj wore became Rasheen's favourite; we all knew that too well. Karan was waiting for me, so I hugged him hello and got back on to the scooter.

We decided to ride till the railway station taking a longer road, enjoying the ride. We chatted on the way, and suddenly Rishabh asked, 'When are we joining tuitions?'

'Why are you so fond of studying?' asked Nayan.

'He isn't fond of studies. He is fond of tuitions,' said Karan.

'Oh, I see, in search of a girlfriend,' I enquired.

'Nayan is the best option. You are neighbours and can romance on the terrace of your house,' said Adhiraaj.

'I wish my girlfriend was my neighbour,' said Karan.

'Girlfriends!' I corrected him.

'My editor,' said Karan.

The chilly breeze was throwing our hair backwards. We loved all that we came across while riding on a smooth road. 'Wow!' said Adhiraaj, pulling my cheeks that had turned pink and icy, and continued, 'I don't want to go home.'

'Where do you want to go?' asked Rasheen, who I called a 'tube light'. She rarely understood anything.

'The weather is lovely, he meant,' I explained to her.

'Would you like to meet Pearl?' said Karan to Adhiraaj, teasing Rasheen.

'Shut up, OK?' she replied to Karan. It was her favourite line.

We stopped at a restaurant named Harry's Kitchen. It was the best Chinese restaurant in the city. We got in and gave our order. I sat with Adhiraaj on one side and Karan on the other. Adhiraaj and I loved the surrounding. The restaurant was half on the road and half above the river that carried water from the mountains. There was a garden opposite to it. I was to pay the bill because it was Granny's birthday the day before. They kept on ordering and eating and overshot the budget. Adhiraaj paid the balance.

'Shall we leave?' asked Karan.

'Go take a couple of rounds in the garden. It helps in digesting food,' announced Adhiraaj as he wanted to sit and talk with me.

Nayan and Rasheen rushed outside while suddenly Karan shouted at Adhiraaj, 'Don't flirt with her, you dog,' and reluctantly left, followed by Rishabh, discussing his shoe collection, which was indeed amazing. Karan gave more time to his shoes than to his girlfriends, which was why he wasn't much appreciated by them.

Adhiraaj and I were discussing our lives. 'What's with Pearl?' I asked.

'I don't know what it is. She rarely talks and is confused with the relationship,' he replied.

'You are still young. There is nothing to worry,' I said and asked, 'Do you love her?'

He didn't reply for thirty seconds; then he smiled, and said, 'She is a good kisser.'

'Ho!' I laughed. 'And that's it?' I enquired.

'Don't make fun of my virginity,' he said.

'Do you love him?' he asked.

'Yes,' I said.

'Who?' he asked.

'Who?' I asked. 'Yes, I love Yuvraj Singh,' I said.

'Karan?' he enquired, and we both started laughing. Everybody thought the same. Therefore, he cracked this joke.

'You stupid girl! How dare you pluck flowers?' We heard somebody shout in the garden.

Another voice argued, 'I didn't pluck. It fell off.'

'Rasheen?' I confirmed.

Karan yelled, mockingly copying the lady, 'How dare you, Rasheen?'

Rasheen came back to us and said, 'I wanted to put the flower in my hair when this gigantic lady came yelling.'

'The fragrance in the garden was yummy,' added Nayan.

'Nothing in this world smells better than Mahi's perfume,' said Adhiraaj, ignoring the rest.

On our way back home, Rishabh saw a leaflet on the wall of a hostel that read, 'Highway King Organising a Fashion Show'.

'Wow!' shouted Rasheen. 'Let's go, Adhiraaj.'

'Do I know you?' he said.

'Karan should go,' I said, and others nodded.

'Are you mad or something?' Karan said.

'You will win! I know, Karan,' I exclaimed.

'Me?' he quizzed again.

Rishabh flashed his yellow teeth as if he was the one we had asked to go. 'You are going, Karan,' I announced. He smiled and I yelled, 'Karaaan, I love you for this. You are the best!'

'I hope Mahima doesn't hear you say this,' said Adhiraaj. Mahima was Karan's girlfriend and never appreciated his company with me.

'I am not scared of Mahima,' I replied.

'Nor am I,' added Karan.

There was another banner we read outside our own school. We stopped and read the matter that said 'Highway King Organising a Fashion Show for Boys Aged Fourteen to Seventeen.' Rasheen was hurt as she wanted to go herself. The rest of it read, 'For more details, login to our website www.eventshwaykings.com.' With the Bollywood actor John Abraham's photo, it read, 'Come win the title The Handsomest.'

I noted all the details on Karan's phone, saved it in drafts, and also sent a message with these details to Granny's phone since I didn't have one. Much later, they dropped me home after dropping Rasheen to her hostel. The day was lovely. I had always loved laughter, treats, funny fights, arguments, and discussions with Adhiraaj on topics like flirting, dating, and romancing.

TWO

A day before new session at school!

I came home at midday with Dad, carrying a bundle of school books with two bundles of notebooks and stationery as I was promoted to class X. My dad was never bothered about things like these, yet he was always after me, telling me 'to make my career'. Each time we came across each other, the only thing he had to say was 'Please study hard and make your career'. I knew I had to, but this just irritated me and forced me to avoid him. Not even once, when we spoke, he acknowledged what I liked doing.

Apart from all these serious topics with Dad, I had an interesting life to live; it was fun to be with Arhaan and observe how he did things. Life was not boring. My brother, Arhaan, came running to explore the packets and ended up swallowing the ink from the refill of the pen for which Dad called him 'an irritating element born by the way'.

I was in my room, ready to put covers on my books and notebooks. Arhaan ran here and there in search for a pair of scissors and a stapler. A helper indeed! What he loved to do was putting name chits on books. Dad bought me chits with sportsmen's photos on them. I also had a few with Yuvraj Singh's picture. He was like a family member who lived on my cupboard in the form of a poster, and on my desktop and Granny's mobile phone as wallpaper. Marrying him was my only thought.

Arhaan was born on Valentine's Day and loved watching only romantic movies, hence he knew well what kissing was and how it was done. Each time a romantic scene played on TV, he became a dead duck with wide eyes. While putting name chits, he came across Yuvraj ones and said, 'Mahi, your man', and continued putting the chit on my lips and then on my cheek. 'Kiss, Mahi, kiss.' I laughed.

By that time, it was evening, and our landline phone rang. Arhaan ran to answer it.

'Hello!' a girl said.
'Love you, babe,' replied Arhaan.

'Who was it?' I knew too well and snatched the phone from him.

'Hey,' I said.
'Are you excited for tomorrow?'
'Of course!'
'I will meet you outside the main gate. We will go together.'
'OK,' said I and disconnected the phone.

It was Rasheen. She was like a family member who often visited us once in every fifteen days, and sometimes we also had a few combined study sessions, which were more of chit-chat sessions. She was from the north-east part of the country. She visited her family just twice a year, or her family visited her at the hostel. She liked living with my family, and we all loved her too.

Beginning of class X!

Either the alarm didn't ring, or I shut the button in my sleep, I didn't know. All I knew was that I was late for school. I reached after the prayer was completed and looked here and there so as to find a way to get in since the gates were closed. I walked slowly on the service lane towards the student entry gate, anticipating Rasheen's reaction for I was late on the first day of the new session. I was excited for the new beginning and also unhappy because it was high school, and I expected that those lectures I had had from teachers and my parents related to studies would be doubled.

Suddenly a voice broke my chain of thoughts. 'Mahi,' it said. I turned back and saw Rasheen coming towards me from the main road. I laughed to myself on seeing her come after me.

'I am sorry I couldn't get up early,' she said, and, instead of telling her what the truth was, I stated, 'It's really irritating to wait for someone who lives near the destination and still is not on time.'

'So sorry,' she said.

'You wasted twenty minutes almost. Now let's get in,' I said nonchalantly, praising my confidence.

'Good morning, Gulab,' we said to the gatekeeper, who was very kind to students, at least to us if not to everyone.

'Congratulations, seniors,' he said as we were in our high school, which was our last year at this school. Strict teachers like Madam Shanta never appreciated him much because 'an enemy's friend is an enemy' as the saying goes. He let us get in quietly, going against the school rules, as it was the first day. We thanked him and quickly rushed upstairs to find our class. We searched the entire upstairs but couldn't find our class.

We went downstairs, and as I opened the gate to the ground floor of the building, we saw that the computer room was newly painted and well organised with new computers and a new carpet. 'This year, we don't have this subject. No use to us,' I said.

'Wow,' said Rasheen, eyes wide open, and got inside.

'It's not the right time to admire it. Come out, you moron,' I yelled at her. I pulled her with her bag and walked further. We selected the right turn and landed outside a big room that read 'Laboratory'.

We stood still outside that room when the sound of a chair being dragged interrupted us. When we looked behind us we saw our classmate Amaar sitting and laughing at us, covering his mouth with his hand. 'This is our class,' said Rasheen.

'It is supposed to be class IX. Amaar had to give three retests, and I am sure he didn't make it to the next session.' I said confidently.

I looked inside and saw our other classmates sitting in the same room, and three of the class toppers were sitting exactly opposite the teacher's table, which assured us that this was supposed to be it. We both looked at each other in excitement, thinking who our new class teacher was, hoping it wasn't Madam Shanta. On deciding who would enter first, I was pushed through the door.

There was a new male teacher sitting on the chair, working on the attendance register. I murmured, 'May we come in?' He was so busy that he didn't hear us seek permission.

'May we come in?' said Rasheen, and he still didn't hear. 'May we please come in?' I said loudly. He heard it finally and looked at us for five seconds from above his specs that were on his nose and ignored us.

'Sir, somebody is at the door,' said Amaar. 'Shut up,' he replied; he looked at me again in the same way and roared, 'What do you want?'

'It's our class,' said Rasheen courageously.

'Yes, sir,' I added.

He looked at us for ten seconds; then, breaking the silence, I wished him, 'A very good morning to you, sir,' and the entire the class started laughing for some reason.

'What is so funny?' he yelled at the class, and they were all quiet. He stood up, looked at us now through his specs, and said, 'First day at school, and you morons are late. Don't you know that first impression is the last impression?'

'I think we have met before,' said I, replying to his statement. When he didn't acknowledge the joke, I apologised.

'Shut up,' he shouted and ordered us to go and get ourselves a chair and a table from the next room. We kept our bags on the floor and went towards the next room.

There were a few chairs and tables kept in that room near the exit door, which was the second door of every class. We took the best furniture and dragged it to our own class through the exit door. 'Back-benchers, get it from the entry door, you fools,' he yelled, pointing at us with his pen. The entire class started laughing at us; we, being the butt of jokes, could only ignore them.

We brought in the tables and chairs from the entry door, and I asked politely, 'Where to place them?'

'Right here in front of me,' he shouted and made us sit in the front row. We didn't mind because we liked to peep outside the classroom, diverting our minds away from boring lectures.

'Thank you, sir,' I said, and we both sat down.

'I didn't ask you to sit,' he yelled. We stood up, wondering if he ever knew what being soft was.

'Just kidding,' he laughed and made us sit. Hearing him laugh, making weird noises by blowing air out, we laughed too and sat down, looking at each other.

'If I wasn't late, this mouse would not have had a chance to embarrass us. It's all because of me,' Rasheen said.

'It's all because of us,' I added.

'What?'

We were asked to give our names for attendance. 'Rasheen Chettri,' Rasheen whispered.

Looking at her being so scared, I gave mine loudly, '*Mahi Arora.*'

'Did you come here to fight a war?' he asked, and the class started laughing.

I then realised that I was extra loud. Ignoring all, I sat, telling Rasheen, 'It's an achievement, our first day of interaction with him, and he would never forget our names.'

He then stood up from his chair and introduced himself. 'Hello, students, my name is Ashwini Pant, and I will teach you disaster management.'

'Are you our new class teacher?' asked Maria, who was our other friend in the class.

'Yes,' he said.

'Really?' I confirmed.

'I know you don't want me,' he said.

'Of course! We always wanted a class teacher like you,' I replied.

'Are you trying to be smart?' he asked.

'We all make mistakes, and teachers have the right to correct us. That's why our parents send us to school so as to learn discipline,' said Rasheen. The class started hooting.

'Do they?' I enquired sarcastically.

That day we were given the timetable with syllabus handouts by our class teacher. He was a very thin, short man, who looked more like a coat hanger. He was a good chatterer, though. We became comfortable with him and had endless laughs with him, discussing our future plans. The toppers wanted to be chartered accountants or engineers. Rasheen wanted to be a singer. I had not decided anything.

The day was good and enjoyable with the mouse. He gave lectures, telling us that we needed to work really hard for it was class X and we were no more juniors, and we thanked him for making us realise that we had grown up.

After the national anthem, on our way back home, Rasheen asked me if I really wanted him to be our class teacher, and I nodded. 'Lucky are we if we have him.'

'How?' she asked.

'You will start liking him more,' I answered.

The following week, early morning in school, a boy named Bilal from a different section led us all to the morning assembly. A sea of students dressed in blue had assembled like a battalion in the large school ground. This was the first time in five years that I actually noticed the strength. A large number indeed! Rasheen was an inch shorter than me and, therefore, stood before me in the second line in the first place.

We were called for choir, where I played the bongo. A lot of students loved the way I played it. The prayer began: . . . 'Walking with the Lord, we are walking with . . . .' Before the beginning of every stanza, I deliberately gave a touch of Indian Punjabi dhol, which the students loved. I was motivated each time I saw my mates smile at me. My music teacher, whose favourite I was, reminded me that it was a school prayer because it sounded more like Punjabi music.

Later, after the national song, we returned to our respective classrooms. Before the class attendance, our class teacher, Mr Pant, introduced us to three new admissions: one boy and two girls.

The boy seemed to be decent, and his name was Ayush; however, both the girls seemed sassy. The school skirt of one girl named Latika was above the knee, which was not allowed. And the other girl named Sheena had worn coloured clips in her hair, which was also not allowed. One similarity between the two girls was that they both made silly faces at the rest of the class. I was the leader of the class gang with about 70 per cent students, including the class toppers Maria and Shyna, supporting me.

It was science class, which was taught by Madam Shanta. I realised that she was staring angrily at me during the prayer. She entered like a giant with no expressions at all. We wished her and sat down. Nobody liked her, and vice versa. Everyone had a different viewpoint on her rude attitude.

1. Some said that her boyfriend hits her at night after consuming alcohol which has made her frustrated.
2. Some said that she doesn't get salary on time which makes her teach and behave rudely. Adding to this, Rasheen said, 'We pay our school fee on time. It's not our fault.'
3. Some said that her mother sent her to a boarding school when she was our age, which makes her feel jealous of us.
4. Some who were always updated with the school news, whether or not it was true, said that she once proposed to Father Edward, our school principal, who refused to accept her, and this makes her behave harshly towards students who are loved by him.

One thing was sure: she hated children. She was unpredictable. It seemed like kids visiting the zoo to see the same animal in different styles. Everyone was scared of her variety in behaviour.

'Come here, you idiot fellow,' she said.

'Go,' I said, laughing, to the newcomer Latika who was sitting behind me.

'I am calling you, idiot,' she yelled, addressing me.

'Me?' I confirmed, trembling with fear. I walked up to her, telling myself to be brave and face her.

'What did I do, madam?' I asked politely. My mates looked left and right as I was on the left and she on the right. I could see the new girl Latika laughing at the situation.

'Go on, it's your first day,' I murmured to her, and then I looked at Rasheen, who was worried, and the minute I turned to madam, I felt pain in my left cheekbone as I got a tight slap.

'Get out of the class right now,' she yelled. I didn't dare to argue, so I did what she asked me to do.

She asked the rest of them to open the biology section of the book and started teaching without wasting time. I kept on moving my jaw to double-check if it was OK. I waited for five minutes until I regained confidence. After all, I was a brave fourteen-year-old. I peeped in and began, 'I am sorry to interrupt, but what's the reason of sending me out?' I asked her respectfully.

'You really enjoy distracting the students during the morning prayer by playing Punjabi music and ruining the school discipline. Don't you dare make fun of God!' she said.

'What is your intention?' she shouted loudly and added, 'Don't you stand dumb. Talk, I want an answer from you, the truth.'

'I did it so as to entertain the students so that instead of yawning and getting bored, they would love the environment,' I replied, looking at the floor.

'Oh! Tell me how many of us were entertained,' she asked. There was a lot of unity amongst us, and we could see nineteen hands raised up.

'Shut up,' she shouted at them. And they put their hands down. The remaining who didn't vote, excluding the bookworms, were the ones who were either scared of her or were neutral.

I was thrown out again with my hand on my left cheek. She started teaching, and after ten minutes, I peeped inside the class and saw Rasheen smiling at me.

'Do you want to join your friend?' she shouted at Rasheen. I quickly stood far from where I could peep in. 'Fourteen-year-olds, and you behave like kids,' she yelled.

'A kid lives in everybody, and we should never let it die. If it does, life will turn out boring,' I said to myself.

Mother Earth couldn't come to save me, but 'Father Earth' did. Our Principal Father Edward was on a round.

'Mahi Arora,' a heavy voice broke the chain of my thoughts.

'Good morning, Father,' I wished him. He didn't seem to understand the reason for the punishment. He was a sensible man who loved children and was liked by everybody. On hearing our conversation, Madam Shanta came out.

'Forgive, Shanta,' said Father and got me inside, holding my arm. Everybody wished him. My peers were happy to see me come back. 'Mahi is a nice girl,' he said, and Madam Shanta asked me to take my seat. She stared at me thrice after she heard me getting praised by Father Edward. I couldn't dare to be rude to her; therefore, I looked at her with innocent eyes that meant apology, and, on the other hand, I hummed in my heart, 'He who wins the lost match is the real hero.'

Madam Shanta was the cruellest creature ever, and the truth was that we were all scared of her. That was why we apologised whenever it was needed, whether or not we meant it truly, and we just hated her. Madam Shanta staring with cruel eyes = apologies needed, whether or not it's your fault. After all, she was our teacher, not a classmate whom we can fight or argue with.

It was time to observe some rag and taunt. One of our friends, Soni, walked up to Latika and asked if she knew how to smile. Soni and Latika were once in the same school but weren't friends. Soni joined us in class IX and had become a close friend. 'She is extra smart is what she thinks,' said Soni.

'Don't worry, Mahi will thrash her with one hand, if needed,' replied Rasheen.

'What are you staring at?' asked Latika.

'Your forehead reads something,' I said. She made stupid faces, but who cared?

'She laughed when Madam Shanta slapped you,' said Rasheen.

'Let it be,' I replied. Shyna came in with the newcomers for some rag.

'Does your father own a fashion accessory shop?' I asked Sheena, who was another newcomer.

'Why?' she asked.

'You wear ten types of hairpins in your hair. The school will not let you be so fashionable,' I explained to her.

'Who the hell are you?' said Latika.

'She is the one in charge,' said Rasheen.

'Ms Latika, you aren't here for modelling. Kindly wear decent clothes to school,' I said.

'What if I don't?'

'You will be explained soon,' I said calmly yet confidently.

The boys seemed to be quietly enjoying the girls' hatred for each other and their arguments. 'Loser, you can go back to your seat,' said Soni to Ayush.

'I will speak to Madam Shanta about this,' said Latika.

'An advice for the newcomers! Remember that Madam Shanta likes no one. None at all,' I said and left.

After a week, for some reason, the sections were merged and mixed. There were some new faces in our class and some faces we had never bothered to see but who had been a part of our school for a couple of years. The strength of our section was more now. The twenty-student united class group, whose boss I was, was left with thirteen in our section, excluding Rishabh, who was sent to a different section.

Rasheen and I were together luckily and, adding to our luck, we still had Soni, Amaar, and a few more with us, and also the three newcomers remained in their original places. A group of unknown boys, who were now a part of our class, were looking at us and smiling, reminding me that I was supposed to have a boyfriend.

We could see around five small groups in the class. There could only be two groups: one in my favour and the other against me. A merry group of guys and girls were entertaining themselves at the cost of the bewildered souls who were still to find their place in the new class. I could see a boy from one of those groups smile at me. I did respond as he was good-looking. Amaar came and introduced him to me. His name was Sagar and he was the captain of the Red House; I welcomed him.

Father Edward had called me for some important news. By the time I came back, it was midday. The students were all settled, and the class was quiet. I had to make an announcement, and I began, 'Good afternoon, friends. My name is Mahi Arora. Being the captain of the school, it's my duty to inform you that our school will have a food canteen from tomorrow onwards. The Monday-to-Thursday menu would include snacks like sandwiches, bread rolls, burgers, patties, hot dogs, and pastries with cold drinks. The Friday and Saturday menu would also include, with the above, chicken nuggets, wings, and chicken popcorn.'

The class started hooting with excitement, and, on hearing 'drinks', Rasheen yelled, 'Three cheers for Bartha Convent! Hip hip hurray! Hip hip hurray! Hip hip hurray!'

And I continued with other necessary information on the piece of paper, given to me by the principal:

1. A few would be assigned duties that are meant to be done efficiently, keeping in mind the school rules.
2. We are not allowed to wear casual dress on birthdays. (The class started laughing.)
3. We are not allowed to bring plastic packets to school. Please bring eatables in lunch box.
4. Rude behaviour in the class will not be tolerated at any cost.
5. Taunting will not be entertained.

I started laughing myself.

And the speech ended. I was in charge of distributing duties amongst the classmates.

It was English class, and an unknown lady walked into our class. We wished her; she seemed to be extremely lenient. We kept on rehearsing and introducing ourselves one by one to every teacher who made an appearance. She was a very fair lady, and soon she was given the name 'Goat' for she had a long thin face with hair on her chin. We talked and laughed for it was our first meet with her. We thought we might enjoy more with her, but she asked us to open the books as she had to complete the syllabus on time.

During zero periods, which were the last class of each day, we sat introducing ourselves to each other. After Sheena, Ayush had become a part of our group, for he became friends with another group member, and in this way, we were almost together except for a few neutrals or statues, including the bookworms.

I had given Rasheen the duty in the walkway that connected all the classes and the stairway, which had one main gate to go to the school ground. I had asked her to make sure that juniors come in a queue without dragging their feet or making any kind of noise.

I was in the corridor myself when I heard students laughing and talking loudly. I went to see if Rasheen was present there. She indeed was but only physically. I walked slowly towards her and saw her peeping inside the boys' toilet, lost completely. 'What was she looking at?' I wondered. It was a very strange occurrence. I could see a boy was peeing and looking at Rasheen through the washbasin mirror behind him. The eye-lock remained till the time he washed his hands thoroughly. They were embarrassed after they saw me noticing them. To cool off the situation, I asked her to come with me, pretending I didn't notice anything.

We were having drinks at the canteen. The same boy came to buy himself one. Rasheen looked at him from the corner of her eye, and when he saw her looking at him, he smiled, looking on the ground, which Rasheen didn't notice, but I noticed. He was of the same age as us but from a different section and was another newcomer. He became friends with Amaar, who was the Santa of our school. He joined us each time we were at the canteen, having food, because he liked Rasheen and vice versa. They both didn't talk but were happy to stare at each other.

Was it the same Rasheen who on Granny's birthday had confidently said that she loved Adhiraaj truly and couldn't date any other boy? I was surprised to notice her fall for this guy.

Rasheen was so lost in him that she didn't bother to laugh at the jokes Amaar cracked—something she was really fond of. She was physically with me but mentally with her new-found love. I had to shake her with her sleeves to check if things were fine. She always replied in a hesitating tone. They never thought of going beyond knowing their names, which they came to know after Amaar introduced them. Therefore, I thought of helping my not-so-brave 'Juliet', Rasheen.

One of our classmates, whom we called 'Newspaper', came up to us and surprised us by telling us that she had heard someone in the staffroom say that Madam Shanta would be our new class teacher. We were all shocked to hear this news. Half of us were dead already, and the other half, including me, wondered if this was really true or was just another rumour.

We called her 'Newspaper' because she came up with news related to everything happening in the school. She knew everything about the personal lives of teachers and also about the students—if they were dating. If she didn't know who was dating whom, she made guesses and spread rumours in the entire campus.

She was the one who helped teachers in distributing notebooks and helped students in submitting them. She was mostly found in the staffroom, helping teachers or their kids. A few teachers liked her to be around so that she could get them a glass of water or some food from the canteen in the absence of the maid. She had no friends in school because most of us didn't like her fake stories about our personal lives.

THREE

The bell had rung, and we all had to gather for the morning assembly. I had the duty of checking if the students were neatly and properly dressed—from hair till the shoes. I so wanted to punish those rude creatures. Time had come! I was lucky enough to be entertained when people paid for their rude acts.

'Come on, you, step out,' I said, addressing Latika.

'Why should I?' she argued.

'Do like you are asked to without questioning much,' I said and ignored her. The length of the skirt was supposed to be below the knee or at max till the knee but definitely not above that. She wore a miniskirt with ankle-length socks so as to flaunt her legs, because of which she stood separate from the rest of the school that day.

I had quit choir by that time because I was in no mood to get beaten up by giants for entertaining my schoolmates, and also this was a more interesting job. The prayer was done, and we waited for our principal's speech to announce the opening and closing hours of our school canteen.

I stood with four students, including Latika and a few who were late and also had to be given punishment. We were very happy to hear him tell us that the canteen would open from the time we stepped into the school till the time we stepped out of the school, instead of only during recess.

Students, all cheering and smiling at each other, lined up in a proper queue to get back to their classes. I asked the latecomers to get inside for their awards. I was in charge and, therefore, could give them punishment according to their potential.

The juniors were made to do sit-ups. A few were asked to take five rounds of the school ground with their bags on their shoulders. Latika laughed loudly when the students did as they were asked. I noticed them making faces at her and hating her. It was our favourite Latika's turn now, and she had to do both of these tasks with one more to entertain the juniors so that they could be comforted before going back to their classes.

The students were done with their punishments and waited for some entertainment. Latika had to start with the third and final punishment. She was already embarrassed. 'I will introduce you to them, and you will add "pull my hair" after every sentence that I say on your behalf. Now, focus your vision on the ground and start,' I said.

I started, 'My name is Latika.'

'Pull my hair,' she added.

'I mistakenly think I am too smart.'

'Pull my hair.'

'I wouldn't dare to mess with anyone.'

'Pull my hair.'

'I am a hypocrite.'

'Pull my hair.'

The juniors burst into a giddy chuckle.

And I continued, 'What an idiot I am!'
'Pull my hair.'

What timing it was! I was impressed, and so were the juniors. And we all went back to our classes. Our Personal Training Instructor had given me this duty, and as he trusted me, he asked me to punish them without harming them. I utilised my position effectively by punishing Latika this way.

That day, our class teacher came in with another student who wanted to change the section as he didn't find the environment in the other section interesting. It was none other than Rasheen's new-found love. 'Was it because of the environment which he didn't appreciate or was it Rasheen that brought him here?' I questioned myself.

The newcomer, Atul, was made to sit in the next row at the third bench and was ready to struggle on his first day in the new section like a cockroach in an overflowing waste pipe. He was looking here and there, making himself comfortable while our other classmates made fun of him without any reason. He seemed to be someone who had never argued in his life, and Rasheen, on the other hand, was someone who loved to create unnecessary brawls; therefore, it seemed an odd combination to me.

During our English period, I was asked to read the chapter. I started reading and stopped when it was our teacher's turn to explain the meaning. Some, including me, instead of paying attention to the teacher, were involved in our own activities. Rasheen was busy gazing at him, and he was gazing at her. They also smiled sometimes but did not look at each other.

Next to that boy sat Sagar, the new joiner, whom we knew better than the others because he was introduced by Amaar. Each time I managed to shift my gaze to Atul to know what they were doing, I ended up looking at Sagar, for Sagar was looking at me, which I mistakenly couldn't notice due to my concentration on Rasheen's situation. I could see them hiding their faces with their textbooks and sharing expressions filled with love. They couldn't catch me looking at them this time.

It was now Rasheen's turn to read, and since she was standing, I couldn't see her lover's reaction. Therefore, I shifted my chair a little backwards so as to view the response clearly. Rasheen read irately as it had interrupted her romantic thoughts. Also she read the words *honey money* as *honeymoon*; we all laughed. I heard someone drag his chair. As I looked up to see from where the sound had come, I saw Sagar making the noise and smiling at me for I didn't know what reason.

Amaar whispered in my ear, 'What's going on, Mahi?'
'Nothing,' I replied, for I thought unless Rasheen and her lover were together, I would not tell anything to anyone about them, though much later I was told that he was talking about me and Sagar.

The eye contact remained till the class ended. They both tried to pretend that they weren't looking at each other. Sagar kept on staring and smiling at me, and I smiled at him too.

The studies had begun already after we were introduced to our new teachers and classmates. We made ourselves comfortable in the environment: listening to lectures by teachers; discussing our future goals with each other, whether or not related to studies; and having fun like pulling each other's leg, teasing, and taunting.

The school was going on well and was enjoyable, and we all had in mind that we had to prepare well for the first-term exams that were to commence in the next few months.

Rasheen and Atul were so dumb that they didn't talk even once with each other. 'What are they doing with their lives? Why the hell are they so slow in proceeding further?' I wondered.

During free time in the class, I could see a few girls laugh with Sagar and Atul, giving high fives. I wanted to show this to Rasheen so that she could learn something from them and be quick where it was needed. But I didn't talk much about this to Rasheen so as to pretend that I wasn't taking this too seriously.

While I was looking at them talking and having fun, I was caught by Sagar, who smiled at me again for his own special reasons. This time, I ignored him, wondering how many times I would respond to his endless smiles. I then thought of making a plan which could make my friend brave and help her take decisions for herself quickly.

The teachers had gone for a meeting, and we were asked to do combined study till recess. None of us actually did so except the bookworms. I was done thinking about the plan, and it was time to execute it. I shouted to Maria that I would be going upstairs with Rasheen to check if the other classes were observing the discipline in the absence of their teachers. Rasheen would stay in the second floor corridor to see that students didn't come out of their classes. And I would check the rest of them. I made sure that Atul listened carefully and went after Rasheen.

It was time to execute the plan. I told Rasheen that I would be waiting in the second-floor corridor for her as I had some important thing to share. Also, I asked her not to leave if I was late as I also needed to check the other classes. I went upstairs to find a place to hide myself and view the scene, moving further. I managed to find a place under the stairs that ended at the terrace building. That was a place where they kept the old answer papers with a lot of books. It seemed so scary, for it was dark and filled with used materials, but it was the best place to hide.

I struggled inside the area to make a small place to watch the movie go on, which had as lead actors my friend Rasheen and her new-found love. I hid myself in the front area so that I could come out easily when needed. I could hear someone walk up the stairs, and that made me so glad and excited.

It was the sound of a boy's shoes, which informed me that it was probably Atul, who might have come in search of Rasheen. And my guess was right. He looked here and there to see where Rasheen was but couldn't find her. He then went to the other side of the building to look for her. I came out of the hiding place and quickly went to the second floor to see where Rasheen was. Our entire class was roaming here and there, making fun of juniors.

There was a lot of noise in the building, which made Madam Shanta check what was happening. 'Newspaper' shouted, informing the students that Madam Shanta was on the round, which scared them. The ones who had their classes upstairs got inside their classes, and the ones who had came in from the ground floor didn't have anything to do apart from hiding themselves as she was coming from downstairs and would catch hold of them if she saw them.

I saw her coming upstairs, and, therefore, I quickly rushed to the same place where I was hiding myself before to observe Rasheen and Atul proceed with their story. She would definitely come here to check, I knew, for this was a place where students did things like smoking cigarettes, drinking, bunking classes, romancing, and so on. I wasn't here for any of these, though.

She went to the terrace to see if any students were bunking or not. I got inside the same area to hide myself behind a big bag that had old books in it. She came back, locked the terrace door, and started walking towards the area where I was hiding myself. I started shifting backwards as she came near to see if things were fine. I fell on somebody's lap. I was scared to hell, and before I could shout for help, the person closed my mouth tightly with his hand and whispered in my ears his name, which was Sagar.

Madam Shanta left, and after five minutes, when we were sure that she wouldn't come back, Sagar made a way for both of us to come out and take long breaths since he had held me so tight from my waist with one hand that I could barely move. I sat on the stairs, enduring the pain I had in my ribs as if someone had hit me hard.

Sagar apologised, took me to the terrace, and made me sit and continued, 'I am sorry to have hurt you, but if you would have shouted after falling on my lap, madam would have dragged both of us out of school.' I was almost crying with pain, and he kept on consoling me.

'What the hell were you doing here?' I asked.

'I was a . . . looking for you,' he replied in a hesitating tone.

'Why me?'

'Just like that,' he said. 'Mahi, I want to talk to you.'

'What? Now you are not singing, are you?'

He paused for five minutes, and I waited to regain my energy.

'I want to say something to you.'

'What?' I asked irately.

'I mean I want to ask you if we can be friends.'

'We aren't enemies, are we?'

'From the first day I saw you playing bongo in the morning assembly, I started liking you.'

'Thanks!'

'Also, you look at me in the class,' he said, 'misunderstanding me—for each time I looked at Atul, he thought I was looking at him as they shared the same table.' I realised why he smiled all that time.

'I don't look at you. You are mistaken.'

'Whatever. I find you beautiful and better than the other girls in the class.' I smiled.

We sat on the terrace, talking to each other; we realised that it had been more than thirty minutes and we had to get back to our class. Sagar closed the door, and I waited for him outside the area where we were hiding. We walked downstairs to the first floor of the building, praising ourselves for not getting caught by Madam Shanta. I was hitting him for fun, and he held my hand to stop me. 'Newspaper' saw us; she was the only one present in the corridor. We looked at each other, ignored her, and went back to our class.

We took our seats, pretending we weren't together, and saw Rasheen with head down on the table.

'Where were you, idiot?' I asked her. She looked at me and said that she was about to come upstairs to see me, but as she heard Madam Shanta was on round, she came back. Madam Shanta never liked students taking care of any junior class, for she didn't find any one disciplined.

'Hey, Sagar, how was it?' asked one of our friends to him.

'What?' he quizzed.

'What were you and Mahi doing, holding hands?' asked Amaar. Sagar looked at me, surprised. 'Newspaper' had begun her job. She had started spreading rumours in the class, adding things like we might have also kissed each other. Our friends started teasing both of us by each other's names. I kept on denying it all, and Sagar couldn't control his smile when people teased him, which made them sure of something that had never happened. I did not like it, but he seemed to be enjoying it.

The bell rang for recess. I dragged Sagar to one side and told him that if he didn't deny the rumours and make people shut their traps, they would create a bigger blunder. His reply to this was that if he argued more, people would spread more stories. I was irritated and asked him not to talk to me. 'Mahi,' he said, holding my hand, and a few of our classmates started staring at us.

'It doesn't matter,' he said.

'It does for me,' I said and pushed him. I did have a 'give no fuck' attitude, but I was bothered as I didn't want to be linked with anyone without any valid reason.

'Wait, you, Newspaper,' I said rudely. 'What do you think of yourself? Stop spreading rumours about me. You are a girl too,' I said. She made an innocent face, pretending she didn't know what I was talking about.

'Who told the class that I was with Sagar?' I questioned.

'How would I know?' she replied.

'You saw us coming together. Who else would spread this?'

'Mahi, we are friends, and I can never do this to you. Please don't blame me,' she said and left.

'Asshole!' I murmured; she heard me, but I didn't care for I was upset because of her.

Rasheen asked me about the matter. 'Nothing,' I said. She asked me to come to the canteen. I asked her to go and I would join her in five minutes. She went out, and Sagar came in to talk to me. There was no one in the class except us.

'Mahi, I am sorry. Please don't behave rudely.'

'What do you expect? I should hug you and celebrate the fake story people are enjoying?' I asked.

'We aren't children, and this happens everywhere. A boy and a girl when caught together are rumoured to have an affair. I can't see you like this, Mahi. Please, honey,' he said and asked me to come to the canteen.

'If I was dating you, I wouldn't mind people talking whatsoever, but I can't accept people talking about something that isn't true,' I said.

'Would you want me to make this true for you?' he said and winked. I asked him to shut up.

We both went to the canteen and sat with a plate of snacks in our hands. I couldn't find any of our friends as they were all missing. I could see Newspaper and Latika argue for some reason. Sagar kept on talking funnily, trying to make me feel good.

Rasheen came running to us with a bottle filled with cold drink, asking us to try a sip. Sagar took one sip and asked if she had mixed hard drink into it. She started laughing, and, out of curiosity, I snatched the bottle from Sagar and took a sip. It was something bitter in taste. She told us that Amaar had brought vodka and that was what they were all drinking. Sagar asked me not to drink much, but I took three more sips from the bottle, ignoring him. He took a few sips himself and handed the bottle to Rasheen, and she went back to our other friends who were drinking.

'I asked you not to drink, Mahi.'

'Who are you to instruct me? Mind your own business,' I replied normally. 'You refuse to tell people the truth about us,' I said.

'Mahi, I have already explained you. Now keep quiet,' he yelled, and I asked him not to shout at me and went back to the classroom.

I sat there, thinking about what had happened today, and he came after me. 'Mahi, do you have guts to tell people the truth?' he asked.

'Yes, I do because I am not scared of any son of a bitch,' I said.

'Are you sure?' he asked.

'Unlike you,' I replied.

He pulled me behind the door; holding me tight from my waist, he brought me closer, kissed me, and said, 'Would you like to date me?' We stood rigidly, facing each other for five minutes. He continued, 'Now go and tell this to people.'

I was left surprised-cum-nervous and kept wondering if he had just proposed to me and kissed. He was a good-looking boy after all but not more than Karan.

I turned my back at him and started walking here and there, having nothing to do. 'Mahi, I know you want to smile,' he said, and I smiled. It was time for the bell to ring, and we thought of going out before we were caught. We went out and joined our friends.

'Where were you?' asked Sagar to Atul.

'With Amaar,' he replied.

'When he likes being with Amaar, he wouldn't come to you,' I said to Sagar. Atul seemed to understand the joke.

The bell rang after a few minutes, and we all got back to our class. It was science class. We all sat quietly with our books open in front of us and waited for Madam Shanta to enter. She came and asked all of us to stand. She was very angry like she always was. She called Newspaper inside the class and asked, 'Who were they?'

She looked at me and then at Sagar and then at the rest of the class. I was shocked to have been caught by Madam Shanta through Newspaper. I thought, 'If I hadn't have called her an asshole, she wouldn't have complained.'

I looked at Sagar with eyes filled with nervousness, but he didn't seem to understand my reason for worrying. Madam Shanta came to know that some students were taking hard drinks mixed with cold drinks at the canteen. I was relaxed to know that it wasn't what I thought it was. But anyways, I was still the one involved. 'Who were they?' asked madam to Newspaper in a rude manner. She said that she only knew that some people were drinking and did not know who they were.

She sent Newspaper back to her seat and asked us to sit. 'Whosoever is caught will be thrown out of my class.' We didn't seem to be drunk, but Latika was feeling tired and so was Atul. Madam Shanta mistakenly believed them to be drunk and threw them out of the class. We still sat confidently without behaving weirdly. Latika and Atul argued with her, telling her that this wasn't the truth, but she didn't seem to appreciate their arguments and ignored them. We drank, and they were thrown out. What a funny coincidence it was! I laughed so much with Amaar. She then started teaching.

'Children, don't you dare misbehave. If I catch any student disobeying the school rules, strict action will be taken. We will not endure such kind of behaviour in the school premises. You are just kids and need to concentrate on your studies, not on such things that could spoil you and your career.' Sometimes she asked us not to behave like kids, and sometimes she said that we were 'just kids'.

'When our principal isn't bothered about us, who is she to interfere?' we wondered. She went on with her lecture. Rasheen felt extremely bad for Atul and thought of telling madam the names of all those who had drunk vodka. I asked her to shut her mouth and why she would do this and for whom. She didn't answer, for she never wanted me to accept that she was serious about Atul. Sagar, on the other hand, smiled at me, moving his lips, and said, 'I love you.' I ignored him, though I had started liking him.

During the zero period, the entire class was on the playground, enjoying and playing games, and some of our friends, including Sagar, were at the basketball court. I thought this was the best time to talk to Rasheen about her situation.

'Hey, Chettri, come here. I want to talk to you on some important topic,' I said, addressing Rasheen. She sat next to me and seemed very nervous. It was not that I was poking my nose into her personal life, but I wanted to help her.

'Would you stop behaving like a newly married Indian bride on her first night?' I said.
'It's nothing like that. Why would I? After all, we are best friends,' she said. I told her that Sagar had proposed. She was surprised to hear that.
'Was that the reason you were both together today?' she asked.
'This was the main part, and I will explain to you the entire story later,' I said.
'Now, tell me what are you up to?' I asked.
'Mahi, we are like sisters, and I've always told you things, whatever they may be,' she said.

'And like always, you also told me about this boy, Atul Sharma,' I said and left that place.

I sat cheering for Sagar, who was playing basketball, when Rasheen came and sat next to me and started the conversation.

'Which boy were you talking about?' she asked.

'I think we shouldn't talk because you are behaving weird,' I replied roughly.

'Sorry, Mahi!'

'Who do look for in the boys' toilet?'

'I don't look into the boys' toilet,' she said, embarrassed.

'And I believe you,' I laughed.

'He looks at me. I don't look at him.'

'You are both dumb because you have been only looking at each other for days.'

'What should I do?'

'You like him, and he likes you too.'

'How do you know that he likes me?'

'I know. Just listen. If you are this way, a day will come when you will look for him in the boys' toilet and wouldn't find him. After a few days, you will see him coming out of the girls' toilet, adjusting his pants with some other girl of our school. And then you can sit and cry all day at school,' I said in a rough tone.

'Mahi, please tell me what to do.'

'Tell him you want to know him more as you like him.'

'I wouldn't. He should propose to me. After all, he is a boy.'

'What on earth do you want me to do to explain that we are equals, boys and girls? What is wrong in doing it yourself?'

'OK, I'll do as you say, Mahi.'

'You better because I am your only well-wisher. This weekend you are coming home, and we will decide what.'

'Surely, Mahi, my caretaker. I love you,' she said, and we headed to our classroom with Sagar, for it was time to leave for home.

We all took our bags and went outside to board vehicles to go back home. Rasheen hugged me and was excited for her new life, and so was I.

'Goodbye, Sagar,' said I, and he came running after me, asking if I was coming to school the next working day.

'Of course,' I replied. He touched my cheek, and we went in our own directions.

FOUR

The school had become more interesting than it usually was due to such happenings. I was happily stretched out in the shine of my boyfriend by being with him most of the time, whether or not in the classroom. We had started bunking classes and spending time alone at the terrace. Sagar whispered in my ears how much he loved me and brought me closer to him, and we kissed a lot.

Also, my mind was reminding me to concentrate on studies as they were the first priority. The studies were going well as I didn't want my personal life to bother my career; though I didn't know what I wanted to become, I knew well that I had to score well in the exams that were about to commence.

We were caught holding hands so many times by our friends in the school campus, mostly at the playground. The news had spread very fast, and every living being who knew either me or Sagar knew that we were together. There was enough of teasing going on in the campus; the juniors also asked me about Sagar, and that surprised me a lot. We still didn't accept that we were together, and life went on the way it had to.

Rasheen, being my best friend, was the only one I had informed about Sagar and most of everything that we did—from kissing to looking deeply into each other' eyes and smiling. I was romantic, but Sagar was much more romantic than me. He wanted to hug me every minute. It was important to me too.

Our class teacher, Mr Pant, took a class on disaster management after too many science classes. He wrote four words on the blackboard: *natural hazards*, *disaster*, *panic*, and *recovery*. He sat on his chair, ordering us to write the meanings of the above in our rough notebooks. All of us wrote in our own language, and he made us stand one by one and read what we had written. Some, like Amaar, wrote nonsense, a few wrote well, and some gave the same definition as the others.

Amaar was caught laughing and smiling at what he had written in his notebook. The teacher snatched his notebook and read to the class what he had written: '*Natural hazards* means a natural occurrence that happens and has a negative effect on the person it has happened with. For instance, Alan forgot to wear a belt on his pants, and when he fought with his enemy, the button of his pants came out, which is termed as a natural hazard.' Now further explaining the term *disaster*, he had written, 'When Alan stood in front of the school, shouting at his enemy, pushing the other students who were there to compromise on his behalf, his pants fell down, which was a disaster as girls were also present there. He shouldn't panic or get scared at this natural occurrence that led to a big disaster; instead, he should run to the staffroom for a safety pin for its recovery.'

The entire class laughed at his joke. The teacher corrected the name from Alan to Amaar and asked him to read his definitions to the class. He confidently read it, and we didn't laugh when he read the definitions with his name replacing 'Alan'. After all, he was a friend. He was then asked to get out of the class. I could see Sagar looking at Amaar with his hand covering his mouth, and Amaar also smiled at us each time he peeped into the class.

'I will not tolerate such behaviour in my class. The next step I will take is throwing you out of the school. Do you understand?' teacher asked. We all nodded. Sagar kept on laughing in the same way, covering his mouth, and seeing him do so, I laughed to myself each time I recalled the way Amaar had written the definitions.

Rasheen followed me keenly and waited for me to spend time with her and help her in deciding the next turn that could bring her close to her love. I knew what I had to do, and she had full faith in me. She worried too much as she didn't want me to get into trouble because of her, but I was confident enough. I had thought that I would talk to Atul once before we could proceed further with our plan, and I did.

Before the social science class, Atul went out, and I followed him and waited in the veranda to talk. Sagar, who was another inquisitive soul, came after me to ask if I was ready to bunk the science class, which was after recess. 'We will talk about this in the class, Sagar. I have some important work. You go, please,' I said. He went, leaving me there. Atul came, and I told him that I wanted to talk to him.

'What?' he quizzed, smiling as if he knew what it could be.

'Hello, Atul.'
'Hi! Your name is Mahi, right? I know you.'
'That's nice. Who else do you know or want to know?'
'I am friends with Amaar and also Sagar,' he said 'Sagar' in a teasing tone. I smiled. 'Anybody else you know?'
'Amaar also introduced me to Maria, Soni, and Sheena.'
'That's it?' I confirmed.
'And a . . . and a . . . ,' he hesitatingly continued, 'There is a girl with a short ponytail.' He knew Rasheen's name but still pretended that he didn't.
'Who?' I pretended as if I couldn't guess who he was talking about. 'You mean the girl with green eyes?' I asked.
'Not that girl. The one I am talking about is in the Red House.'

'That's Twinkle, our friend,' I said.

'No, she is neither Twinkle nor the one with green eyes. The one who is very cute and looks like a doll.'

'Did I just hear him call Rasheen a cute doll?' I said to myself and continued, 'You are talking about someone else because we are not friends with dolls.'

'The girl who is on duty in the corridor,' he said finally.

'You mean the one who looks for you in the boys' loo?' I asked in a funny way. He looked as if I had shot him in his arm. 'Relax! I know it, and nobody else does apart from you both.'

'Please don't tell this to anyone because I don't want people to tease her.'

'Don't worry. I wouldn't. She is my best friend.'

'I like your friend, Mahi,' he said.

'Then talk to her. You both are wasting your time by looking at each other.'

'What if she doesn't want to talk to me?' he asked.

'She will,' I said, and we both went inside the classroom one after the other so that people didn't get wrong signals.

The teacher was waiting to start after giving the same lecture which was 'Get serious, students. It's class X', and things like 'Make notes and understand the meaning of every topic, and don't mug up because if you forget a word, you will forget everything'. We thanked her for informing something we knew better than her as we were students, and we had experienced this lots of times.

During recess, all of us went out together. Nine of us sat together, including Amaar, Maria, Soni, Sheena, Rasheen, Sagar, and I. Amaar had also called Rishabh to join us, and I had invited Atul, and he did come this time and sat next to Sagar. Rasheen looked at me, smiling and thanking me inwardly, I knew. We laughed and discussed what Amaar had done at the disaster management class. Each time he did such things, he was caught. Silly boy! These thirty minutes were spent fighting for chicken nuggets, as it was a Friday, and also drinks; they were soft drinks this time.

We got back to our classes for our next class, which was environment studies, taken by a teacher we knew for almost two years now. She used to merge all the three sections in one big hall in our school and teach. We could sit anywhere we wanted to with whosoever. The room was filled with around 120 students; half of them were with their friends or darlings, and a few were bored and sleeping with open eyes. A few lovers like us bunked the class. Our teacher never bothered to count if all the students were present.

We both went upstairs and got in the same place for that was the safest place to hide for as many times as needed. We could see two more couples in those stairs who were there for the same reason, but we were more decent than them. Sagar sat behind the books, making me sit opposite him. The area was above the stairs that led to the terrace; therefore, we could see the other lovebirds, but they couldn't see us.

One couple was on the stairs near the terrace, and the other was at the different staircase near the door to the second-floor corridor. The area wasn't dark as Sagar had emptied the back side of it for some air and light. He held me in his arms now and hugged me. I kept on pushing him back, but I've told you about Sagar, who was extra romantic. He kept on holding me but lightly this time. One of his legs was folded, and the other was straight, and I sat facing the leg that was folded. He had both my hands in his, and we sat in that position, talking to each other.

'Mahi, you are very beautiful,' he said, looking into my eyes.

I closed my lips tight to control my smile, which led my dimples to get deeper, and I said, 'You are good too, Sagar.'

'I can feel your soft hands in my palms,' he smiled.

I looked into his eyes and at our hands that were stuck together.

'Am I your first boyfriend, Mahi? I know I am. But you aren't my first girlfriend,' said he.

'It's OK till the time you don't double date,' I said, and we laughed.

'What if I do?' he quizzed, smiling at me.

'You will get a hard slap from my soft hands,' I replied.

We heard some girl-like voice shout; it was the same girl who was sitting with her boyfriend in the stairs near the door. She was irritated at her boyfriend as he was touching her breast. I did notice him doing so. She rudely went downstairs, and he accompanied her. We looked at each other and got back to our own world.

'I want to propose to you in a proper romantic way,' he said.

'Now after you have already kissed me many times without my permission?' I laughed.

'So what? You are one girl I would want to propose all my life.'

I wondered if what he was saying was true. I was happy anyways, though I was still not sure about myself because it had just begun.

'Mahi, you are the most beautiful girl I have ever met. I never wanted to be with a girl who is fake to me. You are so genuine. I am lucky to have you in my life. Your brown eyes talk so much. Your dimples make me fall deeper for you every day. I may never find another better than you, and I also like the way you do your hair,' he said and smiled at me.

I felt very happy when he talked about being true and genuine; I felt we might go well. At the same time, I never liked extra of anything. I never wanted to get used to it, but I had to face it, no matter what. I couldn't be scared, wondering what my future would be like and, therefore, got back to where we were.

'What were you thinking, Mahi?'

'Nothing! Just like that,' I replied.

'Are you OK? May I please proceed?'

I smiled.

He had made a flower out of a paper in the time I was busy thinking, handed it to me, and continued, 'Would you like to be with me?'

'Be with you? I am with you already and in this place,' I said.

'Yes, I like this place. It's far from the mess, all alone with you. Our life!'

'We are in the mess,' I said, and we both laughed, and he kissed me.

He was about to touch my breasts when I boldly refused, and suddenly the bell rang, and we got up from the floor, looking at our dress to check if it was clean, and went to the class, realising that we had missed two classes.

I met Rasheen after school and asked her to come home the next evening so that we could decide what to do to get them both to talk. I was so happy because it was a weekend and I could spend some time with Granny, who complained the entire week that I didn't come to her room, not even once, to talk to her. I said goodbyes to all, including Sagar, who was not in a mood to go home. What an idiot he was! I could do anything to meet Granny, for there was not even one place that was peaceful to sit with her and drink. I quickly got into an auto and left for home.

Later that evening, my dad asked me if I had started preparing for my exams. I told him that the session had just begun and I would start it after some time, though I revised all that my teachers taught me. He was always after me, so I didn't much appreciate being with him. I liked being by myself in my room, doing things that kept me going.

He started with his lecture again. 'I don't think you would ever do anything in your life. All you need is money so that you can go with your friends and have fast food. I will stop giving you pocket money. You should concentrate on your future, not on strange life that you spend in your room. Tell me one good thing that you do,' he asked loudly.

I got irritated, looked at him, and said, 'I hate you and your wife,' and went crying to my room. He shouted my name loudly, but I didn't stop. I felt really bad every time this happened. I wanted him to stop making me feel irresponsible all the time; I was helpless.

I liked my school and loved my life outside it too. I rarely liked spending time with the other family members except Granny or sometimes with Arhaan. At night, I went to Granny's room and lay next to her on the bed. I was missing Karan very much that night; I so wanted to go and see him. I was thinking of all that fun we shared together in past. She saw me lying with eyes open and gave me her phone as she knew that I needed it. I dialled Karan's number, and he answered.

'Hello, my clown, my bub.'
I didn't say anything and simply started crying on the phone.
'What happened, bub?'
'Karan, you are a very amazing friend I could ever have.' I kept on wiping my tears and kept on crying. 'I feel needed and loved when I am with you, Karan.' With a runny nose, I continued, 'I love you so much. Thank you for making my life worth living.'
'The last part is too emotional, bub,' he laughed.
I laughed too and added, 'Prep, did I tell you that you look great?' I had said this to him many times before.
'Many times. You look not so bad,' he laughed.
'Thank you. I love you. Goodnight.'
'What happened? You didn't tell me, bub.'
'Nothing, goodnight,' I said and disconnected the phone.

Later, I went back to Karan in my thoughts and remembered the day when we went for ice cream during winters. We both liked the same flavour, and, unfortunately, there was just one available; I took that and teased him. He snatched the ice cream from me, ran in the other direction, and fell on somebody's dog under a small tree. The dog made weird noises and so did his owner.

I went to him, laughing at him, and he came to me and started tickling me as I am very sensitive to being tickled, in fact both of us are ticklish. I jumped and shouted so loudly that an old lady who was on her wheelchair thought he was misbehaving with me by getting physical and started yelling, 'Help! Help!' And before people could come and beat Karan with their shoes, we both ran away.

What a great life we both lived! There were a lot of memories we shared with endless laughs, arguments, talks, and limited food with unlimited hunger.

You might be thinking why I was missing Karan when I had Sagar as my boyfriend. I liked being with Sagar—the way he kissed me and hugged me. I liked the romantic stuff and loved to be loved like every other girl. Sagar was my boyfriend. I liked bunking classes and spending time with him, but Karan was someone who had 'no comparison' at all. He was my favourite conversationalist and my best friend, and I was the happiest when I was with him. He was a hidden part of my superawesome life. I could do anything for him as I loved him the most. Nobody can ever take the place Karan has in my life; he is so precious.

FIVE

Rasheen came to my place on Saturday evening at around 6 p.m. to discuss our next step in her love life. Granny woke me up, announcing her arrival in my room. I sat holding the milkshake glass in my hand, munching chips. Rasheen looked at me with eagerness followed by excitement. I also wanted her to have kisses, hugs, love, and romance in her life like I had.

'I am sure you might have thought something sensible to get us together,' she said.

'You have a lot of expectations from me,' I replied. There was a thirty-second silence, and I was about to finish the shake. She waited for me to continue and quickly reveal the plan.

'I met him and talked about this yesterday,' I said.

'You met Atul?' she enquired.

'Who else? I spoke to him about you.'

Her eyes widened a bit in eagerness to know more. She asked, 'Does he like me?'

'Of course, he called you a doll when I asked him.'

'I like him too.'

'Really! I didn't know this,' I said, replying to her stupid statement.

'Will he propose to me? When?' she enquired.

'It's a coincidence that you are both equally slow and dumb.'

'What do you mean?'

'I mean to say that even if you stay single all your life, he wouldn't come to tell you that he wants to date you.'

'So shy he is,' she said, smiling.

'It is called dumbness to its max.'

She was pissed after I said this about him and looked at the floor, wondering if they would ever be together. 'Hello,' I said, interrupting her thoughts. 'I have decided that you will write a letter to him,' I remarked.

'It is too risky to write a letter. You have gone mad, Mahi,' she said.

'What is the risk?' I asked.

'What if he hands the letter to the principal? I will be thrown out of the school,' she said.

'He wouldn't look at you always if he was to do this,' I said.

'Not at any cost! I won't write a letter to him. I might end up being thrown out of the hostel and the school with insult.'

'Stop getting scared. He likes you, and I would make you write this letter in such a way that you wouldn't be caught, I promise.'

She felt confident on hearing this and was happy about the plan. 'I will write a letter on your behalf,' I said.

And she added, 'I will tell you what to write.' I took her out to the nearest stationery shop to buy an envelope. We reached there, and she started selecting what she thought would be the best glitter pen with a letter pad that had cartoons of teddy bears and hearts. She kept them on the table and asked me to pay for them. I kept the stuff aside, asked the shopkeeper to give us only five envelopes, and handed him a five-rupee coin.

I pulled her by her forearm, and we headed towards my house. 'Why didn't you buy a letter pad and a glitter pen? He would have liked it more.'

'Shut up! It's a letter and not a chart that we made in junior classes.'

'Glitter pen?' she argued.

'I will write it the way I want to, so stay quiet, Rasheen, and stop behaving weird. You have not come with your mom to some toy shop for a toy that you want. I will write it with a ballpoint pen on a paper torn from a rough notebook. Simplicity produces marvellous results.'

We came to my room, kept the envelopes on my study table, and occupied the chairs kept there.

'Why did you buy five envelopes?' she asked.

'We might need them in future,' I said.

'I wouldn't write letter to him always,' she said.

'You might write it to somebody else, for there is no guarantee whether you would stick to him all your life,' I replied.

'You are right, Mahi. We also have opportunities outside school,' she said.

Granny called me to her room. I asked Rasheen to write what she wanted and we would edit it later. When I came back, she was done writing. She was happy to have written it. I was excited to read it, for she was not clever. I took the paper in my hand, and it read like a poem as follows:

To Atul, my teddy,

I like seeing you so much
Simply can't explain how much.
I always expect you to come out of the loo.
And hug me, but you never do.
I look at you all the time.
Hoping you wouldn't mind.

I get nervous when I see you.
I know you get too.
I know you love me but don't say.
You are mine either way.

Your doll Rasheen☺

'This is not supposed to be written in the first letter. We will write a simple letter, and once you are together, you can write your heart out to him.' Rasheen was immature and didn't know the letter *C* of the word *clever*. We had a sisterly kinship; therefore, it was my duty to take care of her in matters like these, and she agreed. 'You can be a poet,' I said, and she laughed.

We both sat and talked about the developments in my friendship or relationship with Sagar. Also, she suggested that we should start watching porn as we had never watched it before. I agreed.

It was time for her to leave for her hostel. She didn't feel like going to her hostel once she was at my place, but she had to. I went to my room, and, without thinking much, I opened my notes and spent some time learning them so that the classes I bunked with Sagar wouldn't hamper my studies as time was passing quickly and our exams were to start in a few weeks. I had started giving at least two hours daily to my studies.

The next week, I went to the school with the letter I had written, keeping in mind all the risky situations that might crop up. I had written it well; I laughed. We all met after two days of holiday. Soni walked up to me and said that the entire school was talking that I was going around with Sagar. I felt a sense of accomplishment after getting linked up with my boyfriend, who kissed me and made me feel good. 'You are mostly outside the class. What's up with you?' she quizzed.

'Things are fine, Soni. Nothing to worry about. Just that people don't let a boy and a girl to be together, so they say such things. I have become close friends with him, and because of such curious ears and eyes that don't allow us to live our personal life, we both like being alone in some private area so that we could make conversations.'

'Is that it? I have often seen you holding hands in the class, and I am not a fool,' she laughed. I smiled at her and told her finally that we were dating. 'That's just too good,' she said.

Our maths teacher, Mr Rana, came in and took his seat. He was glad to see that I was not sitting with Amaar, for he never liked our group. He started teaching, and I was completely concentrating on his explanations as I didn't want to lose my percentage because of one subject. I was in no mood to laugh with my friends. I felt somebody had thrown a piece of paper at my table. I looked here and there to see who it could be. I thought it was Amaar, but it wasn't him. I ignored it and tuned my attention to the teacher.

'Mahi, you remember you had promised me something,' said the maths teacher.

'Of course I do.' I had told him on the report card day that I would take this subject seriously this year. It took me five minutes to recall what was he talking about, but he remembered, for he had a sharp memory and knew the ins and outs of every student. He was smart enough.

He wanted me to be the best as if I were his daughter, and he spent all his time trying to make me a bright student. I never liked people expecting much from me, for I didn't like the pressure of being forced into doing things.

'I am sure you would and everybody should,' he said in a loud voice and started flipping the textbook pages. I got a chit on my face this time; it had something written on it. I opened it and saw 'What's up?' written on it. I looked here and there and caught Sagar smiling at me. I asked him not to do it, for I didn't want a smart man like our maths teacher to catch hold of us.

'Is everything fine?' asked he, and I replied yes in a polite tone. Sagar threw another chit that had 'I love you' written on it. I smiled this time.

We were not all that exhausted after this class. Sagar came to my desk and said that he had brought something for me and was waiting to give it to me. I was happy as it would be the first gift of my love life, no matter what it was. I was excited. Rasheen asked me if I had brought the letter. I had it in my bag. She asked me to give it to her so that she could hand it to the one to whom we had written. I asked her to wait for the right time.

After maths, our class had to go to the library. We went and sat with whomsoever we wanted to. I made Atul sit next to Rasheen, and I sat next to Rasheen with Sagar on my right side. Soni sat opposite me with Shyna. Sagar managed to find himself a magazine that he wanted me to read. Rasheen and Atul sat with the same book in their hands that was kept at the table before we entered. Soni and I went to get a book from the cupboard. I found the novel *Train to Pakistan* by Khushwant Singh, one of the finest Indian authors.

I opened the book and started reading. Sagar asked me if I had come to the library to read, for he wanted to talk. He held my right hand in his left hand and showed me a topic in the magazine which read 'Relationships'. I smiled at him curiously, and he flipped through the pages and ended up at the sub topic 'Boy-Girl Relationship', which came under various levels of relationship. I also had to see what Rasheen was doing and saw that they were both looking at the same page of their books, pretending that they were actually reading it. They both were actually lost.

Sagar interrupted my thoughts about them, and held my hand tighter. I started focusing on what Sagar was trying to make me do. Pointing with his finger, he made me read the main points that suited our situation. One of sentences read, 'This is that relationship which is more commonly taken into consideration in its narrowest sense, and infinite conclusions are drawn.' Before we started being together, people had spread rumours, and the difference was that I got irritated earlier when they used to create news, but now I felt accomplished, for I was spending my time with my boyfriend in school and people could see it.

The next paragraph he pointed with his finger read, 'A healthy boy-girl relationship is selfless and based on the true spirit of love and respect.' He smiled at me, underlining the word *love* and threw a pencil on the floor deliberately. I didn't understand what he was doing. I bent to pick up the pencil, and as I came up, he bent his head and kissed my hand. What a style! I appreciated such surprises.

I looked at Rasheen on my left and could see both of them looking at the same page of the book that had been dangling in their hands for god knew how long. I was smart enough to have planned the idea of writing the letter at the right time, for I could see no developments at all. The match was good as they both were slower than a tortoise.

Sagar was still busy reading the topic and finding the most important points that he wanted me to read. The next point he made me read at least five times was 'Having boyfriends or girlfriends can be very special. It may lead to a lot of good happenings and good times.' I felt good and happy as all that was happening was new to me.

During recess, Rasheen walked up to me and asked when we would give the letter to Atul. I told her that when everybody went out to the canteen, I would send Atul inside, and then she could give it herself; she agreed. Everybody went out except me and Sagar, for he had to give me something that he had brought for me.

I opened the sky-blue envelope and saw a card that had a girl and a boy attached with a heart. It was a very beautiful card. I thanked him, and he was happy to see me feeling good. I kept the card in a big register so that folds wouldn't appear. We both went outside to the canteen.

I went to Rasheen and told her the place where I had kept the letter, and she went inside the class and waited for Atul. I called Atul out of the group and told him that Rasheen was waiting for him, for she had something to give him. He asked what it was. I pretended that I didn't know anything about it, and he went inside to see Rasheen.

Sagar was nowhere to be found. I went to Amaar and asked if he knew where he could be. Rasheen had come back by then, and I diverted my attention towards her and asked if she had given the letter. She told me that she was very nervous so couldn't say anything and had mutely handed over the letter to him. I was glad to know that she had given the letter, and we also saw Atul coming back and joining our table.

Rasheen bought bread rolls for me. I told her that I was waiting for Sagar to come. She told me that she had seen Sagar outside the school kitchen. I went there and saw him having cold drink with Latika. After he saw me, he came running towards me and offered me the cold drink.

I could see Latika pass on silly expressions at me. I told him that I had been waiting, hungry, to have food with him, and he was busy enjoying a cold drink with my enemy. 'She is a nice girl,' he said.

'I don't like her, and whose boyfriend are you?' I asked.

'Mahi, I love you. I only talk to her.'

'Whatever,' I said angrily.

We both sat at the table with our friends and started having bread rolls that Rasheen had bought for me. Latika stood opposite us, smiling at Sagar. He invited her to join us, and she sat next to him. I was irritated, so I got up from the chair and went to the other side where Soni was sitting. 'What happened, Mahi?' asked Sagar.

'You don't know?' I said. I went inside the class, and he came running after me.

'Baby, what is wrong with you?' he asked.

'I just told you that I don't like her. Why did you invite her to join us? Sagar, I always listen to you. Each time you ask me something, I obey you. We rarely are in the class these days, and I argue and fight with the ones who criticise you, and you are becoming friends with the girl who talks nonsense about me.' Soni had told me once that Latika was amongst those who talked nonsense about me and Sagar. 'I do not like it,' I said.

'You need a hug and will feel better.' He came closer to me. I pushed him back and told him not to do this all the time, for I was irritated.

After the school ended, things were normal, and we were both happy. Latika walked up to us when we were outside the school gate, about to leave for home, and said to Sagar that she had fallen in love with him. I asked her to get lost, for he was my boyfriend. She stood there for the next five minutes and said that she found Sagar to be the most handsome boy in school and also outside the school. I too thought that he was the most handsome boy in school, so I was proud of my choice. Outside the school, I thought that Karan was the most handsome boy. Anyways, my choice was awesome as a lot of girls would die to date Karan.

She also wanted to be friends with me, and I refused. Sagar then asked Latika to leave us alone and told her that I was his only love. I was happy to hear this, and Latika left. He kissed me, and I felt pampered, and then I boarded the auto with Soni, and we were on our way back home.

SIX

The next week, one evening, I started looking for competition details. I brought my laptop to the living room and started surfing their website. It had a photograph gallery, which had the view of the resort, the restaurant, and the accessory shops, including toys and stuff like DVDs, music players, and headsets they had in their store. The view was beautiful; they also had artificial trees and waterfalls.

It was dinner time, and the entire family was together in one room except Mom as she was in the kitchen, preparing dinner with our cook. 'What's up?' asked my dad.

'All is well with studies. Highway King is organising a fashion show for boys, so we are planning to send our friend Karan,' I said.

'Who's Karan? The boy with a black bike?' he confirmed.

'Yes, you have got him right,' said Granny, who knew him too well, for she had often seen him drop me home from tuitions. She had always liked him and asked me many times if he was my boyfriend. Unfortunately, we weren't in love.

My brother Arhaan entered the room, wearing a T-shirt and his underwear, and no slippers, which was his favourite summer dress when at home; he was holding a beer mug for Dad. Instead of thanking my little brother, Daddy yelled, 'Where are your slippers? Go wear them.' He went to his room and came out wearing his shoes, for he couldn't find his slippers anywhere, and smiled at everyone, for he thought he was the best-looking person in the room.

What a combination it was! T-shirt with underwear and shoes! I love my brother.

Daddy was busy watching a football match and supporting his favourite team Real Madrid. 'Go and get four beer cans from the fridge,' said Daddy to Arhaan. He went and didn't come back even after five minutes. The opponents hit the first goal. Daddy yelled at them and later at Arhaan. 'Where the hell are you, idiot?' There was no response at all. Daddy shouted his name again, and there still was no reply. I went to look for him and saw him standing on a chair and munching ice from the freezer. 'Oh my God,' I said. He looked at me, worried.

'Goal!' We heard Daddy shout from his room in a happy mood this time. I lifted him from the chair and asked him to give those beer cans to Daddy. I came back, following him.

'Where were you lost, kid?' asked Daddy to Arhaan—this time politely as if he had just realised that Arhaan was his son. Thanks to the Madrid player for the goal that changed Daddy's mood completely.

My little brother looked at the TV and yelled, 'I am a Madrista.'

'It's Madridista,' corrected Granny.

Mom called me from the kitchen to take the chicken soup she had made for me. I came back, holding the bowl with two spoons—the other for Granny. Granny and I started having soup, and because she was lovely, I asked her to buy me a mobile as a surprise gift in front of Mom and Dad, and she agreed.

Granny said to me that she wanted to spend some time with me, talking. I also had to tell Granny about Sagar as I couldn't do earlier. I started eating and ended up emptying the tray.

I heard Shakira's song 'Hips don't lie' playing; it was Granny's mobile's ringtone. Granny put on her specs, checked the number, and guessed it was my friend calling. I saw the number, and it was Karan. I answered the phone.

'Hey, bub,' said Karan to me. He had given me this name.

'Hello, handsomest,' I said, and he started laughing.

'Give me the details, please. I will be filling up the form next week.'

I read to him the details given on the website and reminded him that I had saved other details mentioned in the banner under the drafts menu in his mobile.

'I love you, baby doll,' he said. Another name given by him to the ones he loved.

'If you win, I will get a chance to meet John Abraham,' I said.

'Since when you have started liking him?' he asked.

'You don't know, these celebrities know each other. I can at least ask him to give my regards to Yuvraj Singh.'

'You are so selfish,' he said.

'Not like that. I also like him. After all, he has the best body in Bollywood after Salman Khan.'

'Anyways, how's the preparation going on for exams?' he laughed.

'I already have a father, and you don't need to be another,' I replied.

'Goal!' they yelled.

'Gosh,' I cried. Both of my ears were gone. 'I am not deaf, both of you,' I shouted. With my left ear, I was listening to Karan over the phone, and with my right ear, I could hear Daddy yell from the living room next to me. My father and Karan were both Real Madrid fans. 'Another goal,' they both yelled. Karan asked me to wait.

I waited for two minutes, and then he broke the silence. 'Tell me, I am back,' he said.

'What were you doing?' I enquired.

'I had kept my phone on the table because I had to put some beer in the mug to celebrate and also to show middle fingers to the opponents.'

'You should have been my daddy's son,' I said.

Real Madrid won the match like always, and later we talked about school and the competition we all were excited about. I wished him good luck and continued, 'Get me the banner.'

'I will, baby doll,' he said, and we ended the conversation.

Granny was done having food, and I was about to go to her room for a chit-chat session. She had a separate room in the house. It was a big hall-like place that had the best furniture and the best accessories. Nobody was allowed to disturb her when she was there. Only I could enter without permission, for I was her best friend. She read books during her free time. Also she was fond of talking to her sisters on the phone. Granny had a small bar in her room, for she was really fond of drinks. She had things in balance that constituted visiting the temple, drinking beer, reading books, talking on the phone, cooking food, watching TV, and so on.

She asked me to sit and opened her cupboard to show me a gown her friend had sent her from Shillong. She fell in love with this man when she went to her aunt's place in Shillong. They both loved each other very much. She was unmarried that time when this happened, and because this man never wanted to get married, Granny also decided not to marry anyone, but Granny's father didn't want to see his daughter die alone, so married her off to his friend's son, who was my granddad.

Granny's elder sister was married to my grandfather's elder brother, who lived in London with his family, and her younger sister was unmarried and lived in Delhi.

I sat next to Granny and waited for her to initiate the conversation, and since she didn't, I had to. I began, 'I have a boyfriend, Granny.'

'That's nice. Karan?' she confirmed.

'No, Karan and I are only close friends,' I said.

'Get closer,' she said and poured some beer in a mug for me. I took the mug of chilled beer in my hand and took a sip.

She asked me to tell the story, and I began, 'We have been together for almost two months. The sections were merged, and he was introduced to me by one of my friends. He smiled at me several times. I was trying to hook one of my friends to another boy in our class who sat next to him. Each time I saw the boy passing smiles to my friend, I was caught by him.'

'Who?' she confirmed.

'His name is Sagar, the boy I am with. I don't know whether it was a coincidence or misunderstanding.'

Granny seemed to be excitedly listening to my story and was drinking side by side. 'We started spending time together, bunked classes, and became closer.'

'Is he good-looking,' asked Granny?

'Yes,' I said.

She was done drinking one can, and I was struggling with the same mug in my hand. 'Why have you stopped?' she asked.

'The entire school knows that we are together,' I said.

'No, I meant why have you stopped drinking? Keep going,' she said. I took two sips and could feel the chill beer in my throat, for I was not used to drinking chilled drinks. She asked me to continue the story, and I did. 'The students started spreading this news before we were together, and now their mouths have opened more, but I don't mind now,' I told her.

'It happens, sweetheart, as this is an age that makes you learn so many things. You tend to develop such craze at this age. Don't kill the craze. Keep going. But, my dear, limits—make sure you know them well.'

'Where did you go when you bunked classes?' she asked. I told her that we went to the terrace and talked, holding hands.

'What else did you do?' she asked.

'He kissed me in the library,' I said.

'Don't let him touch you here and there. You don't know boys do such things to girls. Your self-respect should matter to you the most, and kiss only when you want to. Otherwise you will spoil the feeling, and that is the last thing you should do at this age,' explained Granny.

I was enjoying the conversation, as always; she was into her fourth can of chilled beer, and I still had some left in my mug. I then thought of telling her how we met the first time in the area in front of the terrace door when Madam Shanta was on a round. I told her how I fell on his lap and how he closed my mouth and held me so tight by my waist. She said that he shouldn't have held me by my waist, for closing my mouth was enough to keep me quiet.

She interrupted me again and said, 'This isn't love, so if you both break up some day, don't get too emotional, for it is mere attraction.' I listened to her, and, finally, my mug was now empty and so was her fourth can.

'Enjoy this time, for this might never come again in life,' she said.

'I enjoy every moment in school,' I said and laughed, thinking how smart I was, and she interrupted me. 'What are you talking? I am talking about this time when we are together having beer,' she said. She took the fifth can out of the fridge and started pouring it into my mug. I asked her to stop, for my throat had started paining a bit, and she said that we would both divide this, But I refused.

'Another thing, you are only fourteen years of age, so the list of making boyfriends shouldn't stop so early. Life goes on, so keep going, and when the time comes to really fall in love, you will know and make me feel proud, for I don't want you to get into some stupid arranged marriage like I had to,' she said and slept.

The next morning, I didn't get up, for I was unwell. I had coughed all the night and also had a cold. I couldn't sleep well and woke up four times in the night. Granny was there to handle me with care. She gave me a medicine at around 4 a.m. when she found me sitting and sneezing. She slept next to me on my bed and kept on caressing my hair till I fell asleep. I wasn't sent to school. I lay on the bed and asked Granny to send a text to Rasheen's phone, telling her I would not be able to come as I was suffering from bad throat.

At midday, Granny's phone rang, and it was Rasheen. She answered and told her about my health. Then I spoke to Rasheen. She was worried, for Atul had to reply to the letter we had written, and I asked her to take the mobile phone with her and keep messaging me whenever needed; she agreed. Mobile phones were not allowed in our school like any other school, but students brought them so that they could bunk class and talk with their lovers.

Granny took me to the doctor in the morning, and we bought medicines with the worst smell. On our way back, Granny said that it could be because of the chilled beer that I had last night that I had caught cold. But as we weren't emotional, we kept ourselves busy by laughing at Granny's jokes on Granddad on our way back home.

She sat next to me in her room, and I had the medicines while watching TV. Somebody knocked on the door. She opened it, and it was Granddad who had come to ask about my health. 'Everybody, my daughter is fine. Don't bother us by coming to our room,' shouted Granny. Granddad had brought a chicken sandwich for me; Granny snatched it from him and asked him to leave the room. Granddad had become used to her behaviour.

I asked Granny not to be so rude to him, and she replied that it was only because he was the father of her son that he was living in this house; otherwise, she would have thrown him out, for my great-grandmother had given this house to Granny after she died, which was some five years back.

I spent the day resting, revising notes, and having delicious food at home. I was then busy with my dreams of Sagar. Sagar and I didn't have personal mobile phones, so we couldn't talk for hours. He called me on the landline phone to ask about my health, which, I guessed, Rasheen had told him. But I didn't get a call from Rasheen. I wondered if things were fine with her.

On the third day, I suffered from a strong cold; my nose became red and so did my cheeks. I could barely open my eyes, for I was sneezing all the time. I got a call around 8 a.m., and it was Rasheen. I answered the phone and asked if things were fine.

'Things aren't fine,' she said, worried.

'What happened?' I asked. Her mobile phone had stopped working, she said.

'Idiot! I thought something big had happened,' I said.

'What else can be bigger than this? You aren't coming to school, and I can't call you because this mobile phone is almost dying, and I have asked my father to send me some money so that I could buy another mobile,' she said.

I asked if Atul had replied to the letter. 'He didn't come to school yesterday,' she said and told me that Sagar spent the entire day with Latika in the class and people said that they both were dating.

'What rubbish! He is my boyfriend. I will ask him not talk to this girl at all when he calls me up today,' I said. She disconnected the call, saying she would keep me updated about the status.

Granny walked up to me with a thermometer in her hand to check my body temperature; it read 102.

'Fever,' she yelled. I told her that I was fine and asked her not to worry. She brought me some tea and three medicines. I had them all; they had different tastes, but the similarity was that they were all yucky.

I slept, covering myself with a sheet, and Granny switched off the fan while going to the living room so that I would sweat and the fever would disappear. Granny's mobile rang, and I picked it up. It was Rasheen again, and she had called to apologise, for she forgot to ask about my health last time when she had called. I was irritated because of my health, and she was getting emotional. I told her that just because she had forgotten to ask about my health, our friendship hadn't ended and hung up the phone.

I had become so weak that I slept the whole day after taking medicines. I could feel Granny come to my room and caress my hair so as to pamper me. Later, she came with delicious food to change the taste of my mouth, but I didn't feel like eating anything. She came with a cup of tea and a few biscuits so that she could make me eat some medicines, which would help me to get well sooner. I had them and slept at night after waiting long for Sagar's call.

SEVEN

The following week too I didn't go to school, for my health had deteriorated. Everybody in the family was worried, especially Mom as I was missing school due to bad health. Each time Granny came to see me in her room, she felt bad. Dad had gone out of station for some work related to business. Exams were about to begin, and I was unable to give much time to studies because of my health, but I managed.

Rasheen called me from her hostel to keep me updated about what was happening in the school. I told her not to tell the world that I wasn't well as she had a habit of calling everyone to inform them even if any of our friends suffered from a minor headache. She agreed and told me that she had spoken to Atul yesterday. I was happy to know that and asked her what they talked about. She told me that they both had breakfast together at the canteen. I felt happy, for the story had begun. She also asked me if Sagar had called me the previous day, for he hadn't come to school. I told her that I didn't speak to him and asked her to inform me if Sagar was seen in the class. She told me that she couldn't make outgoing calls so would text me any important detail needed.

Granny's mobile rang that morning at around 10 a.m., and it was Karan who had called me to ask about my health. I told him that I was better, for I didn't like telling stories to people, no matter how close I was to them, so as to gain sympathy. Everybody fell sick; I was not the only one. I was becoming weak, but knew I would definitely get well as it was just a fever. I asked him who told him; he said that Rasheen had called all of them to tell them that I wasn't keeping well. Gosh, I didn't like it at all, for I didn't feel like talking to everyone; bad health had irritated me already, though I liked talking to Karan.

I was feeling very hot and kept on sweating all the time, so I took a shower for five minutes. I came back and settled in the living room. I told Mom that I was feeling better after that. I asked her to give me some milkshake; she refused, for I also had a bad throat. I ended up having a cup of tea, something I never liked but had to take because I couldn't take medicines on an empty stomach.

I was in Granny's room when her phone rang, and she asked me to read the number, for I had it with me. She told me that it wasn't anyone she knew, so I answered it. It was Adhiraaj, who had called to ask about my health. I told him that I was well and asked him to message the others not to call me and tell them that I was fine. I told him that I was irritated with Rasheen. He laughed, and we bid goodbye; he was a dear one.

I lay on the bed, thinking about Sagar, the sweet moments, and the silly arguments that we had in school. I was missing him. I found myself either looking at the fan, thinking of him, or, with my eyes closed, thinking about him like what he might be doing and also if he was missing me. I didn't even read the card he had given to me with so much of love. I checked Granny's phone again and again to see if there was a call from Sagar, but there wasn't any; I solely depended on her phone for my calls.

Granny was busy watching a Bollywood movie and admiring the actor and the scenes. I told Granny that I wanted to grab something from my room as she didn't let me go out. I went to my room and I was about to open my bag to get the card, but Mom interrupted me and asked to take rest, so I forcefully came back to Granny's room. I asked her to switch on the AC, for I was feeling hot, and she did but only for ten minutes. The room was now chilled, and I slept well.

At midday, I received a text from Rasheen that woke me up. She had written that she was having a problem and wanted help and asked me to call her. I called her, and she told me that the letter we had written to Atul was caught by none other than Madam Shanta.

I asked how it happened, and she told me that Atul was reading the letter in the science class under his textbook and was caught. 'Who told that idiot to read it in class? We gave it to him last week, so why was he reading it now? What an idiot!' I murmured. Rasheen was almost crying, and I told her to keep her mouth shut and we would not be caught. She said that he might tell her, for Madam Shanta could get anyone to tell the truth.

I suggested her to be brave and not accept at all if she was asked whether she had written the letter or not. She said that the letter had her name at the end, and I explained to her that I had completely changed it and written it in a way that we couldn't be caught. Later, I wondered, 'What was Atul trying to read in the letter, her feelings?' I laughed.

She agreed that no matter how tough the situation was, she wouldn't accept that she had written it. She said it wasn't fair to refuse as she didn't want Atul to suffer. I told her that she would have to do this only if Atul told her name to madam, and if he did, she shouldn't have to be nice to him as it was his own fault that he dared to read it during the science class.

We both forgot to talk about Sagar and hung up the phone. I then received a message from Rasheen, telling me that Sagar was fine and had come to school. I was happy to know that, and I went back to my couch, staring into oblivion with dreamy eyes. I was really missing Sagar. I couldn't tolerate this separation and wanted to spend time with him. I liked it when he kissed me, telling me how much he loved me.

In the evening, I got a call from Sagar, and I was so happy to hear his voice. He asked me about my health and told me how much he had missed me in these four days. He said that he loved me the most. I was enjoying his talk and didn't say much myself. The interesting thing was to remain connected and to conjure mental images of the scene at Sagar's end. The moment was lovely till that time.

I asked him why he didn't go to school yesterday. He replied in a rude tone that he didn't like Rasheen giving me details of what he did and what not. I replied to him that Rasheen wasn't after him to see where he was. 'I asked her, and so she told me this.'

He asked me to change the topic, and I apologised to calm down the moment, and he asked me if I had read the card. I told him that I couldn't read what was written inside. 'I will read it tonight,' I said. He asked me to say that I loved him, and I did in a lower volume as Granny was in the same room.

'How is Latika?' I asked in a funny way so that he would laugh. He started shouting at me, telling me that he liked spending time with her and also that he took Latika to the hospital as she was unwell and that was why he couldn't attend school.

He said he hated Rasheen for this. 'Please don't involve her,' I said.

'Shut up and listen to me, Mahi. I like Latika, and she is a now a close friend.'

'Knowing that she talks nonsense about me?' I asked.

'Whatsoever! That's not my business,' he said. I asked him not to be so rude, and he said that he would do what he wanted to do.

'I don't control you. If I do, you wouldn't be seen anywhere near any girl,' I replied.

'It's OK to flirt with girls,' he said.

'I don't flirt with boys,' I said. Sagar was free to do anything, but, for some reason, I didn't want him to be with her.

Still I apologised to calm down the moment, and we kept quiet; I asked him not to argue today at least. We hadn't met for almost a week. Still he was rude and said that he would talk and spend time with Latika whether or not I liked it and asked me to leave him if I didn't like him flirting with girls.

'It isn't right, Sagar,' I said, and he hung up on me.

I tried dialling the same number, and he disconnected the call. I felt bad that he had created an unnecessary argument. I was also confused if he really loved me or was it because he wanted kisses and hugs that he was with me.

I cried that night, for I didn't expect he would behave in this way. 'Does he want to be with me? Why was he bothered so much about Latika?' I questioned myself. And because I liked him and couldn't let this silly argument ruin it, I consoled myself by saying that maybe he needed some time alone. And I also thought that I would apologise, for it wouldn't make me small, and I wanted us to be happy.

The next morning, Rasheen called me up around 11 a.m. and told me that she would be coming to meet me soon this evening, for she had bought a new-cum-second-hand mobile that also had a camera. I was happy to know that she had got rid of that stupid box that we once called a mobile and which rarely worked. I managed to practise maths for some two hours during the afternoon as every time I grabbed my notebooks, I felt better and less weak.

Dad was back from his tour. Mom came up with Dad to Granny's room to see if I was better and if I was really studying. The medicine had worked, and the fever had dropped. Dad kissed me on my cheek, and I felt loved. Mom had an angry look on her face, for something had happened. I asked her if things were fine. She didn't reply and left the room, asking Dad to come to the living room as she needed to speak to him about something important. I ignored her, for I thought that she must be in a mood to argue with Dad on some personal topic.

Granny prepared chicken for me for lunch. I was glad to have it as it changed the taste after having tea with biscuits, and porridge. And anyways, these items made someone like me feel sicker. I was done having lunch, and Granny asked me why I was crying last night. I told her about the argument I had with Sagar. She was shocked to see me get involved emotionally.

She said, 'It's better to hook up and break up than tolerate a loser all your life. Make boyfriends and keep going. Don't search for love. You will realise that you had it already.'

'Who?' I asked.

'How would I know?' she said. 'Cry only when you achieve, not when you lose because tears have a great worth.'

I did listen to all that she said.

'You are beautiful and can get one any time,' she said. I kept on listening, and she kept on talking.

'You wouldn't regret tomorrow like I don't,' she said.

'Oh!' I said, stretching the word.

'Make, spend, and leave. What is with boys? They aren't getting extinct. Just remember this poem:

> 'Yesterday someone
> Today this one
> Tomorrow many
> The day after—I am still not done

'Enjoy the teenage years, for it's the special part of life. I am not asking you to play with someone's feelings, but don't get too emotional. All the best,' she said.

'You are so lively, Granny,' I said.

Rasheen knocked on the door, and I took her to my room because we had to talk. We sat and started.

'What happened yesterday?' I asked with curiosity.

'Atul is an ass. When he was asked about the letter, he took my name and also added that I sent him proposals and love cards, after he realised he couldn't convince madam. I didn't know he was a liar.'

'Gosh, did he?' I couldn't control my laughter at the way Rasheen said this and gave weird expressions. '*Loser* is a more appropriate word than *liar*,' I said.

'He started crying when I shouted at him for telling a lie.'

I laughed again. 'It did seem an odd combination to me, for you are loud, and we can barely hear his girl-like voice.'

'I also told him to get a sex-change operation done, for he behaved like a girl who was scared of goons after her.'

I enjoyed the way she explained things to me.

'He is a dog,' she said.

'Don't abuse, Rasheen,' I replied.

'*Dog* isn't an abuse.'

'I asked you not to abuse the dog.'

'Madam Shanta read the letter but didn't question me. What did you write?'

I had to explain, 'I just wrote "To you" (with a heart as a drawing) and then "From me".' She wondered, laughing, what he was reading as the letter didn't have anything much.

'Your feelings,' I replied.

'Mahi, what if the letter wasn't caught? He would have proposed to me after reading this,' she said.

'Thank God, he didn't as he is not just a "loser" but a "rich loser".
And I wouldn't want you end up dating a boy with no balls.'

'What balls?'

Changing the topic, she asked if Sagar had called me up.

I told her the entire story, excluding what he spoke about her.

She said that she had seen him going inside the school bus with
Latika. I didn't like it, so I asked her to put a lid on this topic. 'No more
Sagar and Latika. Let him do what he wants to,' I said.

I saw the mobile phone that she had recently bought for Rs. 5,000;
it was a second-hand mobile with MP3 player and camera. I was viewing
the phone menu and clicked the gallery option that had a few wallpapers,
probably put by the old user, and also a few songs.

She told me more about the phone's features, and I liked them, for
they were new. There was a video named *Just Married* in her phone. It
seemed like a wedding movie, and as I opened it, I saw a naked woman
sitting in the Jacuzzi, flaunting her body. We looked at each other with
our eyes wide open and went back to watching it.

A tall man with no T-shirt came and got inside the Jacuzzi, and when
they both came under the shower, the boy wasn't just without T-shirt; he
was without clothes, and they were both totally naked. Because we were
watching it for the first time, we got nervous, and the phone slipped
from my hand and fell on the floor. Rasheen picked it up, and the video
was still playing. She asked me to stop it somehow, and I asked her to
press the red button as it closes all the files. We looked at each other and
discussed that it was a porn movie. We had the craze, so we saw it twice
again without nervousness.

Mom saw us talking politely about it, and we started discussing the
competition of the handsomest so that Mom didn't get a hint of anything

that had happened, and by that time, it was evening and Rasheen had to go back to her hostel.

Later, Mom called me to the living room. I went and saw Mom sitting next to Dad, chopping vegetables.

'Mahi, is there anything you would like to share about your personal life with me and Dad?' she asked.

'No, Mom, Rasheen bought a new phone, and we were discussing its features,' I replied, for I thought she might have heard something.

She pointed the knife at me and said, 'I don't want you to get spoilt at no cost.'

'What happened, Mom?' I asked, worried, thinking she might have caught us watching the porn movie.

'What goes on in your school? Did we send you there for stuff like this?' she confirmed.

Dad was munching chips and looked at me like a policeman looks at a murderer in jail.

'I am studying really,' I asserted. 'Stuff like what? What happened, Mom?'

She threw the card on my face. It was the love card given to me by Sagar. And she shouted, 'What the hell is this nonsense?'

I picked up the card, looked at her, and asked her to stay out of my personal life as I was not the only one who had a boyfriend. I didn't like the way she behaved.

'Mind your language. After I saw this, I realised that you have grown too smart to live and talk such nonsense. I will stop sending you to school if you keep up the same strange way.'

'You can't stop me from doing anything. It's my life,' I said.

'I am your mother.'

'Did you just realise?'

She stood up and slapped me tight. 'Get lost now,' she shouted, and Granny came in.

Looking at the situation that had two carnivorous species staring at me, I couldn't bear to get more slaps, so I left the place, crying and wondering whether I was their own daughter.

I went to Granny's room, worried because I had been caught; I lay on the bed and looked here and there, for the impression my parents had of me had deteriorated to the worst. Now even if I went to meet my friends, they would think that I had gone to see my boyfriend.

It seemed as if I would now be tortured by my parents each time I came across them with another topic added to their favourites, which were 'You don't study', 'Learn something from her', 'Be like him', 'Do this, do that', 'You never listen to us', 'You are spoilt' and so on. I could see my dad's expression which meant that he would kill me. They shouldn't forget that they too had a love marriage. 'What could be written inside the card?' I thought.

Granny walked inside the room, laughing and jumping, reading the card. I got up from the couch and asked her, 'What did Mom say? How did they get this card?' She told me that Mom wanted a paper to write the contact number of the doctor, for I wasn't keeping well, so she took a register out of my bag and saw the card. She took the card out, saw it, and kept it for Dad to read further.

'Didn't she have a diary to write the number that she had to take my register out of my bag?' I argued, and Granny laughed.

We had our dinner in Granny's room, continuing the discussion, and Granny started laughing again. I asked her not to make fun of me, and she said, 'It's normal. Don't worry.'

'Your father read the card and was furious. Don't blame him as it's expected. No father likes to discover that his daughter has a boyfriend who kisses her so much. The dad goes mad after he comes to know that his daughter is dating and might end up getting pregnant. It's not only a love card for him. It's merely a letter by a spy informing him that his daughter has a boyfriend whom she has kissed many times. He thinks she is spoilt.

'Your parents don't want you to get spoilt, so they thought of keeping you in the strictest of custodies with chains so that you are far away from this world that seems to be a world that they hate.'

'They already say that I am spoilt.' I laughed sarcastically.

'He doesn't want you to think that you are not allowed to live your life your way, so he would only observe and silently hate you. This letter has so many things that made your father hate you and behave this way, for it has dangerous things like "darling" and "sweetheart", addressing you,' she said.

I opened the letter, and it read, 'Mahi, I love you very much. I want to be with you all my life. I like your eyes and your lips the most. You are the best gift ever. I want to kiss you all the time. I wish this school never ends. We will sit, holding hands, reading romantic books in the library.'

'Gosh, why did he write all this when he had said this to me already?' I said to Granny, and she laughed.

I was trying to sleep but couldn't, so I looked at the ceiling and thought of all that had happened yesterday and today. I had become something of a silly poet and made a poem, which is as follows:

> He is now into other girls,
> And not this one who has curls,
> I didn't shout; there was a sigh,
> He hung up on me before goodbye,
> Don't worry, Mahi, things will be fine.
>
> You could have got the card but missed the train,
> Mom caught it, for you were late again.

She yelled and did all she could do
And threw you out after 1 before 2.
Let her get angry, Mahi, things will be fine.

So what if Granny came jumping and laughing,
While you were decently walking
All seems too heavy and messed up,
Strong you are and sure will perk up,
It's no big deal, Mahi, things will be fine.

This would go on and on,
You might need to get rid of the moron.
Part of your life which doesn't say,
Remember:
Karan is there for you every day
So stay happy, Mahi, things will be fine.

I lay on my stomach, looked at the right side of the room at the window, and murmured, 'Karaaaaaaan, did I tell you that you make me feel needed? Yeah? I know you do,' I said to myself and slept.

EIGHT

It was 10 p.m., and the competition was over, and the anchor came in with an envelope that had the winner's name on it. He stood on the stage to announce the winner's name. He began, 'The title The Handsomest goes to . . . ,' and stopped for people to guess who it was supposed to be. People shouted their favourite's name and hooted. I was excited to face the surprise, but something inside me had already told me who the winner was.

After guesses, the anchor was finally about to make the announcement. And in one go, he continued, 'The title The Handsomest goes to Karan Kumar.' I shouted on top of my voice, standing on the table, dancing in different yet funny ways in excitement. People who were supporting him also cheered for him with our mates who couldn't stop hugging people whom they didn't even know before. And the noise ceded when the anchor muttered, 'Sshh.'

I could see Karan smile at me, wearing the winner's banner that had HANDSOMEST written on it in bold letters; I was waiting for the next moment, which was, as promised by them, a chance to meet John

Abraham and get a Polaroid with him. John Abraham never came, and, instead, I saw the most sensational Yuvraj Singh going on the stage to congratulate the winner, who was, fortunately, my best friend Karan.

They both shook hands, and Karan took the mike in his hand and said that he would like to dedicate this moment to me and invited me on the stage. I had forgotten how to walk; therefore, I went jumping and jiggling like Karan usually did. Karan waited for me to give him a hug, but I was so lost in thoughts after seeing Yuvraj Singh live in front of me that I ignored him and went towards Yuvraj.

'I love you, Yuvi. Please marry me,' I began. Yuvraj smiled at me. I got motivated and continued with my speech. 'I am not one of your big fans. In fact, I am your biggest fan. Please marry me! I am a true fan of yours because I always cheer for you. Even if you don't score well, I wish you luck and never hate you. People like you only when you play well. I am like someone who is with you during good as well as bad.'

'What?' he asked.

'I love you. Please marry me.'

'I can't hear you,' he said, and I soon realised that my voice was not coming out of my mouth and only my lips were moving.

I was so nervous that I started sweating too much. My face was wet as if it were raining. I was completely wet till my stomach. My hair was all wet, making me untidy. I was also irritated and felt as if I had lost the golden chance of proposing to Yuvraj Singh. Who knows if I would ever meet him again? All I knew was that I was busy scratching my scalp.

I sat on the stage, hiding my face and crying loudly with my eyes closed, because I couldn't bear this loss. I could hear the noise of furniture being dragged, and soon I found that my pillow was wet too. As I opened my eyes, I saw our maid Basanti cleaning the floor of my room; I was lying half dead on the bed. 'It was a good dream until Yuvraj couldn't understand what I meant to say,' I thought. Basanti had switched off the fan so that she could easily clean the floor, and this made me sweat so much.

Mom brought me breakfast and asked if I was feeling better. I apologised to her and told her that I shouldn't have been rude to her. I had thought I would make her happy, for she was my mother. Though I didn't misbehave with them deliberately, it just happened. She was happy to hear me say so but was still not completely satisfied. I got my books from my room to make sure that I was almost done with the preparation. Those two hours of learning daily had helped me during this time when I was in bad health.

Granny seemed to be looking at me with worried eyes. She was a very different human being. She could be rude and scold me any time, make fun and laugh at me, tell me stories, give me suggestions, and also get troubled after seeing me ill, which I realised today. One thing I knew for sure was that she loved me the most and so did I. One part of her was religious and serious, and other was a drunkard and strange yet funny lady.

She then brought me a mug of strawberry shake; knowing that I had a bad throat, she didn't put ice in it. It changed the taste of my mouth, and I felt good. The fever had irritated me too much as it had become stubborn and hadn't left me, but I knew well how to throw it away as it was my body, my right.

She sat on the bed and suggested that we watch TV, for it might change my mood. We watched the Bollywood movie *Dil Chahta Hai*, which was our favourite; my Granny had fallen in love with the actor Aamir Khan. And what a great title song it had! Granny kept on singing the song for the entire day whenever she saw the movie.

In the afternoon, I got a call from Rasheen, telling me that Sagar and Latika both didn't come to school that day. I was worried, for I hadn't spoken to him after the argument.

I tried calling the number Sagar used to call me from. Nobody answered the phone. That made me curious to know what could be the situation. I kept on looking here and there, and negative thoughts emerged in my mind—like maybe I wouldn't get a chance to talk to him ever, or maybe he had broken up with me. I couldn't concentrate on the present; my mind went back, thinking about him.

After many days, Granny allowed me to go to school, for I had to write my first exam. I was still feeling weak, but it had already been many days and I couldn't attend revision classes. I was allowed to go to school, and also Granny asked me to call her up once from school, telling her whether or not I was feeling healthy. I had thought that I would talk to Sagar and clear all the differences, for the time I had spent with him meant a lot to me. It seemed to me as if we had been together for the last few years.

Before leaving for school, I dialled the same number to inform Sagar that I was coming, and there was still no response. I left for school. On my way, I kept on thinking positively. Coincidentally, I met Rasheen at the school gate and called her name, and she came running to me and hugged me tight and told me how happy she felt to see me back. We walked together to our class; we reached fifteen minutes before the morning assembly.

I looked for Sagar but couldn't find him anywhere. Latika was also missing. I wasn't linking Sagar's absence with Latika but was worried. I asked Rasheen if she knew anything about Sagar. 'He was seen on last Saturday,' she replied. It was already the next Wednesday, which meant that he hadn't come to school for three days now.

They all went out for prayer, and Soni sat next to me as she was told by our teacher, for I might need some help.

'What happened, Mahi?' Soni asked. She seemed to be worried; after all, she was another true friend. I managed to tell Soni that I hadn't been able to talk to Sagar for the past couple of days and I'd heard that he hadn't been attending school. My mind was restless and needed some answers urgently.

'That boy isn't meant for you, Mahi. The entire week on your absence, there were rumours about Latika and Sagar spending time alone in the hall behind the basketball court and were caught kissing by Newspaper.' I refused to agree with Soni. 'Whatever, Mahi, after seeing him behave close and personal with Latika, I know that he isn't a loyal boyfriend. Dump him,' she said.

'Welcome back, Mahi. How are you feeling?' asked Newspaper before the start of exam.
'I am fine. How are you?' I asked.
'Mahi, you are a pearl and stay that way,' said Soni, supporting me.
'I am sorry to have hurt you ever, Mahi. I am a changed girl, and I support the truth,' said Newspaper.
'She is right, Mahi. We are all with you.' I was pretty shocked to see them behave in a weird way, consoling me every now and then like people did to a lady whose husband had married another woman in her presence.

Our teacher, whom we called a 'goat', came and distributed sheets and question papers. Sagar and Latika did come for the exam. 'Hi, Sagar,' I said, smiling at him. He looked at me but didn't answer. I smiled at him again and moved my lips to say 'I love you', but he didn't acknowledge.

It was a two-hour exam; we had begun writing, and others discussed with the teacher what our plans were for the last exam day before holidays. After the exam, I realised that I had left a question while I was busy thinking why Sagar hadn't replied. Nothing could be done as we had submitted the papers already, so I ignored my mistake.

I went to the kitchen to fill my sipper as I had to have my medicine. What did I hear? Newspaper came running to me, telling me that she saw

Latika and Sagar going to the terrace. I didn't want to believe her, but something inside me was curious to know what was happening. I took my medicine and went to see if this was true. The terrace door was left open. I saw Sagar. He was all well. I was happy, and then I realised that I hadn't come here to see if Sagar was in good health.

I could hear a girl voice shout, 'I love you, baby.' The girl was Latika. She came, sat next to Sagar, and kissed him. I was angry at her as he was my boyfriend. I kept watching them, and what happened next left me traumatised and embarrassed: Sagar and Latika were caressing each other's bodies, kissing wildly. The minute I saw Sagar kissing her, I was dead at heart. I didn't know what to do. I kept on telling myself that Sagar loved me and he was just being physical with her. I was hurt.

I then heard Sagar say to Latika that he loved her the most, for she was the most beautiful girl he had ever met, and this left me amazed and humiliated. A part of me refused to accept the reality, but I had to. I couldn't control my tears, so I went running to Sagar and hit him many times on his chest, crying louder and louder. Latika disappeared, and all Sagar said to me was sorry many times. I asked Sagar to go away before I pushed him from the terrace and went to jail after murdering him.

I was badly hurt but brave enough to take it. I myself had become a rich loser by letting people hurt my feelings, leaving me crying. I was never like this before; something had gone wrong inside of me. I was braver than this before. I never cried, not after things like these—arguing, getting hurt, and so on. I cried only when I was alone in my room, thinking about me and my life.

Irritation from arguments and fights led to this. I wanted to get rid of this, so later I consoled myself by saying, 'Let go, Mahi. Sagar is an unimaginable bastard.' I controlled my pain and went to the classroom, telling myself that Karan loved me so much.

I had to write the second exam. The same teacher came in, and I waited for the exam to end soon as I had become weaker after seeing what had happened. I kept on writing fast and wrote whatever came to my mind without thinking whether I was writing right or not. I had to get rid of this exam as I was crying inside, badly hurt. After writing the exam hurriedly, I quickly submitted the answer sheet and asked our teacher to send me home as I wasn't keeping well. She went to our class teacher and came back with his permission.

Rasheen dialled Granny's number from our school office and asked her to send the driver, for I was feeling weak. Some fifteen minutes after the exam, she dropped me at the school gate and said that she would call me in the evening, and I left for home.

Granny received me at the main gate and asked me to give her my school bag. I refused, for I wasn't a little kid. I went to her room and lay on the bed, wearing my school dress. Mom came running to see me. I told her I was fine and was just a little weak, adding that the exams went well. She was sent back to her room by Granny, and I was asked to change. Granny was more like a goddess who knew what was going on in my mind.

I came back to her room after changing clothes. She sat next to me and asked, 'What happened with Sagar?'
'He is an unimaginable bastard,' I replied.
She started laughing and asked, 'Who did you fight with?'
'I fought with myself today. I wouldn't go to this school ever.'
'Did you break up with him?'
'I would break him up.'
That tearing pain was provoking me beyond tolerance, and I wanted to kill them.
'Mahi, my brave girl,' she said, smiling at me to build my confidence.
I cried loudly for the next ten minutes.
She was clearly worried now and asked me what happened.

'Nothing! Just feeling weak. I think I should sleep.' I gave an excuse and kept on crying.

'I wouldn't let you till the time you tell me what happened. Did he misbehave with you? Did he try to touch you?' She started guessing. 'What happened?' she asked loudly this time.

'Leave me alone, please,' I said, and she reluctantly excused herself, leaving me to my own threat.

'I would come to see you after thirty minutes,' she said irately.

I spread myself on the bed and talked loudly to myself, looking into the mirror. 'Why did I trust him? I should have known. I was blinded by his fake love. Why couldn't I understand that he was so desperate that he couldn't control his urges for a week? I should have known when he tried to touch me where he is not supposed to. And after singing my praises, he repeated the same to that bitch. All false!'

Suddenly I was transported back in time to those happy moments we shared and all that he did for me—from bringing me food from the canteen to throwing chits with 'What's up?' and 'Love you' written on them. I again realised that it was all false. And I started talking again, 'He wasn't bad, but I was being extra nice to him. He was simply passing his time and wasting my time. I was another name on the list of girls he wanted to flirt with and kiss. Because of him, I have ruined my image at home. I hated my mom when she scolded me because of that bloody card he had given to me. It wasn't love. Granny was right.'

It seemed like a truck hitting a man riding his bike to get his concentration back to his life. My false first love life had come to an end. I was feeling light after I brought this entire stuff out. There was still something missing, and I yelled, 'A day would come when I would kick you hard in between your legs, and you wouldn't dare to do this to any other good girl. And to you bitch, I'll make your life hell. It could be any time when I will be in a mood to run the truck over you. Sagar, you never had a right to take advantage of my trust. I am coming after you, loser.'

'A rich loser,' Granny corrected me, for she was hiding behind the door as she was unwilling to leave me. 'You talked so well. I was enjoying your confidence. Hope you are feeling light now,' she said.

'Yes,' I said.

'Tell me what happened exactly.' I told her the entire story with all the scenes. She asked me to go to school as there was no reason for me to leave the school. Instead, he should leave as I was an old-timer.

It was during the morning of our last day at school when I put a stop to my scattering thoughts and got off the bed to go to school. I had spent the last two days thinking about all this, for I still wanted some time, but I was now completely out of the stress that I had in my mind for being ditched so badly. Ignoring them all, I got ready, and, despite not wasting time, I reached late to school after the prayer.

I was sent to my class without questioning much for the gatekeeper knew that I wasn't feeling well the day before, which was why I had gone early and also hadn't come yesterday for revision.

'May I come in?' I asked my class teacher for his permission. I could see my peers look at me with a smile and a happy look on their face. I could also see someone was not ready to face me. I ignored her and looked at my class teacher, wishing him good morning. He stood from his chair, looked at me, smiled, and said, 'What a style, Mahi Arora! Late on the first day of the session, as well as the last day!' he said in a taunting tone. The class started laughing.

'Not like that,' I apologised.

'Please take your seat. You knew too well that teachers don't teach on the last day of examination. That's why you didn't miss school,' he said. I bowed my head, for he had started his jokes, and he continued, 'Just joking.' I always laughed at his style of saying this.

I said hello to my friends and took my seat while the teacher was distributing answer sheets and question papers. The entire class was busy discussing the exam, and also my group that had me sitting only physically with them. The exam started, and I wrote well, looking here and there to see if he had come. I solved the paper confidently as I had practised maths well, though I left two questions out of eight; 'I will cover it up later,' I promised myself. I was feeling better as the exam came to an end.

Much later, I excused myself, and Soni wished me all the best as she knew what was I about to do.

'Go, fight, Mahi,' said Rasheen. I looked at her, and she was eager to watch what was about to happen.

'Latika, I want to talk to you. Step out of the class.' My hatred made the words sound deadlier than they were intended to. I could see fear in her eyes, for she had thought I would never come to know about their love story.

'I think you are mistaken, Mahi,' she said, fumbling.

'Oh, shut the fuck up,' I shouted. Rasheen and Soni could not control their curiosity to know what was happening, so they went to the laboratory through the door behind and observed the scene from the window, making sure that I didn't see them doing so, but I did.

'Let's not waste time and get to the point. Why did you kiss Sagar, knowing that we were together?' I asked.

'He wanted to kiss me,' she said proudly.

'You don't know what's going inside me,' I exclaimed, asking her not to be so confident of her smartness.

'I am better at it than you, and he knew that always,' she said.

'Ask me to pull your hair. Will you?' I shouted. She got scared and moved away to save herself.

'I saw everything. You seemed to be very desperate,' I said.

'I didn't rape your boyfriend,' she replied.

'Go rape him, for I don't care,' I said and pulled her hair hard.

She was about to cry but seemed eager to confront me and asked, 'Why are you blaming me? I kissed him, but I wasn't aware that Newspaper would tell everyone and spoil my respect,' she said.

'What respect are you talking about?' I said rudely.

'I am a girl,' she said.

I pulled her hair, this time harder than before, and said, 'You spoke nonsense about me in the school. You don't say that you are the only girl who deserves respect.'

'I would complain to the principal that you raised your hand on me,' she said.

'I haven't as yet, and what would you give him as reason?' I asked.

'I am not scared of you,' said she.

'Ask me to pull your hair,' I said boldly. She moved a step away.

'If you had told me that you were dating, I wouldn't have questioned you. I never liked bad surprises.' I pulled her hair harder than before and said, 'You didn't because you are a loser.'

'A rich loser.' I heard Rasheen say and get inside the class with Soni, laughing, for the scene had ended.

I walked inside the class as the last exam was about to begin. Madam Shanta came, distributed sheets and question papers, and did other formalities like signing the sheets. Looking at the question paper with concentration, we started writing the exam as we couldn't dare to look elsewhere in her presence.

A few classmates cheated after they realised Madam Shanta seemed to be surprisingly in a good mood. She also smiled at us after the exam while going out of the class. 'Is she a changed lady now?' we questioned ourselves and reminded each other that she did such things once in a blue moon; otherwise, she was the same cruel giant.

Amaar asked me if I would like to drink. I was surprised and asked how and where in the class. He asked me to say either yes or no. I was not in a mood to get back to those silly thoughts, so I agreed. Rasheen jumped like a kid on his birthday celebration. I could see Sagar hiding his presence from me. I looked at him with eyes full of hatred and anger.

The way Sagar behaved clearly explained that he knew that I wanted to kill him, but his carelessness irritated me, and I wanted to confront him. He should have told me that he wanted another girl as he couldn't control his desperation, and I might have not felt so bad.

He was involving himself with the other mates forcefully, for he didn't want me to think that he was left alone. I wanted to kick his balls, and soon I realised that he didn't have any as he kept on running away from me. I had to control my urges, for I thought I should not waste this day with such a loser.

Abhi, who was another friend from the group, asked him to join us. Amaar interrupted him and said loudly that he didn't want Sagar to be a part of our group, for he was intelligent enough to guess that we weren't together, no matter why. I felt good as I was the first priority. It was expected, for we had spent enough time talking and making fun together in school. Amaar smiled at me.

Rasheen didn't know I was looking at him; she pointed to Sagar and said loudly, 'What a loser!'

'A rich loser,' I corrected, and we started planning our last day.

The bell rang, and we all went out to the canteen as it was recess. We were seven in total. Amaar started buying food from the canteen for our party had to begin. He bought a big tray of nuggets, around ten pastries, ten burgers, French fries, and ten bread rolls. Rasheen was with Amaar and Abhi, collecting the food. I walked up to them, laughing, and asked if we were going for a picnic to a destination that was far away, for the food seemed so much.

I asked Rishabh about the drinks. He opened his bag, and I saw a bottle of vodka. Amaar asked us to get into the school bus parked behind the school building at the burial ground. It was the place where I had lost Rasheen in my dream where I saw Madam Shanta dragging a dead body. I refused to go there, for I didn't want that scary dream to come true. 'Who parties in burial grounds?' I yelled at Amaar.

'Let's experience this exciting activity,' said Rishabh, who was the first person to shit in pants if things went wrong.

'I have seen Madam Shanta visit that place, for she lives nearby,' I said to them.

'Is the plan cancelled?' confirmed Rasheen.

'No way,' I said.

'I hope we aren't partying in the washroom?' said Soni mockingly. Maria and Abhi seemed to be looking at us with eagerness.

We held the eatables, and I walked, followed by them to the school terrace. I opened the last door and asked them to get inside quietly, and I locked the door from inside. 'What a place! Have you come here before?' asked Amaar.

'Yes, a few times,' I replied, and Rasheen smiled at me. We sat down, made a circle, and pulled out the food on paper plates.

We could hear the bell ring. Rishabh looked at me and said with a sad voice, 'The party ended before it could begin.' Soni pulled him by his pants and asked him to sit. He looked at us, and I announced that we would go downstairs at the last bell when the day would end, which was after some two hours. They were all happy except Rishabh.

I looked at him and said, 'You wanted to party at the burial ground, and now when asked to bunk, you have started shitting. What a brave boy!' I said sarcastically. He made faces and started having food with us.

Soni poured vodka in glasses, and Amaar added cold drink. I praised him, and we started having the food. I took a sip of vodka from Rasheen's glass as I couldn't afford to vomit and fall ill again as I didn't like it much. But I ate like Amaar, as if we'd been hungry for ages. Rasheen and I fought for bread rolls like we always did. Soni alone ate four pastries. Seeing this, I reminded her that we also had nuggets, so she could try them too. Maria took an hour to finish a burger, and her glass of vodka was emptied by Amaar, for he had lost his patience to see her hold the can for an hour. Abhi seemed to have emptied the nugget tray with Amaar, leaving a few for me. Rishabh seemed to have tasted all that we had bought except the paper plates. The food that I thought was more than enough seemed to have finished.

I could see Rishabh put the empty vodka bottle and the foil paper with used paper plates in his bag, for there was no dustbin. I asked him to keep the vodka bottle and the waste out, for it was needed as it was our last day and some mischief had to be done.

It was time we went downstairs, and the minute we entered the corridor, the bell rang. We took our bags, bid goodbye to the class, and walked outside together. I asked if they were ready to enjoy some fun. 'What?' they questioned me, and I told them that we would go to Madam Shanta's place, which was behind the burial ground. Rishabh and Maria refused, and I went, accompanied by Soni, Amaar, and Rasheen. Soni asked what we were supposed to do, and I asked her to wait and watch.

We reached outside the small house she lived in. 'It is much scarier than she herself,' said Rasheen to me.

On a piece of paper, I wrote, 'Hate you, giant. We partied today.' I kept those paper plates with foil and other waste at the door. Also I wrote, 'If you are so frustrated in your life, hit hard on your head with these bottles and you will feel good,' and I left the bottles there with the waste. We fixed the paper on her door and ran from there.

We came back laughing, holding our stomachs, appreciating our guts. 'Mahi, your ideas are brilliant,' said Soni, praising me.

'Buy me a phone,' I said mockingly. Rishabh came running after seeing us laugh so much. We bid goodbye to each other. Rasheen said that she would be coming to stay at my place, so she ran to her hostel and brought her bag that Rishabh was ordered to pick up.

Rishabh, Rasheen, and I went back home in the same auto, discussing the competition day and met Adhiraaj on our way. He had come to buy drinks for Karan and himself, for they were to watch a football match together. He gave me two cans of beer as a gift with a pen drive that had something I had asked for.

Rasheen told him that she was going to stay at my place as if he were interested in taking her out that night. Adhiraaj asked her to quit the hostel and give the hostel fee to me as she spent most of her time living in my house. She laughed because Adhiraaj had said it; if somebody else had said it, she would have killed the person.

The night before vacations, after having dinner, we were in my room, talking about Karan and Adhiraaj. Suddenly I reminded myself about the beer cans that were kept in my school bag. I took them out and went to Granny's room. She was sleeping, and I put them on her table and came back to my room.

On my study table, I saw a packet kept. I opened it, and it was a brand new mobile phone that Granny had promised to get for me. What a relationship it was! I had just kept the beer cans as a surprise for her, and a surprise from her was waiting for me too.

I didn't have a mobile but had a SIM card that I used in Rasheen's mobile. It was a good phone with a camera and MP3. I quickly opened the box, put in the battery and the SIM card, and switched it on. 'How did she know I wanted this phone?' This was the latest model in market. I was very happy and so was Rasheen, who kept on exploring the menu.

While we were on the bed at our respective sides, Rasheen asked me why Adhiraaj give me a pen drive and what it had. I quickly got up and switched on the laptop. I told her, 'This has porn, and let's watch it.' We saw the video with eyes wide open, looking at each other; we were surprised on seeing things we had never seen before. The girl wore sexy lingerie, which prompted me to buy one for myself. It was good as I wanted the one which had kisses too.

We watched it twice with eagerness, our hearts beating fast. The sounds they made were funny and also terrible. We were becoming aware about sex and became more curious. After it ended, Rasheen discussed the scenes, asking me if that was how it was done, and I told her to ask Karan as I had never tried these things except kisses.

NINE

It was the second week of our vacations, and things were better in my life. I had forgotten those days with Sagar, and he had become my ex-boyfriend now. My terms with Mom were good as I told her the truth about me and Sagar. She appreciated it when I told her the truth, but there was something that prevented me from sharing each and everything with Mom yet; I would tell her only when I was caught.

Granny came to my room, woke me up, and thanked me for the beer cans I had kept in her room. I hugged her tight and thanked her for the mobile phone she had bought me. I got off the bed and went to brush my teeth, for I was so excited about the mobile phone that I finally owned. The first message I sent was to Granny, thanking her. I already had, but this was a special way. I wrote, 'The first text message from my personal mobile. With you, Granny, now and always. Love.'

The first call from my mobile would be to Karan. I dialled his number, and he picked up the phone.

'Hello.'

I whistled.

'Mahi?'

'Goal,' I shouted.

'What's up, my first love?'

'Stop lying. Madrid is your first love.'

'Oh yes, my bub!'

'Granny bought me a mobile phone,' I said in excitement.

'Wow! Ask her to buy me one too.'

'This is the first call. And I made it to you,' I said happily.

'Who else could be so unlucky as me?' he said, teasing me.

'You don't seem to remember what I did to you last time when you said this,' I said calmly. I had bitten his small finger badly.

'You're the precious girl in my awesome world,' he said lovingly.

'Shut up! How is the preparation going on?'

'I am not getting married so early,' he said mockingly.

'Preparation for the competition, Karan,' I said, trying not to get irritated.

'I have been shortlisted. The second mail was sent much before. Entries are now closed, but I still haven't heard from them.'

'Did you contact them?'

'No.'

'Let's go to their office and check.'

'What time today?' he asked.

'Evening around five,' I confirmed.

'Sorted. See you then.'

'Bye,' I said and disconnected the call.

Dad called me to his room for something I never liked—his irritating lectures. After talking to Dad about my studies, I went to wake Rasheen and asked her to come for breakfast in the living room quickly. Our cook made food only for those three and a half members of our family that included my granddad, my parents, and my brother. Mostly, Granny cooked food for me and herself. We did love a few dishes he was best at. Granny had made Singapore noodles for me for breakfast.

After breakfast, I told Rasheen that we had to meet Karan in the evening. 'Is Adhiraaj coming?' she confirmed.

'No, Karan alone,' I replied.

'I would stay home and watch some movie with Granny,' she said. I didn't like the way she refused and ignored her attitude.

'What are you meeting up for?' she asked.

'That's none of your business,' I said indecently.

Granny asked me why Dad had called me, and I told her that I was asked about my future plans and I had answered, 'Biggest earner.' She laughed and said to me that I didn't need to earn, for she had a lot of property on her name, which would be all mine.

I was happy to know that and expressed myself. 'All that I need is love, for I am one of the richest.'

'You can marry Karan. I like him the most amongst your friends,' said Granny, taunting me.

Also she asked me if I would like to go to Delhi with her to meet her younger sister and told me that Roop had come from London. Roop is my second cousin, who is my granny's elder sister's granddaughter as Granny's sister was married to Granddad's brother. She had come for shopping and for vacations. I was very excited and agreed to it, for there wasn't a better option to spend my vacations.

I lay down on my back on the couch while Granny went on forcing me to date Karan and ended up asking me to invite him for dinner some day. 'What day?' I confirmed.

And she told me, 'When there is nobody at home.'

'Who would Karan enjoy with if there is nobody?' I laughed, and she laughed too.

Granddad, Arhaan, Mom, and Dad were to go out of station in the next few months to attend a wedding of a relative's son and would come after a week.

I was happy to hear that and told her, 'That is the future. We should concentrate on our present.'

'Let me know all that he likes to eat so that I can prepare a good dinner. After all, he could be the son-in-law of our family,' she said and laughed.

'Why don't you marry him?' I asked.

'How can I marry him if I love someone else?' she said and left the room.

'I hope that man wouldn't take a share from your property which is supposed to be all mine,' I said loudly to make fun of her as she did of me, and I could hear her laugh loudly after listening to me.

It was 5 p.m., and I was ready to meet Karan. I got a call from him, asking me to come out, for he was waiting for me. Before stepping out of the house, I went to inform Granny that I was leaving. She followed me till the road where Karan was waiting in his car, so I had to introduce her to Karan. After exchanging hellos and goodbyes, we left. We talked on the way, for the office was at a distance of five kilometres.

'How are your dreams?' asked Karan.

I laughed and told him about the dream I had about this competition that Karan had won and also that instead of John Abraham, it was Yuvraj Singh on stage, and I said so many good things to him and later realised that my voice wasn't audible.

He laughed louder and louder.

I knew it was funny but still asked him not to make fun of me.

'Bub, you and your Yuvraj Singh imaginative love story will never have an end.'

'It's not supposed to,' I said, and we had reached the office.

As we entered the office, we saw a big man sitting at the enquiry window. Karan went to him, and I sat at one of the desks, reading a magazine. After some good thirty minutes, he came back, controlling his laughter, and told me that the competition was over already.

'What? I wanted you to win, Karan,' I said inflexibly.

'Your friend didn't lose. Just his email was left unsent,' said the man who was at the window before and now out of his cabin. I looked at Karan and asked him not to laugh so much.

'It will take place next year, and make sure you have a good Internet connection by then,' he said.

'You don't have to make fun of us,' I said rudely and threw the magazine that I was reading on the table and left with Karan.

I got inside the car and closed the door in anger. Karan seemed to be enjoying my irritation so much that he didn't even bother to talk himself. I could see him laugh at my expression while driving the car. He placed his mobile at the front and took a photograph of us enjoying our own mood. I could see him make fun of me.

'Shut up, Karan,' I said.

'I didn't say anything, bub,' he said politely.

'Stop laughing. Don't you know how much I wanted to enjoy you win this competition, which will now take place next year?' I said, irritated.

'Come on! What if it's cancelled? We can plan something at your farmhouse.'

I looked at him, feeling bad at his carelessness for not checking his mail outbox.

'What happened to you, bub?' he confirmed as I had argued with the man inside the office. I could see him control his laughter.

I kept quiet on the way, and, after about ten minutes, I started laughing loudly. Karan asked me the reason, and I kept on laughing after stopping for every five seconds. 'What a careless bastard you are, Karan!'

'I don't know,' he replied.

I recalled the way I felt and started laughing at myself. 'I know that I wanted you to get me the banner, but winning this silly competition is no big thing to prove that you are handsome. I know you are. You know that you are, and all those girls who want to date you know this.'

'You wanted the banner, and I will get it for you,' he said.

'Where from?'

'Some tailor,' he said, and we laughed.

What happened to me? Why was I behaving like Rasheen? I could have not argued stupidly without a sensible reason.

'You had already seen me win in your dream,' he said, reminding me.

'Let's not deteriorate the plan. I wouldn't tell at home that the competition is cancelled, for they might not allow me to go out in late evening and come back home the next day. Granny wouldn't refuse to let us stay at the farmhouse. We will party,' I said and asked him to inform our other friends.

'I am now taking you to Muffin World,' Karan announced. It was the best bakery shop in the city.

'Thank you, prep, my boy,' I said as I had given him this name.

'You can give me a kiss sometimes,' he said, making me laugh.

Muffin World was owned by a cheerful man named David. He was short with a big tummy and fluffy cheeks. He looked extremely cute and was always very kind to us, for we were his regular customers. He was the first one to ask us if we were dating. Like I told you before, Karan and I were so close that people said so. He was the best baker in the city. The pudding he made especially for me, mentioning Karan's name with jelly to tease me, was the best in the world. David was like our close friend.

We sat and enjoyed pudding and talked about each other's life. I told him about Sagar's story, and he appreciated me for having taken the right decision. Also, he enjoyed listening when I told him what I had done to Latika. He then told me that he had already told Mahima that he didn't want to be with her any more, for she irritated him all the time and didn't let him live.

Changing the topic, we decided to contribute, buy drinks, and enjoy a night at the farmhouse. The six of us were to be a part of it, which included Rasheen, Karan, Adhiraaj, Nayan, Rishabh, and me.

'Anybody else?' I confirmed, kidding.

'Yes, Yuvraj Singh,' he said.

'Too much of happiness,' I said, smiling.

'Too much of imagination,' he replied mockingly.

I walked out of the shop, biding goodbye to David, and Karan stood there, talking with him. I waited near his car, and an unknown voice broke my chain of thoughts. It was Mahima, Karan's girlfriend of that age. 'Hello,' she said in a weird tone, and I replied.

She stared at me thrice from head to toe and said, 'I like your shoes.'

'Thank you,' I replied to her.

Karan had come out of the shop after seeing her talking to me.

'What are you both doing here?' she asked rudely.

'I was teaching Mahi how to kiss as she will soon have a boyfriend,' replied Karan, and I controlled my laughter.

'What happened, baby? Why are you talking rude?' she asked Karan.

'You idiot, what can we do at a bakery shop?' replied Karan and continued, 'How many times do I have to request to leave me and find your own way? We are two completely different people and can't be together. I never believed Adhiraaj when he told me that Mahima was a torture and hated everyone.'

She had tears in her eyes and had to be taken care of. She said that she wanted to talk to me. I waited for her to initiate the conversation, but she stood mutely.

I said, 'Things will be fine. It's just that Karan likes independence and doesn't like to be questioned unnecessarily, just like me. He would respect you if you respect his way of living. If you would fight and argue with him each time when he would want to do things that he loves, he wouldn't like it. You need to give him some space instead of asking him unwanted questions all the time.' I explained to her politely.

She wiped her tears, stared at me, and started shouting angrily, 'I am his girlfriend, and I have a right to question him as many a times as I want. I am very beautiful and can get a better boy than your friend,' she said, raising her eyebrows.

'Go get yourself a better boy than my friend,' I replied.

'You aren't in a relationship, Mahi, so wouldn't understand how it feels.' It reminded me of Sagar, and I wanted to throw her with Sagar in a gutter.

'People have boyfriends, and my friends say that I have an asshole, and I agree,' she said.

'Everyone has at least one,' I said irately, hating her for abusing my friend.

'I respect him so much,' she said.

'That's why you called him an asshole,' I said.

'Why are you getting angry, Mahi? What the hell do you do with somebody else's boyfriend? Are you dating him? I know you told him to dump me. Do you love him? I can see that in your eyes. You are so damn fake, Mahi. You tell him not to talk to me. I hate you, Mahi,' she said.

I was so irritated, for I was wiping her tears but she started screaming at me. I slapped her tight and pulled her hair tighter than Latika's and said, 'You are the bitch of the highest order. Go fuck yourself,' and pushed her away. Karan came running to me, and Mahima started crying louder to pretend whatsoever.

I turned my back to her and got into the car with Karan and shouted, 'I hope I wasn't so rude to you, Miss Psycho.' God saved Karan! On my way back home, I told Karan the entire story. He was irritated and also laughed. Adhiraaj was right; she was weird like she might have fallen from the terrace and lost all sense, for all she had was absolute nonsense.

'You were right. She is a strange question paper anyone can ever solve. She doesn't need a boyfriend. She needs a robot who would work as per the instructions given by her.'

Karan was not meant for her as he was way too far from humbug like this. Karan didn't like the way she behaved with me, for I had nothing to do with it. If I had known her, I would have interrupted them and ended their relationship much earlier as she was a total bitch. I asked Karan how it would be like if Sagar and Mahima were to date as they were both losers.

He laughed and added, 'Indeed a good match it would be.' I looked at him and smiled. 'Bub, I forgot to give you something,' he said.

'What?' I confirmed. He gave me a small packet that had something wrapped with a blue paper.

'You brought me a gift? First time in three years of friendship, I am impressed,' I said. I opened the gift to see what it had.

It was a small bagpack made of leather, and the size was 3 ′ 6 inches. 'Why did you buy this?' I asked. And he reminded me of the day when we both had fought in fun while coming out of the institute and he had caught my bag and pulled me back, tearing the bag. I had shouted at him, for it was my favourite bag, and had asked him to buy me one, and he did, though much smaller in size—3' 6 inches. I laughed and pinched him hard as he said I didn't mention the size.

He dropped me home at around 9 p.m., and Granny came to me and asked how it was. For she always wanted me to be with Karan. 'How was what?' I confirmed and explained that we didn't go for a date; instead, we had gone for work and came to know that the competition had been cancelled.

'Sad,' she said, and I asked her not to tell Dad, for we would spend a night at our farmhouse and party. She acknowledged my plan, and I went to inform the same to Rasheen, who was watching a cartoon with my brother.

I kept my mobile on the bed and went to freshen up. While I was washing my face, I heard my mobile ring. 'It might be Karan,' I said to myself, for he was rarely at the right hour.

'I am coming to you, Karan,' I said and went to answer it, and by that time, it was disconnected. Then I thought I would speak to him once I was totally free.

Granny came to me with strawberry shake after I was done freshening up. The phone rang again, and she told me that it might be Karan. I asked her to read the number, and she told me that the last three digits were 678, which wasn't him. It reminded me that this was the same number where I got stupid good morning and goodnight messages from, and I answered it.

'Hello,' I said.
'Is it Mahi?'
'Who else could it be, moron?' I said for he had already irritated me by sending stupid texts.
'Hello, Mahi, I am Lallan Baabu. Remember?'
'Who the hell?' I enquired.
'Yes, I am the one.' He stopped for five seconds after his silly reply, thinking I might say hurray!
I ignored his stupid reply and said, 'What do you want?'
'Your love! Forever.'
'Fuck you, bastard.'
'Please I would love it.'
'You motherfucker, who the hell are you?'
'I don't have a mother. Yes, I am the one.'
'I don't know you, asshole. Don't you dare call me again.'
'You can know me now. I have given divorce to my wives.'
'Wives? Do you even know who are you talking to?'
'Yes, Mahi you are, I know.'
I got irritated and disconnected the call.

The phone rang again, and I answered it.

'You don't know how hard you would get hurt if I use my knee.'
'Why? You don't have hands?'
'Unlike you, I do, you son of a bitch.'
'I have four hands. Two mine and two yours because you are all mine.'
'What a stubborn rascal!'
'I know, bub. Oops!'
'Karan,' I yelled. 'What the hell are you up to and what the hell is this "Lallan Baabu"?'
'I wanted to have some fun.'
'I would throw you in crocodile's mouth. Get it?'
'Why do you talk to strangers, Mahi? You should have disconnected the call.'
'Are you my boyfriend?'
'No, but you are my girlfriend, and everybody says that.'
'Shut up!'
'I love you, bub,' he said in the weird voice he used when he spoke as Lallan Baabu.
'I love you too, prep.'
'Get lost then,' he said and disconnected the call.

Granny quietly put the glass on the table and said, 'Enjoy strawberry shake', and walked out of the room, leaving me alone for that time.

'Granny,' I called her, and she asked me if I needed something else to eat, pretending innocence. I showed her the gift that Karan gave me; she liked it very much for she liked Karan more than I liked him.

'Such a sweet present he has given you,' she said and got up to go out.

I interrupted her and said, 'I don't mind if you listen to my conversation with whosoever as we are buddies for life.' She was embarrassed to have been caught and smiled and left my room.

Granny had the bigger room, and I was given the other one which was joined with the attic. We always remained connected, for she didn't want me to stay far from her; therefore, our rooms were next to each other. The rest of the family lived on the ground floor. My study room was on the ground floor, next to Mom's room, where I kept my books and school bag. After the card incident, I had brought all my stuff to my room, including the study table.

TEN

I was sleeping peacefully; my mind was without trouble. My life was rolling well and happily reminding me of my family that also included Karan and Rasheen. I didn't have to make an effort to fall asleep like I did the other day when I argued and fought with that rich loser Sagar. I was happy now that it had all ended soon and was ready to go on with my life, spending time with people that meant a lot to me.

The cool air from the window opened my eyes, and I closed my eyes again. My thoughts scattered, and I slept back. Suddenly Rasheen closed the window and woke me up, reminding me that she had to leave for Shillong this evening with her cousin, so she had to go back to her hostel and do the rest of the packing.

I was still in bed, not ready to get up. She stood staring at me as I was in no mood to drop her till the main road. I gave her a high five and bid her goodbye, wishing her a happy journey, and I excitedly informed her that I was leaving for Delhi with Granny tomorrow evening. She then told me that she had heard Granny say that the train tickets weren't available and maybe the plan was cancelled. That woke me up completely, and I ran to Granny, followed by Rasheen, and asked if this was true. She told me that she already had the tickets in her purse. I looked at Rasheen, and she told me that she had said this to wake me up and drop her till the main road.

I then went to drop Rasheen till the main road. She hugged me and was sad as we were to meet only when our school reopened.

After having lunch, Granny and I helped each other in packing our bags. I was in my room with Granny when my mom came and started her favourite thing, interrupting in my life. She didn't want me to go to Delhi and rather wanted me to prepare well for my final exams, which were to take place after months. A part of my life that included only my parents was very irritating. So I wanted to run away from home. I was not patient, which was why I didn't like their suggestions repeated n times, and their zillion questions and comparisons with other kids told me again and again that I was a loser.

They expected so much from me, which I never liked, and I ended up arguing and crying after getting irritated. I also asked Granny if we could live in a separate flat; she laughed. I had thought I would definitely go with Granny, no matter how many times I had to face their instructions. Granny had explained well to Mom about what I should do, and then she couldn't argue. So I was going.

My packing was all done. She asked me if I could get her shirts from the boutique she had given for stitching, and I agreed. Later, I called Karan and asked if he could visit the market with me. He agreed and came to pick me up on his bike. I took my wallet with some money, including the Rs. 1,000 that I managed to get from Dad when Real Madrid won the match. I sat behind him, waving at Granny, who was peeping from the window, and headed towards the market.

It was a spacious boutique with a huge coloured banner announcing 'Ladies Palace'. Karan waited for me outside the showroom, and I went inside, looking for someone to ask about the shirts as I had forgotten the billing slip Granny had given me.

'How may I help you?' asked a fat man who was sitting at the billing counter. I told him that I had come to take Granny's shirts. He asked me about the bill slip. I had forgotten it at home, and he refused to give the shirts without it. I went out, told this to Karan, and dialled Granny's phone and told her the same. She asked me to hand over the phone to that man, and I did.

'Mrs Arora, how are you?' said he to her. 'Yes, sure, and of course' were the three words I heard him say with courtesy. Later, he asked me if I was Mahi and called Karan from outside and made us sit on a sofa. He asked a boy to get cold coffee for us. Karan and I smiled at each other, thinking about Granny's reputation.

I could see a blue-coloured shirt hang on the hanger and asked if this was Granny's as we both liked the colour blue a lot. He said that she liked this very much and wanted to buy this but didn't. I asked Karan if he liked it so that I could give this as a birthday present. It had been six months almost and I hadn't given her a birthday gift. He agreed, and I asked the man to get it packed.

The man was the owner of this ladies' boutique and sat next to us, vomiting good points about his boutique collection. After seeing that we were ignoring him, he started telling us that he had heard about me many times from Granny and also that I had a best friend named Karan. Karan looked at me, surprised, and smiled. I had to tell the man that he was Karan, wondering what else Granny might have said about him.

By that time, a boy informed us that the shirts were on the table, ready. We got up and walked to the main counter. I asked him the price of the shirt I had selected for Granny. He interrupted me, telling me that he would take the money from her whenever she came next, for formality, and later added 'Rs. 1,500', which was the price. I gave him the money, and before he could continue with his stupid greetings, Karan pressed his hand and thanked him, and we went out with two bags. These shopkeepers, I tell you, criticise other showroom collections and lick your brain, forcefully telling you about their collection. It's not worth listening.

We moved towards the other side of the market when Karan stopped outside a showroom, and we got inside. He took me to the first-floor section and showed me two dresses he had chosen for me to buy. One was orange in colour, and the other was blue. I liked both and tried them. The orange dress fitted me perfectly, but the blue one was too short, so we rejected it. Later, he came with another blue dress that was more beautiful than the others. I looked perfect, wearing them, and Karan took them to the counter for billing. I was excited as Karan was buying me those beautiful dresses.

The man read the total price, and I looked at Karan, thinking he would pay for them. 'Rs. 1,800,' said Karan and asked me to pay quickly without wasting time as we also had to go and eat something.

'What? I don't have so much,' I said, and he told me that he had seen that there was money in my wallet. I refused to take the orange dress and kept the other, having no choice, and gave Rs. 999 to the man there and left with the shopping bag without complaining about what Karan had done as he was always like this when we went shopping. How I could forget? Otherwise, he was good at paying restaurant bills, yet not always.

I could see Karan laughing at me. I told him that I was going to Delhi tomorrow and wanted some money. Ignoring the money part, he asked, 'Why are you going to Delhi?' He didn't want me to. I told him that Roop had come and I would come back next week.

What time is the train?' he confirmed and told me that he would come to see me at the railway station. I asked him not to, for the train was at 10 p.m. And then we headed towards the house after a good ride on the road, discussing my life and enjoying the weather when he parked his bike and stood opposite me.

'Bub, what is wrong with you?'

'Nothing.'

'Who else would you talk to if not with me?'

'Am I a loser, Karan?'

'Who dared to say that? Of course not!'

'I don't want to talk about this. It's a bad interruption to our awesome life.'

'Your parents say all that because they want to make you better. Just deal with it.'

'By comparing me with others? I don't like it. I am not bad.'

'You're not bad, bub, just irritated. Relax and think over it from their point of view.'

'Karan, I will stop meeting you if you agree with them.'

'I am not agreeing with anybody. The truth is that I can't see you with tears in your eyes. I am just telling you a way to deal with it. You can't stay like this all your life.'

'They don't let me live freely,' I said and started crying.

'Don't cry. Face the truth.' He held me in his arms, stroked my hair, and said, 'You shouldn't get so angry on silly things like these. Be tactful, and face it with confidence. Once you develop this, nobody will be able to put you in boundaries.'

'I know that I have to study and make my career. I have a life outside this too. I love to write and read, but they don't praise me, and this bothers me.'

'Cry your heart out. You will feel light. Don't kill yourself and your likes ever. And because of this, I wouldn't let you. You don't know how amazing you are and will be. Stay that smart way you have always been. Remember, I love you.'

I was in his arms, feeling loved and needed.

While dropping me home, he asked me if I wanted to go to Delhi as he didn't. I told him that I would meet him first when I came back and gave him a flying kiss, and he left, giving a sad smile, telling me that he wouldn't come to see me if I went.

I lay on my bed, talking to Granny, and soon she excused herself after getting irritated by my endless questions, and I got back to my thoughts, remembering all that Karan had explained to me. I understood what he meant but was not so confident about myself. All I knew was that I had to get rid of this, no matter how. My life had become strange. I never got irritated, and now I rarely was calm.

I also remembered the way Karan asked me to pay at the showroom while buying those dresses, and I laughed at the situation and slept as I enjoyed sleeping.

In the evening, Mom finally confirmed if I had packed all my stuff, including daily essentials, and I nodded. I also confirmed with Granny if she had taken her beer cans, and she told me that she wouldn't drink tonight as Aunt Daisy had planned a night party already.

We were both ready and having food at the dining table when suddenly Dad interrupted, 'Why are you going with Granny?'
I looked at him, and Granny rudely asked him to concentrate on his wife as my parents loved going to dinners together without the children. Dad laughed at Granny's answer, and Granddad said that he would miss me. Granny asked me to ignore him, but I didn't and kissed him on his cheek. Arhaan walked up to me and asked me to get him a watch.

After goodbyes, we got into the car and went to the railway station. Granddad stood at the platform, waiting with us for the train when suddenly I saw Karan coming. I went running to him. He pulled my nose and told me that I was looking cute. After he saw Granny looking at us, he said hello and took me for ice cream.

While having ice cream, he told me that I looked good while wearing the orange dress, and I laughed, pushing him, remembering what had happened at the billing counter. Our train arrived, and we walked, looking for our coach, and got inside, kept our bags, and took our seats.

Before the train was about to leave, Granny also wished a true goodbye to Granddad, and I gave a flying kiss to Karan. The train started moving, and I could see Karan going far with no smile, and I shouted, 'Prep, I will see you soon. Love you.' I could see him look at me without blinking his eye. I stood at the door, looking at him. When he saw me looking at him constantly, he turned towards the exit. And the train left.

We had window seats, and it was a sleeper train. Granny and I had good time together as she told me many things, though I didn't listen to everything as I was lost thinking about Karan and kept on emptying the chips packets that Granddad had bought for me.

Granny thought of watching the movie *Batman Begins* on her laptop, and I told her that this was Karan's all-time favourite and he loved to watch it, and that brought a million-dollar smile on her face; she said that she would see this twice back to back to celebrate our togetherness. Having her around was fun; she knew well how to live every moment happily. I did too, but things had started bothering me. I had to take care of my inner peace.

I liked watching the outside view from the train. It was night, and the train crossed a few villages on the way, and I could see lamps lit in every hut, and they looked beautiful. There were little children sleeping, hugging their mothers in the bed made of wires. Karan was like my mother as I hugged him more than Granny, each time I felt a touch of emptiness. I took my mobile phone out and thought of messaging him.

Before I could write to him, I had his message, waiting to be read, 'Mahi, you shouldn't go. I don't want to miss you.'

I smiled and replied, 'I am on the train, half of the way I've crossed. Do you want me to jump now?'

I got another reply that read, 'We will jump together in some cold-water pond.' We have both been very scared of jumping in chilled water ponds, so we often thought of this.

I laughed and wrote, 'Sunshine, you keep me shining.'
He replied, 'Get lost.'

We reached Delhi railway station at 6 a.m., and Aunt Daisy's place at
7 a.m. Granny was so happy to meet her sister and much more was I to
see Roop after a year almost. At home, Granny and I were busy, talking
with our sisters, also discussing Roop's love life. Aunt Daisy kept on
pulling my cheeks as I was her favourite amongst all children. She called
me Bebu, and Granny admired the way her sister pampered me.

Roop had brought for me two dresses and a soft toy doll from
London. I simply loved them. She was my elder cousin, and every year
we met, she gave me a doll, a soft toy, without thinking whether or not
I played with them. I had collected six soft toy dolls, and this was the
seventh.

After brunch, I went to the room with Roop, and she showed me
my brother-in-law's photographs. She was engaged to him; his name was
Sukruth, and he looked good. Also, she told me that she had met him
when she had gone to the United States for a company trip. They worked
together on same project and fell in love. They were both computer
engineers. She also showed me a few photographs when she had gone to
places with him. He was a south Indian—who they say are intelligent—
and so was my dear sister, though they weren't bookworms.

She also showed me the mobile phone Sukruth had bought her on her
birthday. Though I had myself not come across true love yet, still I advised
her to get married only if it was not attraction. I only had to say this and
did not explain what true love was like. If I was asked, I would have failed
badly. I was happy to hear that she had found the love of her life.

In the evening, I went to the terrace, for I liked being there, watching
the blue sky with the mellow sun. The colours seemed beautiful. I got
involved in it when suddenly a girl from the next house on her terrace

asked if I was Mahi, and I nodded. A common wall connected both the houses, and one could talk and also jump to the other house.

Her name was Jia, and she told me that she was friends with Aunt Daisy. Jia wasn't old; Aunt Daisy had young friends. Jia was of my age, a close neighbour, which was why she knew me and that I was coming. After introductions, she invited me to see her house sometime. I smiled at her and left.

I came back to the room and was told that Granny and Aunt Daisy were going to the market to get drinks and stuff for party that was supposed to take place the day after. Roop was talking to Sukruth on the phone, and I thought of spending some time alone outside the house and watch children playing. While I sat there, adoring children shouting and playing games, fighting and arguing with their friends, it reminded me of my friends. I fought a lot with Karan and argued much with Adhiraaj as they were the only smart people amongst others.

After some time I saw Jia come out of the house with a notebook, giving directions to her house on the phone. I saw a boy coming on his scooter, and it was her classmate.

They were both in the same school, and he had come to borrow Jia's notebook. Jia walked to me with him and introduced us. We exchanged greetings, and he asked from where I was, which grade, which school, and also how my preparation was going on for high school board exams. Oh God, another idiot with study stuff. We were of the same age, and also the syllabus was same. Later, he praised me by calling me beautiful. Jia was surprised to see him talk so much to me and gave him weird looks, maybe regretting that she had introduced us. Whosoever he was, I knew I was in no mood to become friends with him.

Jia seemed to give me extra smiles and continued talking to the boy named Sam. Also she praised him, telling me that he was the best-looking boy in her school and a lot of girls would do anything to date him. I could see him smile, showing his style, which I never appreciated. He looked good, though.

After he left, Jia asked me if I would like to play badminton with her. I could see her talk decently this time without pretending much. I was tired so promised her that I would play some other day. She agreed, and we got into our houses.

I wondered why people behave strangely—like she hated me when her friend Sam praised me while talking and, at the same time, she gave me many smiles. Why do people pretend to be nice? They look better when they behave themselves whether or not good. Anyways, I was not like those girls who come between other girls' personal lives and start dating their boyfriends, so I didn't think I should think much about her and the one whom she called 'very handsome'.

By that time, Granny and Aunt Daisy had come back home, and we had dinner later.

I thought of talking to Karan, so I dialled his number.

'Hello, bub,' said he.

'What's up, prep?'

He ignored my question and asked for the third time, 'When are you coming back?'

I laughed and replied, 'After just six days.'

'Just? All right,' he said sadly and continued, 'Would you like to go on a date with me, bub?'

'Of course not. My first date would be with my first love Yuvraj Singh.'

'You aren't that beautiful,' he said, teasing me.

'And you asked me to date you.'

'Whatever,' he said rudely. 'How are Roop and Aunt Daisy?' he confirmed.

'They are fine.' I told him that Granny liked *Batman Begins* a lot and watched it twice after I told her that he liked it too.

'Wow,' he said after listening to me and continued, 'I have completely broken up with Mahima. No arguments and no cries.'

'Wow! Who's next?' I asked mockingly.

'May be Roop,' he said, kidding me.

'Roop will soon get married to Sukruth.'

'I don't mind,' he said, and we laughed.

'Rasheen might be with her family now,' I said, thinking of her.

'Ask her not to come back,' he laughed.

'Shut up! Why do you both fight so much?'

'I can't share you with anyone,' he said, joking.

'I am not a pizza that you can share.'

'You are a gourmet chocolate. I love having you . . . in my life.'

'Roop has brought me two dresses and a soft toy doll.'

'What did she bring for me?'

'You can wear the black dress as you like the colour,' I laughed.

'I miss your presence so much.'

'I'll come soon, and we will go for ice cream to the same place.'

'You remember?' he said, reminding me of the place where he fell on the dog.

I laughed and got on to the bed, talking to him. And we talked about that day and the lady on the wheelchair who shouted for help.

'I am missing you more now. Go, Mahi.'

'Goodnight, Karan.'

ELEVEN

The next evening, Granny and Aunt Daisy decorated the table on the terrace for the party that was about to take place. It included drinks and food, of course. While Granny poured beer in glasses, Roop was in her room, talking to Sukruth on the phone. I was on the terrace, playing with Aunt Daisy's puppy dog. She had bought it this week, and so the name wasn't decided, and we called him Dogie. He was the cutest creature I had ever seen.

Granny asked me to call Roop from her room. I went downstairs and asked her to join us. She asked me to start and said she would join us after twenty minutes. I informed them about this, and we began.

Aunt Daisy asked me if I was enjoying life, and Granny told her that I was very much involved in pleasant stuff. She then asked me to name the dog when I took him on my lap. I couldn't guess a name, but Granny did. 'Sagar,' she suggested and started laughing and explained to her sister who Sagar was. 'I love the puppy so much,' I replied. I hated Sagar.

'Then name him Karan,' she said, teasing me.

'There are limits to insanity, Granny,' I said and asked her not to involve Karan.

Aunt Daisy seemed to be enjoying the conversation, and Granny started praising Karan, telling her that he came to see us at the railway station. Aunt Daisy knew Karan well and had met him once before. We had started having snacks with drinks at our own speed. I was struggling with the first glass in my hand. Aunt was done with the second, and Granny had the fourth in her hand.

Aunt asked me if I talked to Karan on the phone, and I told her that we did. 'Do you both like talking to each other? Who calls?' she asked.

I told her, 'Karan calls me for long hours, and, of course, we like talking to each other. Otherwise why would we talk?'

'So dumb you are,' said Granny to her.

'Do you talk romantically?' asked Aunt Daisy, sounding curious this time. I could see Granny looking at her sister with a mischievous expression as someone else had become a part of her own acts.

'Get your mind clean. They are just friends,' replied Granny on my behalf to impress me.

And I added, 'Please don't start it again as I am in no mood.'

'What mood are you in? Would you like to talk to Karan? Use my mobile and talk for as many hours you want,' said Aunt Daisy, and they both laughed. There was nothing to laugh about.

These womenfolk talk n times more when they are drunk, especially when they are like these sisters. It had been almost an hour, and Roop was still in her room, talking to Sukruth. Granny got up and shouted to Roop, 'Come and join us quickly or else it's the last time you will be talking to Sukruth.'

I asked Granny when exactly she would learn not to poke her nose.

'I have a right over you,' she said, and I requested her to let Roop spend time alone.

'Oh, yes, when my daughter is here with me why should I be bothered about anybody else?' she said, pretending not to be bothered about Roop.

The terrace was beautiful with lots of plants. I looked around and saw a banner that read 'Let's Get Drunk'. It was hung at the entry wall that I hadn't noticed earlier. I smiled after I read it and looked at those sisters again and saw them enjoy drinking as if they hadn't had it since ages and were strictly following what the banner read. I could see some beer cans get empty. I still had three sips left in the first glass.

Now that I had a personal phone, I could secretly call Karan any time and talk to him for hours without giving explanations to anybody, especially Granny. I sat with them physically but was lost, thinking about my amazing life full of laughter and fun. I could hear the sisters talk about someone sadly. I looked at them and got involved.

'Do you remember Baldeb?' asked Aunt Daisy to Granny. He was amongst the ones who had proposed to Aunt Daisy, but she had refused.
'Of course, the unfortunate man who died before getting married. Very sad,' replied Granny.

Aunt Daisy fell off her chair after listening to this. I pulled her up and made her sit on the chair, thinking why they were talking about dead people at this crazy moment. Aunt started crying louder after listening to this. I offered her some water, but she took the beer can and started drinking in sadness.

Granny consoled her sister saying, 'Thank God, you didn't accept his proposal. Otherwise, you might have burnt yourself along with his dead body.'

I asked Granny, 'Instead of saying that he died so early, why did you say that he died before getting married?'

And she said to me, 'He didn't even have a girl in his life. He died a virgin.'

What was the connection, I didn't know. Later, Granny said, 'He didn't live his life.' he should have otherwise neither would we regret that he died without living life to the fullest nor will he be regretting in hell.

Hell? Heaven, I guessed.

Aunt Daisy seemed to have regained her courage and asked Granny in a soft voice, 'How did he die?'

'In a bike accident,' replied Granny.

'Oh my God! He loved his dog very much, and that is why they both died the same way,' said Aunt.

'When did his dog die?' asked Granny.

'I called you to tell you the other day when he died,' replied Aunt.

'But you told me that Baldeb had died,' retorted Granny.

'I told you that his dog died,' shouted Aunt Daisy. I managed to clear the confusion and explained to them that this meant Baldeb was still alive.

'The lines weren't clear,' said Granny politely to her sister after making her cry so much.

They were badly drunk, and I was full after emptying the cutlet tray. It was 2 a.m. and both the sisters planned to empty a bottle of beer together, sitting on the water tank, which was above the terrace area. This celebration was for Baldeb who was alive in real. 'Get married to Baldeb,' said Granny to her sister.

And Aunt replied, 'I think I should. He is the most loyal lover ever.'

'And so is your doggie,' I said after seeing him look at Aunt Daisy lovingly while she was crying, and they both ended up naming him Baldeb.

I went up to the area near the water tank and sat, observing their acts. Granny started drinking, leaving less than half of beer for her sister. After emptying it, Aunt Daisy took her sister to the corner of the terrace, showed her a man who was sound asleep on his bed on his terrace, and told her that he whistled when he looked at her. And she threw the empty bottle at him, which fortunately fell near his bed, not on him. His son came out, abusing and looking here and there to see who had done this, and I took them back to their rooms downstairs.

Roop came upstairs after the party was over, and I told her about the recent happening. She laughed out loud, and then we both took the things inside, and I excused myself to lie down on the grass on the terrace, watching the sky and the aeroplanes flying. Roop came to me with a floor bed, and I lay on the terrace.

I could feel the fresh air and the fragrance of the plants growing around. After staring at the sky for more than an hour, I fell sound asleep. My phone was vibrating. I could feel the vibration but didn't bother to answer it. I was enjoying my sleep when it vibrated again.

'Hello,' I said sleepily.
'Bub, when are you coming back?' I heard a manly voice ask.
'Never!' I said, getting irritated by the same question and that too when I was enjoying my sleep.
'Hope you weren't asleep,' he said.
'Of course I was.'
'Never mind. I wanted to talk to you, so I called you.'
'You wanted to talk at this time?' I asked and looked at the watch; it was 4 a.m.
'You call me a 4 a.m. friend,' he replied without thinking much.
'Always at the wrong hour,' I replied sleepily.
'I am at the right time now, bub. Get up! How you can sleep if I weep,' he said, and I woke up, worried.
'What happened, prep?' I asked.
'Kidding, bub, just learning to be a poet like you.'
'You are the best of what you are,' I said politely.
'Bub!'
'Yeah, prep.'

'I was thinking about us.'

'What, prep?'

'About you. You don't know how much I like being with you.'

'Prep, I want to be with you always.' And there was silence for a minute.

'The day you get too close, I might drive you away. It's just how it is. We get scared, panic, and react stupidly. Jungle law, I guess.'

I was quietly listening to him.

'But remember this because I am the only awesome guy who will admit to this that you are indeed precious.'

'You make my life worth a billion pounds,' I said, stretching *you*.

'I don't want to miss you,' he said, ignoring my reply.

'I do. I love you,' I said.

'Go away, Mahi.'

Call disconnected!

I was unable to sleep after talking to him, so I called him back after struggling for half an hour on the bed, looking at the sky and imagining things.

The bell rang, and he answered, 'What do you want, bub?'

'Talk to me, prep.'

'I am sleepy, bub. Can't talk.'

'You never listen to me, Karan,' I said, irritated.

'Stop getting irritated so easily. I don't like seeing you that way.'

'I never listen to you, is what I will make you say some day.'

'Ta-ta,' he said, ignoring my reply.

'Get lost! Don't call me ever,' I said and disconnected the call.

Feeling irritated, I covered my face with the sheet and tried to sleep; I couldn't after arguing with him. I got a call from him after some twenty minutes, and I thought of not answering the phone, and I didn't. I lay on the bed, trying to sleep, but couldn't, and my phone rang again. I thought of doing something instead of lying dead on the bed with open eyes, so I answered the phone.

'What the hell do you want?'

'I knew you were still awake,' he said politely.

'I was sleeping soundly,' I said rudely.

'You weren't. Stop lying and wish me goodnight sweetly, though it's morning.'

'Don't bother me.'

'Sweetly say goodnight if you want to sleep well,' he exclaimed.

I got off, took my bed inside the room on the terrace, locked the door, and lay.

'If you don't say it, we will both be unable to sleep, bub.'

I smiled and said, 'Goodnight, Karan.'

'Night, bub.'

It worked, and we finally slept.

I woke up the next evening around 4 p.m. and went down to Granny with my mobile phone, after organising the bed well. I could see Jia sitting next to Aunt, having tea, when Aunt asked if I would like to watch a movie. I asked the show time; it was at 10.50 p.m., so I refused as I thought I would speak to Karan for at least an hour. 'You wanted to see it,' said Granny and I told her that I would see it in the afternoon some day. Jia said that she would take me the day after with her, and I agreed— to get rid of the matter.

When I came back after taking a shower, Jia was waiting for me with a sweet and true smile this time and a glass of chocolate shake. 'Are you my granny?' I asked her, and she laughed. She asked me about my friends, and I told her about the others and Karan.

'Is he handsome?' she asked.

'Of course,' I replied, feeling proud of him.

'I don't have a boyfriend,' she said sadly, wanting me to get her to talk to Karan.

'He has a lot of girlfriends, though,' I laughed, and she changed the topic.

'Would you like to play badminton?' she asked and added, 'Sam would come too.'

'Only if you don't hate me this time for talking to your friend,' I said.

'It's not like that,' she replied.

'Were you being normal when you made hateful faces at me? If yes, then I wouldn't question the real you.'

She felt bad, apologised, and told me that she liked him and wanted to date him and didn't like it when he talked to other girls.

Another Mahima! I laughed and knew too well that the end would be the same as Mahima's.

'Don't worry. I have a better-looking boy in my life, and also I never come in between two lovers.' She appreciated that and asked about badminton.

'Sure, what time?'

'9.30 p.m.' she replied and took my number to give me a buzz.

While the others were having dinner, I was watching TV, and the doorbell rang. I was in my shorts, ready for badminton. It was Sam, the same guy Jia had introduced me to the day I came here. He asked me to come out for badminton, and I did.

Jia was inside her house, getting the rackets and shuttle. I stood outside with Sam, accepting compliments that I looked good. Also he asked stupid questions like 'Any boyfriends?' I replied no, and by that time, Jia came, gave us the rackets and went inside again.

'Where all did you go after coming to Delhi?' he asked.

'Nowhere,' I replied.

'Are you friends with any boys?' he asked.

'Of course,' I said.

'How can you be single then?' So many questions. I asked if he was Mahima's brother (Karan's ex-girlfriend Mahima!)

'What?' he quizzed.

'Is your sister named Mahima?'

'What?' he asked, confused, and I started laughing as only I knew the joke.

We had started playing badminton after ten, and Granny and Aunt had left for the movie. I played with Jia and gave the racket to her when Sam came to play opposite me. I sent a message to Karan: 'Let me know when you are free. We will talk'.

'Mahi, whom are you messaging?' asked Sam.

'Not your business,' I replied.

'Would you like to date me?' he asked, joking.

'What rubbish!' I said, and Jia started giving him those hateful looks. He apologised and said that he was kidding, and I told him that I didn't take such people like him seriously.

I could see him smile at me continuously. I stopped looking at him, bid them goodbye, and got into the house after two hours almost. I checked my phone, and there was no reply from Karan. He rarely replied when his reply was needed the most. 'Well, this is not true,' I said as I was irritated with myself for missing Karan so much. I wanted to talk to him.

I checked the fridge, got some fruits in a plate, had them, and checked my phone again for Karan's message. I thought of calling him up. And when the bell rang, he picked up the phone and, without letting me say hello, he said hurriedly, 'I am busy. I am busy. Will call you back in some time,' and disconnected the call.

I waited for his call, but he didn't call as he was with his family, and by that time, the other family members had come. Roop told me that she might take me tomorrow to a place nearby on her bicycle like she did during our childhood. I agreed as this was something special rather than just shopping at malls.

The next day was the second-last day in Delhi. It was raining heavily in the afternoon, and Jia asked me if I would like to enjoy the rain. I agreed and went to the terrace. It was midday, and Jia joined me. We took bath in the rain for an hour, and the cool breeze brought me peace.

We danced and sang under the heavy rain when Jia's mother asked her to come back. I didn't mind her going back as I preferred to be alone with nature. I was missing someone. Who? I didn't know. I remembered those losers I had come across in my life and how my parents were after me all the time.

Enjoying the rain had made me forget them, but there was something inside which was bothering me. It stopped raining, and I still lay on the terrace garden for a few hours, thinking of good memories and smiling at the sky, which was beautiful.

Roop came in and asked if I would like to go for a ride. I wanted to, so I quickly got ready and left for a ride. She took the bike out, and we left for the ride, accompanied by Jia, who sat behind Sam.

'Mahi, you look great,' said Jia. I looked behind and saw both of them coming behind. I asked Roop if she had invited them; she said no. The bike jumped off a big stone, and I realised what a pathetic coincidence it was! This time I wanted to be with Roop only. She took me to the fire brigade area. There were so many water tanks, and also the road seemed uneven and had become a swimming pool. The water wasn't dirty, so I asked Roop to ride through the water, and she did. I could feel the waves of water on the left and the right side as we rode in between. I enjoyed it a lot.

We were in a different area, and Jia was at some other place, luckily not with us as I didn't like interruptions, though she had stopped pretending. Roop and I stopped at a canteen and sat, having some snacks and drinks. Granny had called Roop to remind me that I had left my phone at home; I knew it. We discussed our lives. I told her about Sagar, and like Granny and her sister, even she liked Karan.

She asked me if I remembered those days when she was in India and I used to visit her place with Granny. I told her that I did, and we started recalling those days. I used to roam with her friends, who were much older than me, and her tutor was a kind man. I liked talking to him. He used to come on a bicycle to teach them at home, and when I asked him why he came on his cycle, he told me that he had an Opel Astra car. Once when he took it to the market to buy some stuff from a showroom, somebody stole his car and left this bicycle in its place, and from that day onwards, he rode the bicycle as he didn't have enough money to buy the same car again. We both laughed.

She started asking me about my childhood.

'Do you remember the boy who wanted to marry you?'

'Ah, Sahil,' I confirmed, and she nodded. He was my classmate in junior school, and we were both really fond of each other. 'I used to hit the boys who bullied him,' I told her and laughed, adding, 'He has grown up very handsome, though I haven't met him but saw him once in the market and luckily recognised him.'

'Mahi, do you remember the boy who hit you with a stone? You cried loudly, getting the colony people out of their houses.'

He was older than me, and I called him a donkey. He lived near Aunt Daisy's old house. Nobody was at our home, and so his mother came to me with some sweets for me so that I would stop crying, but I didn't accept them and pushed her away. At night, I went with a chalk and drew a donkey peeing at a wall of his house near the entry gate and came back. His mother came to catch hold of me but was affronted by Granny as I wanted to take revenge.

She also asked me if I remembered my childhood friend named Vicky, and I explained to her that I could never forget that idiot who always broke some toy or the other. And once when he tried to hit the street dog Moti, who was my friend, I bit his hand and pulled his hair hard. Later he got his hair length shortened so that I couldn't pull them, but he didn't dare to bother Moti. She laughed loudly.

Jia and Sam had come to the canteen, and we were about to leave as it was evening, and we did. Granny had called on Roop's phone to ask when we were coming back as a guest had come. I was excited about the guest, as there was suspense about his identity till the time we reached home. The four of us came back together, enjoying the beautiful dark sky and the fresh air in our own ways by making the bike jump on big stones and the uneven road.

We reached home at around 8 p.m., and I was asked to stay out for some time with Jia, and she asked me if Karan was my boyfriend. They would not understand what was between me and Karan. I knew that, so I nodded yes. Sam said that he always knew it—the uninvited. Who was he to poke his nose? And she asked me if we had kissed. I asked her to excuse me. She then shouted when I was leaving, and I replied, 'Tomorrow'. I could see her give silly expressions this time also, as Sam looked at me as if I was his girlfriend and was going far away.

I got inside the house, wondering who could have come. On the same table at the same place where we used to get drunk, strictly following what was written on the banner 'Let's Get Drunk' by Aunt Daisy, I could see a man sitting next to Granny but didn't know who he was. 'Meet my granddaughter, Mahi,' introduced Granny to him.

'Hello,' I said and got myself a chair. He looked very simple. He was wearing a shirt, not tucked in, with pants and formal slippers and had brought an old tape recorder with him for some reason.

'What would you like to try, Baldeb?' asked Aunt Daisy, smiling at him. I got it then. He was the same Baldeb who proposed to her and the one these sisters were talking about the other day. I could see Granny ask her sister to come along, and Aunt Daisy went downstairs with Granny, leaving me with Baldeb. He asked me about my studies. I told him that they were going great.

We discussed many things, and I introduced the puppy to him. 'Baldeb, this is Baldeb.' He looked at me, confused. I didn't bother to clear his doubt, and he told me that he loved dogs and asked whose dog was it. 'It's Aunt Daisy's dog,' I replied.

After hearing that it was Aunt Daisy's, he looked at the dog like a mother would look at her newborn. I asked him if he ever had a dog; I knew he did. He told me that he loved three living beings in his life—his mother, his dog, and . . . He didn't name the third person. It was Aunt Daisy, I guessed myself. The first two beings were in heaven. 'Did you ever love a girl?' I asked.

'Yes,' he said, smiling like a newly married Indian village bride.

'Who?' I asked, and he didn't reply. I asked him if he would mind if I told him something about Aunt Daisy. He got interested and asked what it was.

'You love dogs, right?'

'Yes,' he said.

'Aunt Daisy loves you, and that is why she named her dog Baldeb,' I said. He took the puppy in his lap and hugged him like a father hugs his child after his wife's delivery. 'Baldeb junior,' he laughed and kissed the puppy again. I was really enjoying the scene, so I told him that the puppy's nose was like his nose, and he smiled widely this time. He was madly drunk already.

I suggested that he propose to Aunt Daisy today as they would make a good couple and should get married. Also I told him that the other day when Granny and Aunt Daisy thought that he was dead, Aunt slipped from her chair after hearing the shocking news. 'Is she all right?' he asked. And I reminded him that she fell from her chair, not from the building, and also she was all right as he had seen her a couple of minutes before.

'The weather is romantic tonight. You should propose to her,' I said. I could see Baldeb hold the puppy again and whisper something in his ears when I interrupted and asked the dog, 'Should Daddy propose to Mummy?' and Baldeb agreed to propose to her. There were no limits to insanity, but all I knew was that I was enjoying it. Granny came back with Aunt Daisy and Roop. I wished Baldeb good luck.

Granny poured whisky in all the glasses, and they started drinking, eating snacks side by side. I got off from my chair and made Aunt Daisy sit next to him. I could see them lost into each other's eyes, and I helped them find a way by whispering in Baldeb's ears if he had come here to have free drinks or to get her love. 'Granny, don't you think Aunt looks good with Baldeb?' I asked.

'They look great together,' replied Roop, and I could see Granny smile like a mother does when her daughter finally gets the right man after rejecting *n* number of men.

They kept on drinking, and I could see Aunt hold Baldeb's arm, romantically looking into his eyes, wanting him to kiss her. 'I love you,' whispered Baldeb finally, and Granny was happier than Baldeb himself.

'I was about to say this to you, Baldeb, that I love you,' said Aunt politely to him.

'What a miracle!' I announced, and she smiled, hiding her face behind his shoulder, and I went on with the same glass of cold drink while the others were having their third peg.

'Get married, Baldeb, before you die,' said Granny, drunk. I corrected her statement and explained that she wanted them to get married sooner and have babies.

'We wouldn't have babies, Baldeb. I can't deteriorate my figure and go with that pain,' said Aunt who had nothing but fat in her body.

'You are my baby. I don't need any another baby,' he replied to that fifty-year-old lady.

'What an understanding! Baldeb, what about Baldeb junior?' I asked, pointing a finger at the puppy.

'I will adopt him for Mahi. Otherwise he wouldn't let you spend time alone,' said Granny to Baldeb. Roop went away, laughing at the conversation that the three of them thought was very serious.

'The first time I saw you, you had a bigger butt,' said a drunk Baldeb to Aunt. It was time to excuse them to allow them talk about personal matters. But I thought of observing them when Granny sent them to the place near the water tank and took Roop with her downstairs; I remained at the same place, waiting for them to talk whatsoever.

Aunt Daisy started crying louder, and I went to see what had happened but came to know that she was crying in happiness.

'Let's get married,' she said.

'How about a live-in relationship?' asked Baldeb, teasing.

Aunt Daisy was finding a way to hug Baldeb.

'You are such a down-to-earth man, Baldeb. I am lucky to have you in my life.'

'You are the most beautiful girl I have ever come across,' said Baldeb.

'Girl?' I confirmed to myself and continued to observe them.

'So are you, Baldeb, beautiful at heart,' said she and hugged him tight this time.

'I promise, I would wash all the clothes and cook food on time,' he said.

'Just this?' confirmed Aunt Daisy.

'And I will love you very much,' he replied romantically.

'I mean, you also have to clean the house and give me leg massage,' she said.

'Of course,' he said.

I stood there, thinking what Aunt Daisy was up to. 'After rejecting so many men, she has luckily found the one who loves her, and look at the way she is behaving. Strange and overconfident!'

She caught me hiding and asked me what I was doing there. I told her that Baldeb had brought a tape recorder and I had come to give it to him.

'Thank you, baby,' said Aunt to me.

'If she hadn't been here, we wouldn't have been together,' said Baldeb emotionally to Aunt.

'It's destiny. God wanted you to be together. Who am I?' I said to them.

'You are Mahi,' said Aunt Daisy, thinking I was overdrunk and had forgotten my name.

'Daisy, she didn't mean what you understood,' said Baldeb, who seemed smarter than Aunt Daisy.

'Aunt, you are lucky that a man like Baldeb loves you. Make sure that you respect him and help him in all kinds of work as life might steal him away from you,' I said.

She seemed to understand every bit of what I said, but in her own sense, and continued, 'I won't leave hair on the washbasin and also I will buy fewer clothes.'

'You should help him clean the house and wash clothes,' I suggested.

'I would also wash your underwear if needed, but promise me you will never leave me, Baldeb.'

Baldeb seemed to be very emotional and had teary eyes this time as washing underwear was a big promise, he thought.

'I love you, Daisy,' he said, wiping off his tears.

'I love you too, Baldeb.'

I came to the terrace garden area, and Baldeb played some regional song on his tape recorder, and they both danced, holding each other in their arms, badly drunk.

I looked at the strange ways of life, but they were together. I disguised laughs into coughs and grunts. I went to the same room where I had slept the other day and also saw them get inside Aunt's room as it was midnight.

I lay on the bed, thinking about my past—the time I spent with Sagar. When I hugged him, he kissed me, telling me that he loved me very much, which was all false, and that brought tears in my eyes when I remembered how he had left me for a girl like Latika. I didn't know what kind of person I had become.

I was enjoying Baldeb and Aunt Daisy's love story, and now I was feeling lonely, teary, and weak. I got angry very easily those days. I liked Granny the most because she was the one who supported me in every way, and I had a belief that my mom didn't give much time to me and, in fact, was the first one to shout at me and keep me in strict custodies, and so was my dad.

Also, I thought that I would speak to Sagar at least once as I was feeling very angry and didn't know now what 'forget and forgive' meant in my life. I kept on crying, thinking about my parents, who, I thought, did not love me; rather they kept me in a world which I didn't like. I wanted to kill them and all those losers I had met in my life. I angrily cried a lot. I lay on my bed and kept on consoling myself by saying, 'What is there if they don't love me? Karan does.'

TWELVE

After crying for God knows how long, I didn't know when I slept. I forgot to talk to Karan and also didn't check my mobile phone. I was sleeping like a corpse. Suddenly I heard the window of my room shut with a loud noise, louder than the sound of a bomb. The weather was cold, and the chilly wind blew in while I was sleeping. I would have got a heart attack, but fortunately I was alive. I never liked being woken up like that. I closed the window and saw Granny walking up to me with a million-dollar smile with Aunt's mobile phone in her hand.

It was the last day in Delhi, and our train was at 11 p.m. that night. She told me that there was an important call for me from an unknown number.

'Hello,' I said, unclearly.
'Is it Mahi?'
It was someone I had never spoken with before.
'No, I am Heena, moron,' I said for he had already irritated me by calling me up when I just woke up.

'Hello, Mahi, I am Sam Hudda. Remember?'

'Jia's friend?' I enquired.

'Yes, you are right.'

'Yes, tell me.'

'I had called to apologise.'

'For what?' I enquired.

'You didn't like it when I said that I knew Karan was your boyfriend. I didn't mean to hurt you.'

'I don't get hurt on such stupid scenarios,' I said.

'That means you aren't angry?' he asked.

'I never was. I am irritated by your weirdness.'

'I am sorry to have irritated you,' he said.

'I will talk to you later.' I could see Granny cleaning my bed and pretending that she wasn't listening to this conversation and was busy with her thoughts.

He asked me to wait for a minute for he wasn't finished.

'If I hadn't said that, we would have become friends by now,' he said.

I laughed like people do just for the heck of replying when they don't have anything to say.

'Hope you aren't irritated now,' he said.

'Does it bother you?'

'Of course,' he said weirdly. I wondered why he was being so nice to me.

'I can't talk more. I have things to do.'

'Goodbye, Mahi, I will call you sometime.'

'Bye,' I said and hung up.

Granny said that she had done all the packing and also that I could talk more to this boy if I wanted, and I refused, rudely telling her not to come up with such stupid phone calls, calling them important and ruining my morning time. She laughed at my answer and clapped like a thunderbolt, making fun of me. I liked being with myself after waking up, not coming across any stupid, weird, irritating, or negative thing—in fact, nothing.

'It was good to see your face in the morning,' I said, and she smiled at me as she was praised. I lay on the bed again when she hit on my butt, reminding me that it was already afternoon. I got up and went for a shower and other procedures.

She then sat on my bed, checking my mobile phone and ordering Aunt Daisy to make breakfast for me. While taking a shower and singing *Dil Chahta Hai* title song, I thought about my friends, and that reminded me that I hadn't spoken to Karan and Rasheen also had not called me when she was supposed to. I was also thinking about Adhiraaj as I hadn't spoken to him after the day he had called me to ask about my health. We were all to meet sooner, therefore.

I came to my room and saw Granny so involved in my mobile phone.

'What are you doing? Checking messages if there are any from Karan?' I enquired.

'Why? You got scared?' she asked childishly.

'What a waste of question, Granny,' I said.

'Did you fight with him?' she asked.

'We both love each other to eternity and never fight,' I said, laughing at her interest in Karan and me.

'Why didn't you pick his calls last night? Four missed calls,' she announced. 'When did you sleep?' she asked.

'Late midnight,' I answered and told her that Karan wouldn't mind if I told him that I forgot to talk to him.

We both went downstairs, and I had brunch with them, while they were having lunch. I dialled Karan's phone, and he answered.

'Hello, prep,' I said.

'Bub, what's up?'

'Great, I couldn't speak to you for some reason. I am sorry, pearl . . .'

'How do you know?'

'What do I know, prep?'

'About what Adhiraaj's girlfriend Pearl did?'

'I called you a pearl, idiot. What happened to her?'

'She called me up yesterday and was crying that she really loved . . .'

'Adhiraaj? Wow, finally. I am glad to hear her say so.'

'Shut up, bub! She told me that she is in love with me.'

'What? What the hell?' I said, shocked. 'Bitch!'

'Yes, she got my name tattooed on her arm, though not real.'

'Oh my God! Does Adhiraaj know about it?'

'I went with Adhiraaj as he wanted to see her. She said this then and there.'

'What did Adhiraaj do?'

'He got into the car embarrassed and said that I could do whatever I felt like.'

'Did he?' I felt really bad as Adhiraaj never fought or argued with anyone.

'She held me and said that she would like to date me. Also she took my hand and touched her waist.'

'She is a desperate bitch. I knew already. She rarely spoke to Adhiraaj and was always eager to kiss his pink lips.'

'Pink?' he quizzed. 'I would have touched her everywhere if she wasn't his girlfriend,' he said, laughing. 'But I pushed her away and got into the car, telling Adhiraaj that he meant much more to me than my real brother and advised him to date Rasheen, and he started getting irritated as always.

'Was he very sad? Give him a slap if he ever cries for that bitch. He is so precious to me,' I said sensitively.

'He wouldn't cry ever, but you might, bub,' he said, laughing.

'Why the hell will I cry? Sagar and Pearl are both rich losers. Flush them in a gutter I will some day, and I will talk to Adhiraaj once I get back.'

'When are you coming back, bub?'

'Just five more days.'

'Bitch! You are supposed to board the train tonight, I know.'

'Why did you ask when you knew it?'

'Shut up! Anyways what did you do last night?'

'After the dinner party I lay, thinking about my past.'

'Why did you cry? I asked you not to, and if you do again, I wouldn't talk to you ever.'

'How do you know?'

'Who on earth wouldn't know? Don't cry, my charming bub. Talk, I may listen,' he said in his style.

'May? Or will?'

He laughed, and I called him an asshole.

'Promise that you will stay like this Karan,' I said sensitively.

'With you now and always, bub,' he said, repeating what I had said to him during our early years of friendship, and laughed, calling me an emotional fool.

'Talk properly or don't talk.'

'All right, goodbye, bub,' he said and hung up on me.

I dialled his number again, and he answered, 'I can't talk properly, bub,' making fun of me.

'Shut up! I will talk, and you better listen,' I said strictly.

'I *may* listen,' he said, interrupting me.

'You can never get rid of me, remember. Of course, you are my friend. I love you, and I would want you in my life,' I said arguably in a louder voice and apologised later.

After breaking the silence, he continued, 'Never apologise for showing feelings when you do so. You apologise for the truth,' he said seriously and started laughing loudly after sensing that I was irritated by his stupid statement. 'I don't like girlfriends like you who get stuck and don't go away easily.'

'Get lost, boyfriend,' I shouted.

'Goodbye, girlfriend,' he replied unusually and disconnected the call.

I could see that Jia had come and was staring at me while I was talking to Karan. 'Why are you giving strange looks?' I asked.

'I didn't understand what you mean,' she replied.

'Nothing, forget it. What have you come for? Sugar or salt?' I asked, laughing.

'What?' she quizzed.

'Neighbours like you come to borrow such things,' I replied.

'I have come to see you, Mahi,' she said.

'Did you dream of me being unwell?' I asked.

'Stop it, Mahi,' said Roop.

She seemed an OK girl but acted weirdly at times. 'I don't like such stupid people with weird attitudes. They are not likable at all,' I said to myself.

'When are you leaving, Mahi?'

'Tonight, girl,' I answered.

'I saw a good friend in you,' she said.

'Did you?' I said.

'What do you mean, Mahi?' she asked.

'You don't get things easily? I meant I know I am all good, but which quality in me you liked the most?' I asked curiously this time.

'You are perfect from head to toe,' she said, praising me.

'Another Sagar,' I whispered. 'Definitely a rich loser if not now, maybe next time.' I could sense that she was praising me falsely.

In the evening, we were to leave for home, and Aunt Daisy and Roop went to drop us at the train station. Aunt Daisy gave me Rs. 1,000 as she couldn't buy me a gift. We left for the station, and, on our way, we picked up Baldeb, and I had to sit on Granny's lap—something I hated doing—as we were six people including the driver. I felt bad as I had really enjoyed being with Aunt Daisy and, of course, Baldeb, and the bicycle ride with Roop. At the same time, I was happy as I was to meet Karan.

We reached the railway station, hired a coolie, and handed over all our bags to him. We had come with an attaché case and a bag, but we were going with two more bags that had our shopping stuff in them. Granny walked, holding Roop's and her sister's hands, whereas I was holding Baldeb's hand because of the rush. I had started liking Baldeb; he had that innocence hidden behind what I called stupidity. He was a good man at heart. We had reached the platform with the coolie, but those three ladies hadn't.

'Do they know the platform number?' Baldeb enquired of our driver, and he said, 'Yes. Granny does know the platform number.' He was asked to wait for them near the luggage, and Baldeb took me to a small canteen and bought me chocolates, juices, chips, sandwiches, and other eatables to have on the way. I was being pampered like a kid, and I liked that. Apart from this, I wanted Baldeb and Aunt Daisy to get married as he truly loved her.

We stood near the driver, looking for Granny here and there. I asked Baldeb to visit us as he was a part of our family now. He agreed. I could see his expressions and his eyes that were so true. He was a kind-hearted man, and I would stay in touch with him, I decided. I asked him to give me his number. I saved it.

After a couple of minutes, they announced that the train was about to come in the next five minutes, with the very common music tuu . . . nuu . . . nuu . . . that came after the announcement at the railway stations of our country. Baldeb was busy pulling my cheeks, and I showed him those three women coming towards us. I could see Aunt Daisy giving hateful expressions and Granny murmuring something, and Roop was not bothered and just held their hands.

'Where were you lost?' I asked.
'An old man whistled at Aunt Daisy,' she said.
'Eve teasing,' added Aunt.
'What happened?' asked Baldeb.
'That old man with his one leg in the coffin whistled and passed comments on Daisy,' said Granny.
'He commented on my clothes,' said Aunt.
'Who told you to wear a skirt and come to the Old Delhi railway train station?' said Baldeb politely.
'Shut up, Baldeb,' shouted Aunt.

'Uncle is right,' I announced, calling him 'uncle' for the first time, and angrily said, 'What makes you to be so rude to he who loves you the most?' Aunt was quiet. Granny added, lifting up her eyebrow, 'Behave, Daisy,' and she politely apologised to Baldeb. Granny shared her bravery by telling us that she hit the old man with her slippers on his face and by that time, people had come to save him from her.

'Who bought you so many things?' asked Granny, and by that time, our train had come.

'Baldeb,' I replied, and we headed towards our coach with the coolie. We walked and got inside our coach. The coolie kept our luggage, took the money, and went away. They all took their seats as there was some time for the train to depart. I told Granny that I liked Baldeb more than Aunt Daisy. Aunt was happy to see us all happy at their decision to live together, but they had both decided that they would marry after a year or two.

I could see Jia come with Sam Hudda, holding a flower bouquet. 'A bad interruption again,' I said to myself. Jia came inside the train and hugged me tight. Ah, I didn't want to, and Sam gave me that bouquet of white flowers. Granny was smiling, seeing boys fond of her granddaughter. I handed over the bouquet to her. They bid goodbye as it was already late, and they had to go home. They stayed for not even five minutes; I didn't mind as I was happy they were going.

'We had already got food packed. Why did you get so many things, Baldeb? Don't waste money,' said Granny to him.

'It's OK,' replied Aunt on his behalf. Roop was quietly observing the scene. The sound of the train's horn announced its departure. And they were about to get off, leaving us. I hugged Roop and wished her good luck for her love life. Aunt Daisy and Granny cried, getting separated. I could see the way Baldeb consoled Aunt Daisy. Granny touched her sister's cheek and wiped off her tears. They were crying like an Indian bride and her mother cry when the bride leaves for her husband's home.

Roop jumped off the train; train had started moving. Baldeb was on the platform too, but Aunt was scared to jump off and the train had started moving. 'Somebody, pull the chain,' yelled Aunt.

'Jump on Baldeb, Daisy,' said Granny to her sister. She still was at the door, waiting for Mother Earth. She finally jumped and bumped into Baldeb, who was walking with the train.

Granny and I watched the romantic scene, and I shouted, 'Take good care of uncle. He loves you the most. Bye, Aunt Daisy, bye Roop, bye Baldeb Uncle, love you.'

'Karan, I am coming back.' And the train left the station.

We were on the train. I felt like hugging Granny in excitement. 'I like Baldeb. He is a kind man, but why is Aunt Daisy so rude to him always?' I asked her.

'I will take care of this,' she said.

'What?' I confirmed.

'Daisy is supposed to be sweet to Baldeb,' she said and I nodded, smiling.

'Did you speak to Karan?'

'Yes, I did. A sweetheart,' I said, and she smiled, taunting me.

After some time, she opened the bag, and we had food—delicious mutton curry with chapattis. I could see two men staring at us, strangers. One of them stared at Granny, giving strange expressions, teasing her. Granny abused the man, and he started misbehaving and threw our bag on the floor. I got scared, and the other man started shouting at him, trying to be nice or maybe he was really, I didn't know. I picked the bag and kept it on my seat. A lot of other people had come to our coach after listening to them shouting at each other.

'Why did they interrupt us while we were having food?' I murmured.

The man who had misbehaved shouted at the one who stood by us, 'The next station is Muradabad, and it's my city,' he said. 'And I am the don of this city.'

'What do you mean?' asked the other man, pushing him.

'I will ask my people to hit you hard,' said the goon.

'What do you think that I am alone?' He laughed and retorted, 'The next three coaches are filled with my goon friends.'. I clapped louder than a bomb, and they both left after arguing because of Granny.

I laughed louder and continued having food. Granny observed what I was doing. I thought I would tell Karan about this for some fun—a laugh with him.

Granny decided to watch a movie named *Socha Na Tha* on her laptop, and I thought of sleeping. We both always enjoyed the train journey. I had never slept before in the train; this time I did. I got a call from Karan, confirming if I was actually on the train or not. I asked him to wait and listen to the honk of the train, and then he was certain we were on the train and bid goodbye, telling me that he would pick me tomorrow evening for a treat, and I agreed.

I woke up after two hours when Granny was almost done watching the movie. She rewound the last part of the movie, showing that the hero and heroine run away after being scared of not being accepted by their families.

'You and Karan can run away from your families even if we all accept you both. It's really interesting to do it. You hide yourself, have adventures, and spend time together,' she said, looking at the floor as if she had done it at her age.

'Did you try this?'

'Of course.' She smiled and asked me not to question so much.

After reaching our house, keeping the luggage, and meeting the other family members, we slept. We were both very fond of sleeping; the best sleep was in Granny's bed, which was softer than a baby's skin.

I got a call from Karan in the afternoon, reminding me that he would come around 5 p.m. to pick me, and I told him that I knew.

I was ready to leave the house and meet Karan. Granny told me that she heard the honk of his car. I ran outside, and there was no one. She came, laughing at me. 'Stupid joke!' I said and walked away, laughing at myself. Suddenly I got a call from him, asking me to come out. I did and saw Adhiraaj sitting in the front seat as they were both coming from some work. I sat behind after greeting my darlings.

Adhiraaj asked me if I would like to sit next to Karan and laughed. 'Don't worry, I will throw you out after some time, and then she can sit next to me,' said Karan, replying to Adhiraaj.

'You will throw your brother out for a girl?' asked Adhiraaj, sounding emotional. 'Who else?' said Karan.

'Fuck you,' said Adhiraaj.

'Mahi, if you weren't dating my brother-like friend Karan, you would have been all mine,' said Adhiraaj, teasing.

'You are saying this now when Pearl dumped you,' I laughed.

'I always loved your fragrance, Mahi.'

'Dog,' said Karan.

'Give me a hug, Mahi.'

I did, and he said, 'What a relief!'

'Bastard, get away,' said Karan.

Adhiraaj laughed and said, 'I would have felt this way if you had agreed to date Pearl, but you didn't. Brothers!'

'Once you get totally away from her, I wouldn't leave this opportunity,' laughed Karan.

'I hope you weren't emotionally attached. You can get a better girl, just any girl. Life goes on,' I said.

'Any girl except Mahi,' corrected Karan before Adhiraaj could say anything.

'I am glad you broke up,' I said, and Adhiraaj looked at me as if I was putting salt on his wounds, and I explained him that she was a rich loser. And the combination was odd.

Adhiraaj's house had come, and he had to leave the front seat for me. He got off, teasing Karan by touching my cheeks and ordering Karan, 'Don't you kiss her as it's my right.' He laughed and ran away.

I got inside, and Karan murmured, 'It was better when he was with Pearl. I think I should get them together.'

After dropping Adhiraaj, we went to the ice cream parlour. Suddenly Karan stopped the car outside Muffin World and looked at me. I was happy to see him after a week, and so was he. We looked at each other and smiled when he hugged me tight, and we stayed that way for the next five minutes as we had missed each other very much.

I knew too well that whether or not I had a boyfriend. I had him, and he meant so much to me. He was not letting me go, and I wanted to stay that way, but I had to bite his shoulder as people who were passing by were looking inside the car with a lot of interest, and I didn't want to create a scene.

He ignored the ones who stared at us and asked me to wait. He gave me a packet, and what was it? It was the dress that I couldn't buy the other day because there was not enough money in my wallet—the same orange dress he had bought for me. 'Wow, this is beautiful,' I said.

'I know you said it the other day also,' he replied.

'It's so beautiful of you get me this,' I added.

'You can give me a kiss.' He winked, and we laughed. Karan never had perverted thoughts about me, he said.

He took me to Muffin World, and we had pudding together. I loved everything that day. It was the happiest of all those days, though there was less fun, but something lovely happened inside me. Karan had become a special part of my life, and there was a fear hidden inside of losing him. When I thought of this fear, coincidentally Karan called me an emotional fool, and I laughed and got back to the real me, who was fearless, and concentrated on the present.

Mahima was sitting with her friends at the same place, and when she saw us, she gave us weird looks and so did her friends, who were murmuring something about Karan and me. Karan never liked getting into quarrels. It never bothered him, and also people never dared to talk nonsense to him.

While David took Karan out to a gift gallery, which was next to Muffin World, I waited alone at the table, having pudding. Mahima stood up, pointed a finger at me, and said, 'Friends, this is Mahi Arora, who is dating Karan presently.' Her stupid friends laughed.

'What more have you done with him apart from hugging him tight?' she asked, and the two girls who were sitting with her laughed and added, 'What else?'

'Unlike you who forces boys to have sex and then says "They used me", bloody frustrated single,' I replied.

She shouted abuses at me; half of her voice didn't come out due to her overexcitement of fighting with me. I ignored her stupid comment, and they thought I was scared.

'Mahima, you don't deserve Karan. He is an idiot,' said one of the boys from her group, and I looked at that son of a bitch angrily.

He showed me his middle finger, and I replied, 'Did you take this inside of you?' and he made strange faces, thinking he was being cool. What a loser!

'You both deserve each other,' said Mahima, teasing me stupidly.

And I replied, 'Like they say, "throw away the odd and get the even". I am so glad that he dumped you,' I said, making fun of her.

'I can kill him once I get my revolver,' said her friend, who was nearly four feet ten inches.

'Revolver might throw your little ass far into pieces,' I replied, and he got furious.

'Relax, guys,' said the same boy who had showed me the middle finger and abused Karan, adding, 'He is a real bastard.' This got me furious.

'How dare you abuse Karan?' I threw the empty glass of shake at his face. 'Talk to me,' I shouted. 'Don't you say a word against Karan. What do you think you are, bloody narrow-minded souls? You are two boys and three girls. Are you all dating, and which boy is dating two girls amongst three of these?' I questioned.

'Whether or not we are dating, we aren't answerable to anyone. We are independent souls who think about our lives and not others. What makes you get involved into our personal life?'

I was angry till the core, and I had to do this to avoid such occurrences in future.

'Who the hell are you to abuse a person like him?' I said, holding that boy's collar. 'Even if you rub your ass a hundred times, then also you can never be like Karan. Respect him! You better,' I said and gave a punch on his mouth. He got angry and hit me on my forehead. I got hurt, though it didn't bleed. I pushed him hard, and he bumped into the pastry fridge.

Everyone else present at the bakery shop stared at me, enjoying the fight. I was so angry that I couldn't control myself from hitting Mahima hard on her face. The other girls stood far away from me. 'How could a boy stay happy with a frustrated girl like you? What makes you think that you are the best?' I yelled, hitting her head hard this time.

Karan had come after listening to abuses and shouts and asked, 'What happened?' I went on with the fight as it was needed that time.

I looked at those stupid girls who were her friends, out of which one had started crying after seeing Mahima look like a jungle girl with her hair rough and untidy, her cheeks that had my fingerprints on them. I felt pain in my forehead, and that made me go and hit the same boy again, and I did. He hit me on my mouth, and my lip started bleeding, and I kicked him on his stomach. The shot didn't land at the right place.

Karan irately held me from my waist and took me out. I kept on abusing them. They were all now ready to leave for their houses. 'All you fools wouldn't have to go to the toilet for shit as you have already brought it out from your mouth,' I shouted at them. I could see that boy hold his stomach, and I yelled again, 'I ain't a doll-type of girl.' He had hit me hard, but I could take care of myself. They started the unwanted, and I didn't leave the opportunity of ending it.

David came up to me and asked, 'What happened?'
'Nothing,' I said, smiling at him.
'If this is nothing, Mahi, I wonder what will "something" be like.' And I laughed. It was 9 p.m., and Karan got me into his car this time with more civility by opening the car gate at my side and making me sit. He looked at me seriously and asked if I was fine.
'Of course,' I replied boldly, and he told me not to fight with anyone who talked whatsoever about him. I didn't like his advice and asked him to stay out of it.

He started the car, and I looked away from him, feeling bad, not because I fought with them. I wasn't regretting the fight. I didn't want to have such things in my life, and also tears came out of my eyes. I didn't know why but definitely not because of that boy who beat me.

My house had come, but he didn't drop me; rather, he told me that he was taking me for a drive somewhere. I asked him to drop me home, and he refused. He stopped near a club and asked me if I was fine. I told him that I was OK, and he said unless I told him what was going inside me, he wouldn't drop me home.

'Tell me, I may listen. Involve me. I will help you get rid of it,' said Karan to me, concerned.

I looked at him and started crying, irritated. He stroked my hair lovingly, and I kept on crying for the next five minutes. I hugged him and didn't leave him until I thought I should.

What's the matter, bub? Bring it out. Don't hide it inside,' he said.

And I began, 'Sagar ditched me, knowing that I really loved him. I was not supposed to be played for fun. He left me crying for hours and days and didn't bother to talk to me once. Was I that bad?' I cried while Karan caressed my hair. 'He left me for a girl like Latika. Is she better than me in looks? Even if she is, she didn't love Sagar as much as I did. He wasn't bold like me. If he had told me that he wanted to be with Latika, I wouldn't have refused and rather would have stayed away. Such a liar and a loser who didn't have guts to speak the truth. You take good care of me. I like being with you, and people don't let us live peacefully,' I said, crying.

'Where is your "give-no-fuck" attitude lost, bub? I am irritated at your behaviour,' he said, and I wondered.

After the five minutes' silence, I added, 'I miss Sagar and cry for him after being explained by Granny that I shouldn't be so emotional. I can't control my tears, but he doesn't bother to call me and apologise. I hate him.' I cried louder. Karan was peacefully holding me in his arms.

'And my parents, who gave birth to me, left me in my room to live alone and forced me to live my life the way they wanted to. I would leave this house and will never come back. Why is everybody behaving rude to me? I deserve love. I have never harmed anyone. Mahima and her friends spoke all nonsense about me and you. Why? Five of them started the quarrel, creating a scene in front of these people who were there. I couldn't take it, so I had to be harsh with them. She wasn't lucky enough to be a part of your life. I am, so she is jealous of me. But I don't want these things in my life any more. I am upset because things are not fine around me,' I said.

'Bub, don't find faults. Find a remedy and get rid of it,' he replied, and I stopped crying, though I enjoyed being pampered in his arms. Something inside me was unhappy and wanted answers.

I stopped talking and still was in his arms, feeling rested, and I felt each of my breaths. I was in that position for a few minutes, and, then breaking the silence, I said in his ears, 'I didn't do it. It just happened.'

'Bub, you should do what you think is right and get what you want to have. It's also good to cry as it makes you feel light, and you don't get pimples on your face,' he said, laughing. I laughed, pinching him on his waist, and he shouted in my ears. 'Also you look cute when you cry, bub,' he said, and I looked at him.

Granny called on my phone, asking me when would I come back home as I was late. I told her, 'After an hour.' She agreed.

'I am glad that Granny secretly allows me for things like these. I love her.' My life was changing, and things I never liked were becoming a part of it—like fighting.

To change the mood, he took me to the same place where we had ice cream. He went running to the stall so that if there was one cone left, he could have it all. I followed him, shouting, and luckily there were two cones left. We took our own and walked towards the park-like place where he had fallen on a dog.

There was a small marble chair under the shed that had lamps lit. We tried to get inside, and suddenly Karan's foot slipped and his cone fell on the ground. He looked at me like an innocent baby, feeling bad to have dropped his ice cream. I couldn't stop laughing.

I didn't share my cone and loved observing him look at me like a hungry beggar. Karan had innocent eyes, a sharp nose, sweet pink lips, and short hair. I loved his face; it had something that brought a smile.

He then sat tickling me. I had learnt how to control feeling ticklish, but he didn't know. It was my turn to tickle him. He started running, and I was behind him. He looked at me and made faces, and I caught him and pushed him on the ground. I jumped on him, and he kept on shouting. I tickled him, enjoying his discomfort.

He asked me to stop, but I didn't. He was shouting so loudly that it brought a young lady out of her house. She looked at us angrily and said, 'Don't do physical things here. It's a reputed society.' I looked at Karan, who was lying down, laughing at what she said. I dragged him by his right leg to the park. The lady abused us, and I abused her even more, and before the entire society could call the police and catch hold of us, we got into the car and sped away.

After we were done laughing, he said that this place seemed unlucky for him. I nodded, holding my stomach, which was paining badly due to the laughs, and added that it had just been twice as people were about to catch hold of us. He said that next time when he got me here, he would wear a wig or something so that people wouldn't recognise him.

It was winter, and we loved the chilly air. He drove fast, and I asked him to drive slowly. He ignored me, and I said, 'You never listen to me, Karan, and mark my words, "I never listen to you" is what I will make you say some day.'

'What's wrong, bub?' he said.
'Do you know how to drive?' I asked, and he replied, 'I will drive you crazy tonight, bub. I am sure you will enjoy the drive.'
I didn't reply, and on seeing this, he said, in a weird voice like that of a girl, 'You never listen to me, bub.' I laughed, and by that time, we had reached my home.

I waited, looking at him, and said, 'You have a fake driving licence, I know.' He had turned fifteen with me this year but had a different date of birth mentioned on his documents as he had to be eighteen to get a licence.

'What are you waiting for? I hope you won't kiss me, Mahi,' he laughed.

'Fuck you, Karan.'

'Your house has come. Get lost now,' he replied.

I slapped him in jest and got off the car and went towards the gate without saying goodbye. He came behind me without making a noise, tickled me, and kissed me, biting on my cheek, and ran away, leaving me surprised at the situation.

Granny opened the door, and he was gone. I got inside the house, holding the packet that had the dress he had given me and walked up the stairs, whistling. I lay on my bed, thinking about the situation and laughing to myself when Granny asked what the matter was.

'Things are changed. People whistle and get kisses these days,' she said, taunting me. I looked at her surprised and told her that it was bad manners to notice somebody's private things.

She laughed and reminded me that Baldeb had called to wish good luck as it was the first day at school tomorrow after vacations. I was surprised at myself as I had forgotten. I checked my school dress and my bag to see if they were all ready. Granny helped me so much.

I quickly changed when she came up to me and asked if I had fought with anyone as my forehead had a little blue mark after the boy had beaten me. She got furious and started scolding me, telling me that I was not supposed to get violent. I didn't feel bad as it was Granny. She rarely scolded me. I was experiencing confidence crisis by becoming irritated and angry. Things weren't in my control. I needed some time alone.

THIRTEEN

The same alarm clock woke me up, and it was the same school dress, the same hairstyle, the same school bag, and the same transport, that is, an auto that I boarded to go to school. The auto driver removed the front mirror after I got in, for what reason I didn't know. I could only see his back. I enjoyed the chilly wind while enjoying the auto ride all alone. I was feeling very light after a big break from school and was happy inside.

I reached my school, and after paying the auto fare, I walked towards the entry gate and realised that it was the same auto driver who was staring at Mom in the front mirror. That was when I understood why he had removed it so that I couldn't see him.

I turned back and walked towards him. He kick-started the auto. It coughed but didn't work. He was scared of me walking towards him. I went towards him, looking at him, and suddenly he hid his face and asked me not to spoil his million-dollar face, which seemed to me not even worth fifty paisa. I told him that I wouldn't hit him, and he apologised for what he had done the other day.

My school was some twenty steps from the main road, and as I walked to the school carrying my bag, I felt excited that I would meet my school friends as we loved being together.

I got inside my school, looking here and there for my peers but couldn't find any, and suddenly I saw my school building, which had changed completely. Everything from its texture to its colour seemed to have been altered during the vacations. It seemed so new and fresh; suddenly I saw Sagar get in from the gate, looking at me and giving a light smile. I then felt a light pain inside me when I saw him looking at me.

I walked into my class, wished my class teacher, and said, 'I am on time today.'

'Thank you,' he said tauntingly, and I took my seat. He was a jolly teacher like a friend. Only a few friends had come; our group was missing. The morning assembly had to begin, and a classmate told me that Rasheen was outside to see where they all were.

I looked at Sagar who was sitting next to our table this time. I felt some kind of pain each time I looked at him, and something had to be done to get rid of it. I felt that I was crying a little inside; though I had Karan with me, I still felt bad after remembering all that he had done to me.

I heard Amaar laughing in the corridor like a man with a heavy voice that could lead people die of heart attack. Our class teacher went out and got them inside. All my buddies were together—Amaar, Soni, Maria, Abhi, Shyna, and Rasheen. Rishabh came with them and went to his section, carrying his school bag. Soni and I hugged each other and the others.

Amaar came in excitedly, stepping on others' feet, saying 'Let's get drunk,' explaining to me that we would drink today as they had planned already. Also he told me that he had something personal to share with me.

'Personal?' I enquired.

'Yes,' he said, rubbing the left part of his chest, indicating his heart. I winked and told him that I would love to hear him.

The bell had rung, and I had to go out to do my duty. 'Amaar in love?' I asked myself and took my position. Students came in queues, and I saw Latika without a blazer. I asked her to step out. She ignored me and kept walking. Suddenly her rude attitude was interrupted by a tight slap given by Madam Shanta, and she had to stand next to me for punishment.

I checked the other students to see if they were all dressed properly. A junior whom I didn't know said, 'Mahi, you look great.' I smiled, thinking she might be in my house, and she added, 'Your friends are good too.' I looked at her and then asked her not to talk as it wasn't allowed. I picked all the students who weren't dressed properly, as well as the latecomers, and asked them all to step aside.

I looked at Latika's forehead, and she asked me, 'What are you looking at?'

'Your forehead reads something,' I said.

'But what?' she argued as I had said this a few times before.

'What makes you so rude and stubborn?' I asked, making fun of her. She got angry and started gnashing her teeth. I showed her my hand and said, 'Do you see this? It's two times heavier than before. You better remember.'

'What would you do?' she asked politely.

'Game over!' I said and made her stand with the others.

The prayer had begun, and I sang with the rest of the school. I could see Father Edward smiling at us. He had to give a lecture as it was the first day after vacations. We appreciated him a lot. Amaar was making weird faces at Madam Shanta, and we all recalled the last day when we threw the used plates and vodka bottle outside her house door with a short note. I saw her staring at our class, taking deep breaths, and her nostrils had widened. I asked them not to make fun of her as if she caught hold of anyone of us, the entire group would get into trouble.

After Father Edward's lecture, the assembly was done, and the students started getting inside their classes, and by that time, the latecomers were brought inside and had to be punished. One of the juniors amongst them was hit on his back by Latika. I asked the reason rudely, and I was told that he had murmured, 'Pull your hair, Latika.' I remembered that he was the same boy I had punished earlier with Latika. I asked him, 'How many times have you been punished?' I told him to behave himself. He apologised later.

There was a little kindness in my heart; therefore, I thought of not punishing them today. The juniors went away, giving smiles, thanking me, and Latika got inside the class with me.

Later that day, after two classes, Newspaper informed us that Madam Shanta might take two classes today, the third and the fifth class. We had to trust her as we could see in the morning assembly how eager Madam Shanta looked to meet us. The bell had rung for the third period, and some of the students took out the science books and some, who didn't, had social study books kept on their table.

She walked inside, and there was at pin-drop silence in the class. We wished her, and she yelled, 'Why do you hate me?' She shouted like a witch in a horror movie, and her voice echoed like we were in the movie hall, watching a horror movie.

'You started hating us first,' murmured Rasheen slowly like a child does to take revenge. I pinched her to shut her mouth. I looked here and there, pretending I was searching for the culprit.

'Who is fond of getting drunk?' she asked in a louder voice, breaking the sudden silence. I looked at Latika, and she threw her out of the class;

like once before, Madam Shanta mistook us for Atul and Latika. I could see Atul look at me, trying to tell Madam Shanta about us when suddenly I confidently informed madam that Atul had got drunken one day. 'He drinks, madam. The other day you sent him out of the class, he was drunk.' I had to do this; he was behaving cleverly, taking our names.

She threw both of them out of the class and asked us all to stand while she continued teaching the syllabus that was to be completed in the session. She made an innocent face and said, 'I am strict with you not because I don't love you, but because I want you to concentrate on your studies. I don't mind if you like drinking, but don't embarrass me by doing things you are not supposed to do.' She was hinting at the vodka bottle and used plates with a note, which we had kept outside her house.

I could see Rasheen get emotional and murmur, 'She isn't a bad teacher,' and I asked her to shut her mouth. Amaar and I knew very well that she was pretending to be nice so that idiots like Rasheen would vomit the truth to her. Nobody except us knew the truth. She taught a chapter and asked us to stand with our hands raised.

Also, she threw a book in Soni's face, and a few others were beaten by her when they moved their faces away from the books; I asked Rasheen, 'Still do you think Madam Shanta isn't bad?'

She corrected her stupid statement made in a hurry and said, 'I meant she isn't a bad teacher. In fact, she is a very bad teacher.'

'Stupid cleverness,' I said to myself.

Suddenly she went out, brought a stick, and hit all of us four times on our knuckles to vent her anger. We cried, consoling each other as we could feel the worst pain in our fingers. 'She indeed is a witch,' I murmured.

Fire was burning inside madam. It was winter, but we could still feel the heat of that fire. 'Fire brigade' had to be called; we couldn't dare to behave casually as she was mad to such extent that even if anyone of us said anything, she would listen. She would drag that student out of the class. So we thought of silently observing her.

Father Edward was on round in the school. As he came in, we all wished him, and he asked madam about the ones who were sent out and also why we were all asked to stand. She gave her never-ending explanations to him sweetly as always, but he seemed to get irritated and reacted as if his heart was saying 'Shanta, you rude element, when will you improve?' He made us sit and brought those morons inside.

During recess, Amaar and Abhi planned a party as we had met after vacations. Amaar had brought a bottle of vodka, and the rest of us accompanied him to the school terrace. I was waiting for Maria inside the class, and the others were gathering eatables in packets. Sagar called my name. I looked back and saw him smiling at me. I turned my back to him but, he shouted that he wanted to talk to me. I ignored him as I didn't want to spoil my day. I'd cried a lot for him already and was in no mood to bring back the false love whatsoever. I went towards the canteen to join my friends. I wanted to confront him, but not now.

When I reached the canteen, none of my friends were there. I looked here and there and suddenly I saw Newspaper, who had become a good friend, not because of sympathy but because she hated the ones I did. I asked her if she had seen any of those idiots. She said no, adding that she had recently heard that Madam Shanta had gone home and wouldn't take our class. I thanked her for giving me the news, which hopefully was true as madam so needed to give her throat some rest because she rarely talked but shouted all the time.

I went upstairs and opened the door. I saw them sitting there and distributing paper plates and plastic glasses. I joined them, and we started drinking and having food. Amaar had brought chocolate cake from home, especially for me. He knew that I liked it, but I was shocked to see him control his hunger and save a big piece of cake for me.

Amaar took me to the other side of the terrace with a big tray that had snacks and two glasses of vodka for us. I told him that I couldn't eat so much. He reminded me that he could, and I added, 'Of course.'

He also reminded me that he had to tell me about his personal life. I was trying to have the glass of vodka mixed with cold drink, and he was focusing on emptying the tray. And the conversation began.

'Mahi, your friend is in love,' he said.

'I knew it already. Wow!'

'That's true friendship, which is why I thought of telling you before telling the others.'

'Who wants to die seeking food?' I said after I saw the speed at which he was eating.

'She eats the same way,' he laughed.

'I am feeling bad for your parents.'

'Come on, Mahi, listen to my love story.'

'Oh yeah! How did it happen? Where did you meet her?'

'She came with her father to my meat shop to buy chicken. I was at the shop with Dad. She got in and smiled at me, and you know how well-mannered I am, so I acknowledged her.'

I was listening to him patiently.

He added, 'She forced her dad to buy two chickens as she wanted to have four leg pieces, but that idiot left her daughter crying for two leg pieces. I couldn't see her cry as it was love at first sight, and we had already got soft corners for each other the minute we saw each other.'

'You are speedy everywhere. Don't you think so?' I enquired.

'I am a man, Mahi. If I love someone, I would go and tell without hesitating.'

'Man! A huge man,' I said, raising my eyebrows and nodding my head.

The rest of them asked us to wrap up quickly as the next class would be Madam Shanta's, and I informed them that she wouldn't come. They asked questions, but I was not allowed to avoid Amaar's story.

'How did you propose to her?' I asked.

'In a very special way. No other lover would have done this ever.'

I looked at him and asked him to go on quickly.

'If I tell you the story quickly, it wouldn't sound interesting,' he said.

I was losing patience.

He began, 'She sat behind her father's scooter, facing backwards. She had in her hand the packet that had chicken in it. I went behind her scooter, running, and gave her two more leg pieces I had stolen from the freezer at my shop. She smiled at me lovingly and thanked me. I said to her that I loved her and wanted her to love me too. She gave me a flying kiss and went away.'

'That's so new. I have never heard of such love story,' I said mockingly. I actually kind of enjoyed it.

'I am an innovative man, Mahi. You should know.'

'You are indeed,' I added. He had a lot of confidence in him, no matter for what situation. I clapped after listening to his story.

'It's not complete, Mahi,' he said. 'The girl called on the shop phone, telling my dad that she was my school friend and wanted to talk about studies.'

'Where did she get that number from?' I asked.

'The address of the shop and the number are mentioned on the packet. Don't you know, Mahi?' He sounded smart.

'Oh yes, I forgot. That's nice,' I said politely.

'I quickly gave her the home landline number so that my father doesn't catch hold of me. The next day onwards, she started calling me on my landline, and I called her from a PCO somewhat far from my place so that my parents don't come to know about it. I have also kissed her four times, and the fourth time was the best. She loves me a lot, and the day when I kissed her for the fourth time, she didn't let me go home early, and I came back around 11 p.m., lost, thinking about her.'

The story was getting funny and interesting bit by bit, and, with eagerness, I kept listening to him.

He continued, 'When I reached home, my romantic thoughts were interrupted by a shoe I felt in my face. It was my father's. He shouted at me, "You used to steal money from the shop counter. Since when have you started stealing chicken pieces?" I didn't know that my father counted chicken pieces kept in the freezer. I looked at my mom with innocent eyes, telling her that I didn't know anything and maybe the chicken was born without legs. He then hit me with his shoe for an hour and threw me out of the house. I spent my night at a neighbour's place. The people were helpful as they knew I was a good child. I still feel pain in my shoulders and my head.'

'That is not correct. Your father shouldn't have behaved this way,' I said, consoling him.

'It's OK, Mahi. Everything is fair in love.'

'Which school is she in?' I asked.

'Guess?' He looked at me for thirty seconds and said that she was in our school. I asked him if it was Rabila or Sheena or a girl from a different section.

He said that the girl was in class VII.

'Class VII?' I enquired. 'A child she would be. Why are you with a girl younger than you?' I asked.

'She does things that girls of our age can't do. She isn't a child. And it's good to be with a girl younger than you as you can keep her in control and be like a man.'

I gave him a surprising look, and by that time, the fifth period had ended. We shook hands, and all of us were ready to go downstairs.

We all walked together downstairs and threw the garbage in the dustbin near the canteen, and we saw Madam Shanta go upstairs to see if there were drunkards. We quickly hid those bottles in the washroom as we still needed and got back to our class.

The entire class was empty. We quickly opened our books and started pretending as if we were revising the syllabus. Some of our classmates were at the school canteen, some were at the basketball court, and some were chit-chatting with their friends in the ground. Newspaper came running, announcing that madam would soon come to see if we were studying or wasting time, and by that time, a few more students had come in. Latika and Atul were still missing.

After struggling for some ten minutes, searching for clues, she finally came back to our class. I saw her crossing the staffroom and asked the class to concentrate on the books. There was pin-drop silence as she entered. We could see her staring like a witch as if she would tear us all.

We stood up, pretending we were so busy revising that we didn't notice when she had come in. She took a round, checking what all we were studying, and shouted, 'Where is the rest of the class?' We replied that we didn't know. There were only fifteen children in the class.

She went out and came back after five minutes with the rest of the class and punished all of us again. This time, she asked us all to remove our blazers and hit us hard on our arms. I had decided that I would complain to Father Edward. We all rubbed our arms and were very angry with her. She was a rich loser who hated us always; in fact, she hated everyone.

I got angry and told my friends that we would have to take a strict action against it, and they nodded. We could never forgive such a cruel person who called herself a believer of God. False world it was: on the one hand, you are in the church, praying to God, and on the other hand, you harm people and do bad deeds. What kind of humanity was it? 'We would have listened to you, if you had ever been like a mother to us. We make mistakes, but who gives you the right to hit us?' I murmured to my friends, addressing madam as I couldn't dare to say this directly to her.

After school, we had planned to meet at the terrace of the hostel building next. The school workers lived in that hostel. Maria and Shyna had left with Rishabh as they couldn't afford to take the risk of getting beaten up by Madam Shanta again. Also, they had decided they would quit drinking in school. We didn't force them as they had a right to do whatsoever.

I also asked Rasheen to go back home as what we were about to do was riskier than what we had done before. She was scared inside but had promised to be with me during easy and tough times. Soni came with us, scared, and, at the same time, excited to see what we were up to. Amaar and I were the bravest of all. I made the plan and thought of executing it on behalf of our class.

I took the empty vodka bottle and put inside a paper that read a note, 'Rich loser, who gives you the right to hit innocent children like us? What have we done to you? Why do you hate us? This is the reason God gives you no happiness in your life. Stay this way and die in a gutter.' I asked the others to move backwards as we might not have much time to run away. Also, I thought of adding another note, and I did. It read, 'Does it pain inside?' I was to throw this bottle on her bed. Whether or not she got hurt by this bottle, she would be upset after reading the notes.

I was hiding inside the hostel opposite her house. The countdown had begun, and then I threw the bottle inside her house, almost at her. I hadn't thought of throwing the bottle at her; it just happened. Without looking behind, we ran towards the school exit gate and were safely on the main road in some two minutes. We were smarter this time. Otherwise she would have come running after us, and we would have been all dead; also, we were lucky to stay alive as that building was so old that it seemed like it might fall off any time, but it didn't.

Rasheen started taking deep breaths. Soni was proud of me like always, and Amaar shook my hand, praising me. We had thought that we would not tell anyone about what we just did, not even the rest of our friends as the four of us were confident that no matter what happened, we wouldn't accept that we had done it. Rasheen was the only one who could be easily convinced by people, but because I had done it, she would try not to utter a word.

I was on the main road with Amaar, waiting for an auto, when suddenly a white car stopped and Pearl came out and walked towards me. I didn't bother to smile because she was a loser who had dumped the best boy ever, my dearest friend Adhiraaj. I ignored her and walked towards the other side.

She called my name, and I looked at her. 'Mahi, I have come to warn you to stay away from Karan as I want him to date me,' she said, stretching the words *date me*.

I said, 'What a rich loser you are! You don't know what you have lost. You will never get another Adhiraaj, though I am glad that you aren't together as he deserves the best. You are not even an "OK" material.'

She looked at me, pissed, and said, 'I might run my car over you, Mahi.' By that time, Amaar had stopped an auto. I looked towards my left and my right. I broke a headlight with my feet and ran away. I am sure she might have stood there, thinking, 'What happened in ten seconds?'

I reached home and went running inside, laughing as I had to tell Granny about my brave acts. 'Granny,' I shouted, and she came running to me, smiling lovingly. I wasn't smiling, though, but started the story. I told her about the vodka bottle and the note I threw at Madam Shanta from her window. She didn't appreciate this and asked about the rashes and cuts I had on my arms. I told her that Madam Shanta had hit the entire class. 'Unbelievable!' She was shocked to see the bruises and said that she would speak to the school principal about it. I requested her not to, telling her that this might affect my respect amongst my friends; after all, we were in class X and by now fifteen-year-olds, not from junior school.

That evening, Karan called me to ask how was the day, and I told him about Pearl and all that she had said to me. He didn't like her and asked me to ignore her. I continued telling him that Pearl said that she would run her car over me and that I kicked the headlight. He laughed.

Granny came and sat next to me. Holding my left arm, she put an antiseptic cream on my rashes. Karan told me that he was going out of station for some work with his mother after a few days, so he might come to pick me from school and drop me home once before that. I agreed, and the conversation was done.

Granny looked at me with worried eyes and asked if I had started the fight. I told her that we started drinking in school from this year, but Madam Shanta had always hated everyone without any reason. And I was all set mentally so couldn't dare to fight with the cruellest creature, who was almost triple my age and my size.

Much later, it was time to sleep, and Granny kept on caressing my hair till she was awake. I couldn't sleep properly. I looked at the ceiling and thought about the fights I had with people as things weren't going well, and I had to do get rid of this stuff.

I was feeling some pain in my arms and knuckles, but I consoled myself by saying, 'What else are we supposed to accept from witches like Madam Shanta?' I was feeling very bad and felt weird as I had never come across such idiots in my life before. I didn't like fighting with anyone, but it just happened, and I couldn't stop anything.

When I didn't respond to their rude behaviour, I felt like a loser inside, and when I did so, I felt I was not ready to accept this and had to get rid of it as a part of me never encouraged such behaviour—because I didn't want to become like them. I was very brave when I fought with them, and later I felt irritated and wanted to cry to lighten my heart.

I hit people when they got on my nerves. The 'smart me' inside didn't want to let such occurrences take place, so I thought of changing myself and not allow people to bother and interrupt me.

I wanted harmony in my life once again as such quarrels irritated me; I wanted to live a great life. There was a time when I used to tell Karan that we have lived these years of our lives so well and hopefully would do so till we die and God would surely give us both a 'Noble Prize' when we die for living life to the fullest.

The time had come to start the change needed to bring back the old, happy life. It was mine, and I needed to stay calm and make it.

FOURTEEN

The school was going well. Results of the exams before vacations had been declared already. I had done well in all the subjects except science. Our subject teachers had started distributing unsolved test papers to help us prepare for the final exams. The session was coming to an end, and revision was going on. The entire class was happy to see that Madam Shanta was not coming to school, but the question was 'Where was she, and why wasn't she coming to school?' I was worried, but later I asked my kind heart not to interfere in such matters, and I didn't care.

It had been some ten to fifteen days that Madam Shanta wasn't seen in school or anywhere by anybody. Even Newspaper had no clue about her. The entire class was happy. Latika came to me, saying that she wanted to talk to me. I told her that we should let go of whatever had happened between us as I didn't want to argue or fight with anyone anymore, and I left.

Our English teacher came to engage our class. The syllabus was completed, so she distributed some practice papers. She had been nice to us the entire year. She asked us about our personal lives and was eager to know the truth from everybody. I didn't tell her anything about me and asked Rasheen not to discuss anything about Atul, and Amaar was smart enough to take care of himself.

Later, she asked us if we drank daily. We refused, telling her that we hadn't drunk in school till now. She seemed to be behaving in a different way today, like a spy. A few idiots from our class told her many things from bunking classes to smoking cigarettes in the school. Amaar looked at me, and we informed each other not to utter a word about anything that we had done, and all our friends nodded.

During the maths class that day, while the teacher was distributing exam papers to each one of us, Sagar threw a chit at me that read, 'Sorry'. I knew too well that it was him, but ignored him as each time he reminded me of his presence, I felt pain inside. Our teacher was happy to see me improve and asked me to practise more. The entire class had done well. Our studies were going on well but not our personal lives. Rasheen was still single, and her terms with Adhiraaj had to be improved as he avoided her always.

Soni was going through fights with her boyfriend, who lived in a different city, though Rasheen had informed her that distant relationships wouldn't go well. I was single too, but the most important thing was that I had to get rid of tantrums as I felt heavy inside. The high school was coming to an end, and we all had to join different schools for the last two years of schooling as this wasn't a senior secondary school.

Sagar kept on throwing chits at me till the recess. I kept on ignoring him. The bell had rung, and we were about to join our friends at the canteen. Latika called me from behind, and I told her that I didn't want to get into fights with anyone as I already had enough of it. She then requested me to stay as she wanted to apologise for dating my boyfriend. I stood and listened to her. 'Mahi, I am sorry to have hurt you. I shouldn't have misbehaved with you,' she said.

I looked at her as she was very fake, and I replied, 'Latika, speak the truth if you feel that you should.' I didn't trust her crocodile tears; I left the place, and joined my friends.

We were all at the canteen when suddenly Amaar came with his newly found love and introduced her to the group. She was the same girl who that day had said 'Mahi, you look great' and 'Your friends are good too'. I got it then what she had meant when she praised my friends; she was praising Amaar.

She looked like a IV-class student—thin and short—and Amaar had a big, fat tummy. They both looked like father and daughter, but who cared as I could see how happy Amaar was with her. He was my friend, after all, and whosoever was his girlfriend, I would stand by him. They walked the school ground, holding hands, like a father takes his little child to the park to play with other kids.

After some time, he came with his girlfriend as she wanted to have some food. She took a bread roll from Rasheen's plate, and Rasheen kicked her and snatched back the bread roll. It was her favourite. I told her that she was Amaar's girlfriend. She shouted, 'So what? She is not my girlfriend.' Amaar seemed to be consoling his girlfriend by politely telling her that Rasheen wasn't bad, and it was just that she loved bread rolls and didn't share them with anyone.

Later, he came to Rasheen, telling her that if Adhiraaj needed something from him, he would surely help him as he was Rasheen's love. On listening to this, Rasheen got emotional and gave a full bread roll to his girlfriend. I laughed as I stood observing them.

During the last class that day, which was taken by a not-so-strict teacher, Sagar started throwing chits at me that had 'Sorry' written on them. He did it four times, and before he could continue, I wrote 'Fuck off' on a rough register and threw it in his face. It took some five minutes for him to adjust his nose and make sure that he was fine. Later, he smiled at me, opened the register, read it, and asked another classmate to give it back to me. He then looked at his right side.

We bunked the zero period and went to the terrace. Amaar had called his girlfriend to join us, and she was brave enough to join us. Rasheen had brought her mobile phone upstairs, and we sat listening to songs. Rasheen then dialled Adhiraaj's phone, and they both talked to each other. I wondered if Adhiraaj had started liking her and whether he was not going to school these days. What a coincidence it was! Soni was busy with her boyfriend on phone. Maria and Rishabh were playing some weird games.

Amaar was busy talking to his girlfriend. I was happy for him as I had never seen him smile so much. I could see him kiss her by opening his mouth so big as if he might swallow her in a second. She was no less; she sat on his lap and kept on hugging him all the time. I thought it was not good to stare at someone while he or she was getting physical, so I ignored them and sat watching the sky that I always loved doing.

I heard the sound of knocking on the door. Somebody had knocked on the terrace door. I looked through the hole and saw that it was Sagar. I went out as I didn't want people to know that he had come. He asked me to sit on the stairs as he wanted to talk something serious. He apologised to me for what he had done. I told him that I had already had enough of fake things and was in no mood to take any more. I opened the terrace door and got inside, and when I was about to close the door, he kept his hand on the door and said, 'Mahi, I told you that I want to spend my life with you.' I looked at him and could feel the pain that reminded me of all that happened in the past. He politely added, 'I am sorry that I couldn't keep my promise.'

I gave him a tight slap as I desperately wanted to and replied, 'I kept my promise,' and closed the door in his face.

I had told him once that if he tried to date some other girl in my presence, I would give him a slap. I was feeling lighter than before, but I was not finished with him. I needed some time.

The bell had rung, and we were all still at the terrace, busy in our own worlds. I had tears in my eyes. Rasheen was done talking to Adhiraaj and came running from the corner of the terrace, informing all of us to go downstairs. I quickly wiped my tears and got back to them when suddenly Amaar shouted, 'No, we will do it after marriage,' to his girlfriend, and this made me laugh—the way he said it in a girly voice, shouting for help. I looked at the funny surroundings, and we went back to the class for our bags.

We were together outside the school gate when suddenly I heard the honk of a car. It was Pearl again. I looked at it from the corner of my eye but was in no mood to argue or fight again. She had got the headlight fixed and was sitting in the driver's seat with her friends. Rasheen was with me. I was wondering whether I should tell her about what Pearl had done to me. She might leave nothing the way it was; rather it would break everything, including Pearl, into pieces.

I didn't like Pearl because she had dumped Adhiraaj. Rasheen never liked her as she was Adhiraaj's girlfriend. She was Rasheen's worst enemy. I didn't tell Rasheen anything. I saw Karan walking towards me. He had come to pick me up and drop me home after spending some time with me as he was leaving for Mumbai the next day.

We met. He was in his school dress too, and he looked great, wearing blue pants. We walked towards the other gate of the school where he had parked his car. Rasheen stood talking to Karan, and for the first time, I felt that they both were happily talking to each other. There was a boy hiding with a girl behind a small shop near our school. They were wearing our school dress and were from our school. Later, I saw the girl push the boy on the wall, and they were kissing.

Rasheen had to go, and she bid goodbye and left for her hostel. Karan was in his car, waiting for me to get inside. I looked at them again curiously but couldn't see their faces. This time the girl was on the outside, and the boy pulled her hair and kissed her. Karan pressed the car's horn, signalling me to get in. This interrupted them, and they both came out—Latika and Sagar. I looked at them, irritated, as they had apologised to me, and I was smart enough not to take their apology.

Latika looked at the ground, embarrassed, and Sagar looked into my eyes. I got inside the car. Karan asked me who they were and confirmed if it was Sagar and Latika. I nodded. Sagar was looking inside the car and staring at Karan, and suddenly Karan asked me if I wanted him to make Sagar feel jealous by kissing him. I looked at Karan. He was laughing already, and I joined his laughing session and we left the place.

I was all quiet and was thinking about what I had just seen. I laughed after recalling the scene when Sagar pulled Latika's hair. 'Pull my hair. I am Latika' was my favourite dialogue I shared with Karan, and he laughed.

'Bub, my cute clown, did I tell you that you look great?' he said.
'Karan, did I tell you that you were a copycat just now?'
'Copycat, I fear. I edited it, though.'
'I would like to tell you something,' I said seriously.
'What, bub?'
'I don't want it any more because it was never a part of my life before, and I don't want it to be,' I said, lost in my thoughts.
'What happened, bub?'
'I don't want to be with you, Karan. I don't want to get used to it,' I replied after looking at him as he didn't understand after knowing everything.
He stopped the car and said, 'What the hell are you talking?' He looked serious and later confirmed if I was joking.
I laughed louder after seeing him looking at me worried and continued, 'You idiot, I meant that I don't want fights and arguments in

my life, never. It bothers me, and I don't want such brawls to spoil my happy life.'

He seemed to have released the breath he had held and said, 'Bub, you have a bad habit of fighting with the ones who abuse me. You don't have to.'

'You don't tell me what and what not to do, Karan.'

'Stop behaving rudely. Listen to me. Be a little more realistic, and start saying no more often. Say no to yourself. You know you don't like fighting, but you do, and later you become irritated, angry, and sad. This interrupts your laughter that spreads like music, and you end up crying.'

I looked at him as I had always respected his suggestions. Karan would always be one man whom I would share things with. He was smart.

'But if you ever get irritated extremely, then go for it, burst out the anger, and fuck the world, but then you shouldn't feel bad for it. Do what you think you should. You know how to play sensible. Fights don't lead you anywhere. Fuck and dump. Don't take things seriously and interrupt your happy living. Be a quick and sensible player. Do it your way, Mahi. Your way, highway,' he laughed.

I smiled at him when he said so. 'Karan is Batman for me,' I said to myself. 'I will have to get rid of this strongly so that I can destroy such unwanted stuff any time in my life, if needed, and resume my happiness.'

'You don't sleep too much either, bub. You don't realise how important this is,' he said, ignoring the previous comments.

'Do I have dark circles?' I asked.

'No, you send me messages late night. I like them, so keep sending them, but not at the wrong hour when you are supposed to sleep.'

'Now where does this come from?' I said as it had no relation with the above.

'It is related to you,' he replied confidently.

I smiled at him and said, 'You are my saviour, and I love you, Karan.' I hugged him.

'I love you too.' He held my hand, kissed it, and said, 'Will you marry me?' mockingly.

'If that happens, I will win the world,' I said, replying funnily.

'Eh!'

'I hate your "ehs" as much as I hate those rich losers.'

'You hate everyone, bub, always complaining and crying,' he said, making fun of me.

'I don't hate you, Karan. What's this?' I asked, placing my hand opposite his face.

'That's your leg, Mahi,' he said, making fun of me.

'And I kick you, Karan,' I said and slapped him.

It was time to go home, and he dropped me. 'I will miss you, Mahi. I'll come back soon after meeting my aunt,' he said and left. I stood on the road, looking at him going, and got inside when his car was nowhere to be seen.

I got inside the house and went to see Granny. She was talking to Baldeb. She handed me the phone, and I spoke to him for like five minutes, asking if Aunt Daisy behaved well with him. He told that my aunt had changed a lot and helped him in doing house work, which I didn't think she did. He was a man who never complained and just moved on with his life happily. I praised him and asked how their son was—the dog Aunt Daisy had named Baldeb. 'Daisy and both the Baldebs are in good health,' Granny confirmed and snatched the phone.

She spoke to her sister while I went to freshen up, and the call was done. Granny came to me and asked if things were going well in school and if Madam Shanta hit us again. I told her that she had not come to school for the last ten days. 'That's good,' she said and brought me the lunch.

She looked at me till I was done eating and asked if I spoke with Karan. 'Granny,' I said loudly.

'Baby,' she said politely.

'What time do I come from school?' I asked.

'About 2 p.m.', she replied.

'What time did I come today?'

'At 4 p.m.', she replied and looked at me, expecting something interesting.

'It means that I met Karan and spent time with him, and he dropped me home.'

'That is good news,' she said and laughed, looking at me, expecting I would respond to her excitement, which I didn't.

It was the fourth day after that day.

For some reason, we didn't go outside to the ground for prayer; rather we prayed in our classes. Our class teacher seemed to be the happiest man on the planet that day. He kept on looking at the ground, thinking of something and laughing again and again. He took our attendance and started discussing about his subject, disaster management. He asked us how the revision was going on with other subjects and also if we were studying at home for our final exams that were to commence soon.

Newspaper informed us that she had heard a junior class teacher discuss with another teacher that Madam Shanta and our class teacher had an argument on some topic, a bad argument. Suddenly after he was done with his laughs, he got serious and said that he loved his class more than anything else in this school and wouldn't like if teachers complained to him that we misbehaved or were disobedient.

He asked us if science classes were going well and also if the syllabus was completed. We told him that one chapter was still left. Later, he told us the reason behind his smile, which was that he was soon to be the vice-principal, and we congratulated him. Madam Shanta was supposed to be the vice-principal but for some reason, she couldn't—like they say. 'May the best man win'.

He asked us the reason why Madam Shanta hit us the other day as he had come to know from Newspaper. We told him that Madam Shanta didn't need a reason to hit us and she had been like that always. He was another teacher, but we talked our heart out to him without thinking much. Later, we told him that she always found some mistake or the other, even if there wasn't any. Also, we asked him to speak to Father Edward as she was becoming violent and we weren't kids any more. I added that she hit us on our knuckles and also on our arms after asking us to remove our blazers. I wondered, 'Who does that?' And my heart answered, 'Madam Shanta.'

He was listening to us seriously. We complained like kids. Rasheen added to it, 'We all make mistakes, and teachers have the right to correct us. That's why our parents send us to school, so as to learn discipline.' The class started hooting.

'Do they?' confirmed our class teacher, mockingly, as she had said this to him on the first day of our school. He was a jolly-natured person, and we didn't mind even if he shouted at us.

During recess, Amaar had planned to drink as it had been days since we had any. Rishabh refused to join us, saying that madam was back and that if we were caught, she wouldn't leave us alive. I dragged him upstairs with us. They had brought pastry cakes, beer cans were bought by Rasheen this time, and I paid for snacks that we had bought from the canteen. It was indeed a big day for us as our school was coming to an end. We might never get this opportunity as life went on, so we thought we would make the celebration special.

Maria had stopped coming to school as she was preparing for the final exams at home and so was Shyna. It was me, Abhi, Amaar, Soni, Rasheen, and Rishabh. There was a helper who was cleaning the terrace. Amaar went on moving and dragging his feet and spreading the mud everywhere. The helper boy was older to us. We were sitting on the terrace when he asked Amaar not to drag his feet. Amaar lifted him up a foot from the ground and warned him that if he dared to talk like this, he would be thrown from the terrace.

The boy, when he got on the ground, said that he would complain to Madam Shanta about this and she would see what she needed to do with Amaar. I shouted at Amaar and apologised to the boy. Rasheen knew him well as he was the one who had put the beer cans in the fridge in the school kitchen. She talked to him and asked him not to talk anything with any of the teachers, and he agreed. Amaar apologised to the boy, and he went away to do his work.

We sat talking to each other when Rasheen asked me about the watch I was wearing. 'Dad bought it for me,' I said. She borrowed it and wore it on her hand. Also, she asked Amaar to give her his locket that was in the shape of a skull as she loved such things, but he refused.

Amaar announced that because it was the last day, he would drink more than two cans and the others would drink just one. I refused to accept it as he wouldn't leave anything for us. Before we could put the cutlets in the plates, Amaar had already started having it from the packet. 'This giant will finish it all,' shouted Rasheen and snatched the packet from him. He made innocent faces at her, requesting her to give him just one last cutlet; as expected, she didn't. Also Rishabh said that we should divide the food and drinks equally among the ones present.

I had a can of beer with two cutlets. Rishabh could only have half a can as Amaar couldn't stop himself from snatching the can, which was struggling in Rishabh's hand for the last half and hour. Soni, Rasheen, and Abhi had one and a half can of chilled beer. Also, they decided to do weird things like putting beer in their mouths and spitting on the school ground. I warned them not to waste it, and also if we are caught, we would be thrown out of the school. Rasheen said if any one of us was caught, we wouldn't name the others, which was expected as we had unity.

Rishabh requested us to play some game, so I went to the other side of the terrace, brought a stone, wrapped it with all the foil paper we had, and made it into a ball. I then placed the empty beer cans as pins. I threw the ball at the cans and tried to drop the beer cans. 'Buds at bowling! What an idea! I love it,' said Soni.

'Don't insult the game, bowling.' We named it "baaling", which didn't mean anything.

'Just a word,' I replied. We started playing it. Abhi got in the position to throw the ball. As he pulled his hand backwards to throw it with force, Rasheen snatched it from him.

'This is cheating,' he shouted, but no one seemed to be listening to him. Rasheen threw the ball but didn't hit any pin. Abhi laughed childishly. Rishabh threw the ball, but it didn't reach till the pins and stopped at the middle, and he was embarrassed. Soni managed to strike the pins by fluke. Amaar threw it with such a force that the foil was torn and the stone came out. I hated him for his stupidity, and I didn't get a chance, but we all enjoyed the game and making fun of each other.

Rishabh took all the empty cans and put them in a bag as we might need them for Madam Shanta, as suggested by Rasheen The fifth period was coming to an end, so we were all ready to go back and join the class. Amaar suggested that we take water in the mouth, wash our teeth, and spit it on the ground, and we agreed as we might not get another chance to do it.

We took the bottle, filled our mouths with water, and spit it on the ground; it landed on Madam Shanta mistakenly. She looked up, and we hid ourselves. Quickly, I asked them to go downstairs, and we did. Rishabh, in a scared voice, said, 'Amaar brings trouble always,' and Amaar gave him a punch on his stomach. We got inside our class; it was the last class, environment studies, the class where the sections were merged.

We took the books out and joined with the rest of our classmates in the school hall where the teacher taught us. The teacher had begun teaching when Madam Shanta came inside with stitches on her forehead, which could be due to the bottle I had thrown at the window of her house. 'What a shot, Mahi!' said Amaar, giving a pat on my back after seeing her stitches.

Rasheen praised me by saying, 'If we have people like you in our country, people wouldn't dare to harm innocent people.' I was shocked and was not proud of it. 'Did I hit her?' I asked myself.

She asked our subject teacher if all the students were present, and she nodded after counting the strength, excluding the ones who were absent. Later, she asked Madam Shanta how she got hurt. She informed her that she had fallen from the stairs on the floor. 'Poor floor,' murmured Amaar, and Rasheen laughed. I asked them to stop the nonsense.

She stood there, looking at us with scary eyes, and suddenly she showed a watch and asked, 'Whose is this?' She had found it outside the class. I looked at the watch; it was mine. I looked at Rasheen, who had left it outside the class. I raised my hand and went to get my watch. As I thanked her, she gave me two slaps without stopping. I got hurt on my right eye by her nail, and she shouted, 'What the hell was this watch doing on the terrace?'

I needed some time to open my eye and look at her. She pulled me out by the collar of my blazer, brought a stick from the other section, and started hitting me on my legs. My eye was paining badly, and I shouted, apologising, and she took me to the principal's room.

She hit me on my knuckles. I was still rubbing my eye. I was crying with pain, and that was the first day after junior school that I cried so much. The bell had rung and the students had started coming out from their classes, heading towards the assembly ground for the national anthem.

After the anthem, I could see Amaar, Rasheen, and Soni looking for me here and there. They saw me standing outside the principal's office.

Rasheen started crying after seeing my red and swollen eye. Soni said that they would accept and surrender, and I asked them not to do anything unless I asked them, and forcefully I sent them back home. Amaar came back and said, 'Count the times she hits you. I will take a strong revenge. She will pay for the pain you will go through.' He went away, kicking the door angrily.

The students had gone home, while I stood there, waiting for I didn't know how long. The boy who cleaned the terrace had seen madam hitting me. He asked me what happened, and I asked him to leave me alone and not to put salt on my wounds. I could see him express sympathy, but I didn't need it. I had wiped my tears and stood, waiting for her to come with the principal.

I could see some teachers come and enjoy the scene, looking at me like people watched the animals in a zoo. They were all gone while the boy still stood, observing me, and the gate was closed. She came back after an hour, gave me a tight slap, and said, 'Were you drinking on the terrace?' I looked at her, shocked, as if I was mistaken for the culprit, but I was confident enough to refuse.

'Are you amongst the ones who threw the bottle with a note at my window? Are you the one who kept the waste stuff with the whisky bottle outside my house?'

'What an idiot!' I thought. It was a vodka bottle we had kept, and its label said that clearly. I refused to accept anything and listened to her in shock, adding that I didn't do such bad things, and she shouted, 'Were you sleeping on the terrace and left your watch?' I didn't respond to her. 'I will make your life hell, remember,' she said and went inside.

It was 4 p.m., and I wasn't allowed to go home. After some time, she came back with a register and took down my full name, roll number, and section with my class teacher's name. She asked me to name the ones who were with me. I refused, telling her again and again that I wasn't a drunkard and had gone alone to the terrace to bunk the class. I got a tight slap on the same side that had already swollen because of her heavy giant-like hand. I couldn't find a better answer as this wasn't an innocent answer but had to be accepted by her.

She came back after some ten minutes and threw a paper on my face that read 'Restricted'. I wasn't left so brave to get more slaps and beatings, so I took the paper in my hand, and she continued, 'I will make sure that you don't come to school for ten days and also that you aren't allowed to sit for the final exams.' I stood there, listening to her just as I was asked to, and by that time, that boy was asked to get my school bag from my class, and I was asked to leave.

I stood remembering what Karan had said: 'If you get extremely irritated by something, burst the anger and fuck what the world says.' I was planning how to get back at her in a way she wouldn't come to know who did it. But I knew it wasn't possible till I was a student in this school; she was a teacher, not a schoolmate I could fight with, a cruel teacher indeed. My hands were shivering as my knuckles were paining. I was strong enough to endure the pain and the swollen eye. The boy came and informed me that my friend had taken my bag.

As I went out, I saw Rasheen sitting on roadside with my school bag and her own, wearing the school dress. She hadn't gone to her hostel and was waiting for me outside the school gate. All the others had gone back home. It was such a moment of true friendship. I was in this problem because Rasheen had left my watch on the terrace. Otherwise, we wouldn't have been caught. She knew how loyal I was and would never take her name even if I was caught on her behalf. She was waiting for me and was tired of holding two heavy bags.

I hugged her tight. I could feel her crying inside, but I consoled her, telling her that things were fine. She pushed me back and started shouting, 'She hit on your knuckles in a way not even an enemy hits, and you are telling me that things are fine. She hit you on your face many times, leaving your eye swollen, and you are telling me things are fine!'

'What do you expect her to do—hug me and say, "Baby, you left your watch on the terrace while you were trying spitting after you were done drinking"?' I laughed, trying to make her laugh, but she didn't.

We headed towards the main road, and I told her that madam also asked if we left bottle and notes outside her house and if we were the ones who had thrown the bottle at her window the other day. Rasheen was pissed and said that she would accept that it was her mistake tomorrow in school. 'You don't know what to talk and how to deal tactfully. If you do this, you will get us all into trouble, so shut your mouth. She will also drag you for the letter we wrote for Atul as you were lucky to have been left innocent that day,' I shouted.

'So what? I don't care, Mahi. I can't see her hit you so much and so badly,' she said.

'Close your eyes if you can't see it,' I said, irritated.

'I am in no mood to laugh at your silly jokes, Mahi,' she yelled, getting angry.

'Oh! Go on with your good jokes, please,' I said to her.

'Mahi, please, we will all surrender tomorrow. You can't take all this alone,' she said.

'You don't have to get idiotically emotional, for God's sake. If anyone of you utters anything, mark my words. I will not have relation with any of you, nor will I ever talk to you,' I replied.

'You can't do this, Mahi,' she shouted louder this time.

'He who is smart will get over it, and that's me,' I said politely to her. 'I have not accepted anything that we did from throwing the waste paper plates to spitting at her from the terrace. I just said that I was alone, bunking, on the school terrace and, therefore, I left my watch. Also, if you all surrender, she would not give us admit cards to appear in the final exams. Amaar wouldn't get it for sure, and nor will you. Father Edward has a good impression of me, so I will get mine, I am sure. So let it be the way it is going. Simply keep your mouth shut.

'It's not that we are scared, so we aren't telling her the truth. I am sure nobody would want to waste a year and not be allowed to sit in the examination hall. I will play it tactfully and smartly as I need to, so you all stay out of it. After the exams are done and we get our mark sheets, you can do whatsoever with her,' I explained.

She seemed to have understood what I meant and promised me that she wouldn't let any of them say anything. She didn't want to do it but had to as I requested, for this was the only way we could be safe. We went to our respective homes.

As I reached home, Granny came out jumping, asking me how my day was with Karan. As I was late again, she thought I had met Karan. I told her that I had some work in the school and Karan had gone out of station.

As I came back from the washroom, wearing casuals, she saw me and started shouting, 'What the hell is this?' She pointed at my eye. I told her that I had fallen from the stairs in school. 'What hit you in your eye?' she asked.

'The iron railing, but I am fine. Don't worry, Granny.'

'Why shouldn't I worry?' she said, louder.

'Please, I am in no mood to argue with you,' I said.

'I will cut your tongue if you do,' she yelled and asked if I had fought with someone. I refused politely, telling her that I really fell off the stairs. She didn't seem to believe this, and I lay on the bed to give some rest to my body, which was struggling with pain as if I'd got bitten by red ants. I had scratches on my hands, and my knuckles were all red.

Around 9 p.m., she came to my room and woke me up as I had slept while taking rest. I got up and had my food and strawberry shake with my eyes half open, and my body felt weak.

Granny looked at me with worried eyes and said, 'These days are unlucky for my little one.' She was referring to me. 'Your teacher hit you hard that day, and today you fell from the stairs and got an eye swollen,' said she. I was in my sleep while having food. When I was done, I slept again like a lazy bum not belonging to any other world but to a world of my own thoughts.

FIFTEEN

The golden radiance of the afternoon lightened my room. I tried getting back to my sweet dreams but couldn't, and after trying for some minutes, I got up by the smell of something delicious Mom was cooking in the kitchen. I couldn't wait to try that yummy whatever, and my mouth started watering. I quickly went to brush my teeth in the bathroom downstairs as mine was being cleaned.

I heard a child singing songs and realised that it could be my little brother Arhaan as he was the only kid in our family. He was bathing and dancing, holding the soap in his hand, making moves and singing songs in I didn't know which language. He was spreading water everywhere and also at me, not deliberately.

After I was done brushing, I admired my face in the mirror, checking if there was some improvement in my eye that had swollen because of that giant-like teacher. The swelling wasn't there, but the spot of red colour had changed to purple colour in the last couple of days. The change had begun—for my life also. I thought of ignoring nonsense and stayed happily involved in things I loved doing.

I was very hungry, so I went and stood outside the kitchen. I waited for Mom to give me whatever she was cooking in a plate, but she didn't, and this didn't let me keep my patience.

'What are you cooking, Mom?' I asked eagerly.

'Are you done brushing?' she asked.

'Yes, Mom.' I looked at her, smiling, and told her that if the smell was so good, how delicious that would be to eat.

She removed the plate from above the frying pan, and I saw kebabs getting brown. She smiled at me as she knew I was fond of kebabs and asked me to settle at the dining table.

They looked so appetising and I thought of having them immediately. She said that she was bringing the casserole to the dining table when suddenly Granny called my name, saying that my phone had rung. 'Who the hell is that?' I shouted and asked her to leave it. She came to the veranda and looked at me, smiling with eyes wide open and using her hands in a way to express 'wow', and I understood she meant Karan.

I forgot the food and went running to talk to Karan as he had called after some days since he had gone to Mumbai.

'It's Jill. Time to say hurray!' I yelled, laughing, copying a cartoon that Arhaan liked watching.

I answered the call.

'Prep, I know that I am so nice that you can't ever get tired of me,' I said, praising myself funnily.

'Put away the niceness. I am so fond of you that I might accompany you for endless treats until the end of life,' he replied.

'Now that is what makes you priceless, Karan.'

'Bub, you are the real non-stop music, and I like listening to you.'

'Eh!' I said, copying him this time, like he did when I told him how much he meant to me.

'Ah, bub, I hope you aren't left alone after I have come to visit here.'

'You are a part of me, prep. I feel that you are always with me,' I said, stretching the word *always*. 'That's why I get irritated so much,' I said, making fun of him.

'Oh! Weird, you smart me,' he replied.

'So true! Weird *you* smart me.'

'How are things in school? Did you speak to Sagar or anybody?'

'I have started avoiding rich losers, except for one as she caught hold of my collar and restricted me from coming to school.'

'What?'

'You remember that giant-like teacher? She hit me badly when she found my watch on the terrace the day we got drunk.'

'Really? How hard did she hit you?'

'What do you mean?'

'You are lucky enough. If I was there, I would have given you a punch for leaving your watch. You should have been smart enough, bub.'

'It's long story, prep. I will tell you some time.'

'What an ass you are! Bloody idiot!'

'I already have a father, and you don't need to be another. Thank you.'

'Stop getting irritated. You should know how much I care for you, and also I am so fond of you.'

'I know I am as irresistible as hot chocolate,' I said, praising myself.

'And I love having you . . . in my life,' he added.

'I so want to see you, prep. Come soon, please.'

'No way, I hate you.'

'Of course! Life is awesome with you, Karan,' I added.

'Bub, I miss you.'

'A flying kiss for you, Karan.'

'Go away now!'

And he disconnected the call.

I looked at my mobile to recheck if the call was disconnected, and it was indeed. I went downstairs to have food.

In the evening, Mom came and sat next to me in the living room. 'Mahi, what happened on your cheek and eye?' she asked.

'I fell from the stairs, Mom.'

'I don't believe. It's like somebody has hit you. Did you fight with someone?'

'No, Mom, I fell from the stairs and bumped into the iron railing.'

'Oh!' she said, worried. 'Do you have pain?'

'No, Mom, I am fine.'

'OK,' she said, smiling at me, and added, 'If you're fine, then you should go to school from tomorrow.'

'This is not why I am not going to school. It is because the course is finished, and there is nothing much to do in school apart from revising, and I like doing it at home when I am alone. I study well.'

'Good, all the best,' she said and went to her room.

I had told Granny the same thing as I didn't want her to go and fight with Madam Shanta for all that had happened. I was happy to stay at home as I had enough time to sleep and also study. I gave five hours a day to my studies as exams were commencing in the next few weeks. I kept going through notes and assured myself that I would do well as it was class X, which meant that my percentage would get me admission in another good school like Bartha, where I was studying.

The next day in the evening, I went to the market to buy stationery as I had to get ready for my final exams and had to have all that was needed. Pearl had come to the same stationery shop. I ignored her, selected my stuff, paid the bill, and got out of the shop.

I could see her staring at me. I was in no mood to fight as I was a changed girl now. I went towards the main road to board an auto for home when suddenly she came in her car behind me, hit me on my legs, and went away.

I could feel a very bad pain in my legs and my forehead as I fell on the road. A man came and helped me get up. My clothes were all dirty with mud, and the stationery packet was torn and all the stuff lay here and there on the road. I quickly got up, picked up all the things, and put them in the same packet, holding it properly so that the stuff didn't fall. I had scratches in my elbow and my knees, and my forehead was fine but paining. I thanked the man who helped me. I cleaned my clothes, removing the dirt, and stood at the roadside.

A few more shopkeepers had seen me fall as a car hit me. They asked me if I was fine. They brought water for me. I thanked them, and one of them asked if I wanted him to drop me home. I refused.

Luckily, I could see a yellow bike on the road that a policeman rode. I shouted, 'Sir, I need your help.' He came towards me and looked at my clothes and my elbow, which was bleeding. I told him that somebody hit me with her car from behind and ran away. He asked me if I had the number of the car. I said no and told him the colour and the model. He was on a round in the market as it was a crowded place. He asked me if I knew who that person was. I told him Pearl's name, adding that she was fifteen years old and didn't have a licence. He waited with me when I asked him to excuse me, and I called Adhiraaj.

'Hey, Adhiraaj.'
'Mahi, what's up?'
'I am good. I need your help.'
'Of course, anything for you.'
'Do you remember the number of Pearl's white car?'
'Yes, why do you need it?'
'Just let me know the number. I will tell you the story later.'
He gave the number.
'Thank you, bye.'
'What happened, Mahi? Are you OK?'
'Yeah, I am fine, goodbye.'

I disconnected the call and gave this number to the policeman. He took my number and informed me that he would call me after investigating further. It was a small city, and I knew that they would catch hold of her soon. I reminded him again that she was fifteen years old and didn't have a driving licence and still drove the car. He asked me to visit him at the police station the next day; he was a helpful man who was doing his duty properly. He asked me if he should take me to the doctor. I thanked him and went away after taking his mobile number.

It was late by then, and I left for home. I didn't want to fight but wanted to punish her as one couldn't just hit anyone. Everybody has a right to live. In this place, police was what I had to take help from, and I did. I was smart enough to do so. I praised myself and got inside the house, forgetting the pain I felt on my body due to this.

The minute I got inside the house, my mom dragged me to Dad, who was standing rigidly and looking at me with angry eyes. 'Oh my God, now what?' I said to myself. 'So you are not going to school?' he said.

'Yes, because there is nothing much happening. I am studying at home,' I replied. Dad kept on staring at me, hating me for I didn't know what reason as I was studying seriously—something that he always wanted me to do.

'When is the next Madrid match?' I asked Dad, smiling and changing the topic. He didn't respond, but Mom did.

She came closer, looked at me angrily, and gave me a tight slap. I looked at her, wanting an answer, and she retorted, 'Since when have you started getting drunk in school? You are restricted from going to school, and you lied to me. How dare you? Is this what I taught you? You are spoilt, Mahi.'

Dad came near and shouted, 'I will make sure that you don't go anywhere. Where are you coming from?'

I kept on wondering if I was the unlucky girl who was caught doing things. Mom started shouting again. I didn't know what to say. All I knew was that I didn't want to live with them. I hated them; they wouldn't let me live. So what if I was restricted? I was not the only one. There were many more in different schools. They couldn't rule over my independent life. I was unlucky that I was caught, and I thought of not telling a lie, so I stood listening to them and crying. I wondered if she had become a spy, checking my school bag, to see if there was something which was not supposed to be there.

'Do you also smoke?' asked Mom angrily.

'No,' I replied politely.

She held my hand and shouted with tears in her eyes, 'Another lie.'

I told her that it was true; I never smoked. She didn't seem to be listening to anything I was saying. Though I didn't like her hitting me, I never wanted her to cry.

'Please don't cry, Mom. I swear on you, I don't smoke,' I said. She asked me to go away, and I got into my room, wiping my tears because I didn't want Granny to argue with them as she had never liked anybody scolding or beating me since my childhood.

Granny came and asked me how I got my clothes dirty. I didn't reply, and she saw my elbow bleeding. 'What happened, baby?' She checked my face properly, getting tensed. 'Your knee is bleeding too. What happened? Did you fight with someone?' she asked, worried.

'What do you think I am so weak that people can beat me and leave me bleeding?' I replied confidently.

She looked at me, worried, and wanted an answer. I told her that I fell on the road. 'How could you?' she asked.

'Like anybody can,' I replied nonchalantly.

'Shut up,' she shouted seriously this time. I looked at her and told her that I fell as I wasn't walking properly and the road was bumpy.

'It seems like somebody has pushed you, leaving your body bleeding from scratches.'

'No, Granny, I fell as I didn't notice that the road was uneven.'

I went to the washroom to clean my body and came back wearing my night suit. Granny was waiting for me with eyes that looked worried and was holding a medical kit in her hands. She pulled my hand and made me sit on the bed. She sat next to me, keeping my leg on her lap, and cleaned the wounds with an antiseptic liquid and her love dialogues. 'You don't know how much I love you. You're the world to me, and I can't see you getting hurt. Never! You are my child,' she said, stretching the word *my*.

'Your parents got married at an early age and gave birth to you the next year. I have taken care of you always. You grew up in my arms. You are my child, and no mother can see her child getting hurt. Don't you ever fight with anyone. I know you do.' She went on with her emotional dialogues, and I had to listen. 'Fighting is not the solution for anything. I saw it on TV that four students of your age fought and one of them died.' She had tears in her eyes, and I couldn't control my laughter.

'You ask me not to get emotional, and then what happened to you? It's a minor injury, and I am fine, Granny,' I said and hugged her.

'Granny, my life is all fun and . . . fights sometimes. I don't get into serious fights that lead to killing someone, so relax,' I said, consoling her.

'I think Reenu is right when she asks you to forgive and forget,' she said.

'It's a new world, and such things don't work,' I said. Reenu is my mother's name by the way. 'Granny, in my life, there is nothing like forgiveness or anything like killing, and I promise. I am sleepy. Goodnight,' I said and lay on the bed.

'So early? It's only 9 p.m.', she confirmed.

'Sleep has no time, Granny.'

I lay on the bed, feeling bad about my family. 'I have to be a better child,' I thought, but I never did things deliberately or to hurt them. My parents said that I told lies to them. True that was; I was never so comfortable in telling the truth because they never appreciated the 'true' me. They never understood me. They wanted me to be like others who just sat at home and studied, wearing big specs. I wanted a well-balanced life with family, friends, and school. I wouldn't like being off balance, focusing on just one thing, no matter what.

My parents would never understand me, nor would these rich losers who thought they were right in everything they did and said that I was all wrong and untrue. 'I will have to do something to make them know, like Karan suggested, and find a remedy instead of faults. Thank you, destiny, I still have Granny and Karan, who make my life worth living.'

The next morning, while I was sleeping soundly, I felt raindrops on my face. I loved the feeling as it was awesome. I took my hand and my legs out of the blanket and felt those drops of rain on me. I so enjoyed it. I was half awake and half sleeping. I loved nature. I was not ready to open my eyes as it might throw away my sleep that I loved so much, and I might have to wake up completely. The drops falling on my body made me wet.

I felt the raindrops for some minutes on the part of my body that was not covered—my neck, my arms, my legs from below the knee, and my face. Though it was winter, I didn't like wearing a sweater, and also my sweatshirt was torn at my elbow last evening. I felt pain as I stretched my body. Suddenly I felt raindrops only on my face and nowhere else. I thought maybe it was raining from some part of the sky and my face lay under the part where it was raining, and that the rest of my body was under the part of the sky from where it wasn't raining. I then realised that I was sleeping on my bed in my room. Then where was the rain coming from? I couldn't accept that the roof might be broken or leaking, so I opened my eyes finally.

What I saw was unexpected and unseen. I saw Granny standing with her eyes closed, her head covered with a scarf; she was murmuring something. And in her hand, she had a small bottle with holy water in it. She was chanting some prayer and sprinkling holy water on my face. I looked here and there. I was in my room at the same place where I had slept last night, and I made double sure that I wasn't dreaming; it was reality. She kept on doing it for some some more minutes, and I lay there enjoying the water drops.

When she was done, she opened her eyes and looked upwards like how people thank God. She looked at me and wished me good morning, and I smiled at her.

I got up and asked, 'What were you doing, Granny?'

'You don't need to know that,' she replied.

'It was very weird,' I said and looked into her eyes that were gazing at me.

'That is why you don't need to know what it was,' she replied angrily.

'I am sorry,' I said politely as I had hurt her religious sentiments.

She said, 'The time isn't good for you, and also you have started telling lies, which you never did before.'

'You have always told me the truth?'

'Everything,' she said louder.

'What lie did I say?' I asked. She ignored me and left the room.

I freshened up and went to the living room. Granny brought breakfast for me and herself, along with strawberry shake. I held my plate, and she looked as if she was hurt.

I also saw Mom, who stared at me and was in no mood to smile. She went to her room, and I thought of not bringing on arguments again.

'What is the matter? Will you please tell me?' I asked politely.

'Your school teacher gave a punch on your face and hit you very hard, making your face and eye swollen, and you told me that you fell from the stairs and bumped into the window,' she said rudely, bringing her eyebrows together.

'I told you that I bumped into the iron railing, not the window,' I corrected her.

'Whatsoever,' she yelled. 'It wasn't the truth.'

'You might have fought with someone yesterday and somebody might have hit you. And you said that the road was uneven and you fell off. Were you running on the bumpy road that you scratched your knees and elbow?' she shouted. She looked as if I had ditched her. I had, according to her. I apologised truly.

'I met with an accident yesterday,' I replied.

'What kind of accident was it?' she quizzed.

'A bike bumped into me,' I said and kept on eating breakfast.

'What do you think, I am stupid?' she asked.

'Of course,' I said. She got up from the chair and went to her room. I called her several times, but she didn't listen to me. I looked at our plates: mine was empty and hers was full of food. She hadn't eaten a bite. I took her plate and my shake mug in my hands and went upstairs to her room.

I opened the door of her room with my knee and got inside, holding the plate and shake mug.

'Why are you behaving weirdly?' I asked.

'I will cut this word *weird* into pieces if you say it again,' she replied.

'I have grown up. That is why I thought of not telling you such silly things,' I said.

'You have grown up so much that you called your grandmother stupid,' she replied.

'Ho, ho, *stupid* stands for "smart talented unique person in demand".'

'What rubbish!' she said.

'Granny, I am sorry to have hurt you, and yes, it was Madam Shanta who hit me, but she didn't punch me all right,' I said, correcting her.

'What did she do? Kiss you?'

'Just some five tight slaps,' I said confidently.

'I knew it too well already.'

'I didn't tell you as I didn't want you to go to my school and complain like junior students' parents do.'

'I would go to your school and talk to the principal. No teacher is allowed to hit the children and that too so badly,' she said.

'Who told you about this?'

'Rasheen called up yesterday to ask about your health and also told me that she came to know from a source that you were restricted from coming to school. And you told me that you wanted to sit and study at home. Another lie!' she said, raising her eyebrow.

'She should have called on my number,' I said to myself. 'My dumb fellow, Rasheen.'

'She had called on your number, and I received the call.'

'It's bad manners, Granny,' I said, surprised.

'Shut up. I am your grandmother. I have a right. Do you know the girl who bumped her bike into you? Oops, it was a car,' she said sarcastically and was irritated at me.

I looked at her, shocked. 'Who told you about this?'

'Do you know her?' she asked, ignoring my reply.

I had to reply, and I did, 'Yes, I do.'

'The policeman had called to inform that you were supposed to visit him at the police station around 6 p.m. I mean, we have to visit the police station,' she said, stretching the word *we*.

'I have stopped creating blunders out of silly fights with rich losers, and this is the only reason I didn't tell you. Otherwise I would have. If I can tell you about the very important part of my life, which is Karan, I wouldn't mind telling you such nonsense.'

She smiled after hearing Karan's name and continued, 'It is not a small issue. Your teacher hit you badly in your eye. What if it had led to some serious problem? What if you had a serious injury in your leg when that girl bumped her car?'

I looked at her, and she was serious when she continued, 'You are supposed to inform me, everything. A parent deserves to know what his child is up to. You aren't grown up so much that you take such decisions on your own. An action is required. If you keep up the same way, and tomorrow if you are in some problem and need us, how would we know the truth? We deserve to know everything about your life. You are our children. You are answerable to us for everything that you do and what you don't do. A child, no matter how old he is, remains a child for his parents always. Do you understand?' I was listening seriously to her. 'You got it, Mahi?' I nodded. 'If you don't tell me about everything, you make me fake and not related,' she said.

'I promise that I will tell you about everything,' I said seriously, and she appreciated it.

Around 6 p.m., I went to the police station with Granny, identified Pearl, and informed the policeman that this was the girl. He made her father sit outside, and we were with him in his cabin. He started scolding her, and I realised that Granny was talking to another policeman in a different cabin. She had come with me, and she always seemed to have friends anywhere. I guess she had found another lost friend as a policeman in the station.

The policeman who promised to help me said to Pearl, 'You are kids and getting so angry and smashing people with your car. is a crime. Do you know that? If you spoil some innocent person's life, you spoil your life as well.' I liked his statement when he called me 'innocent'. Pearl started abusing him, thinking he wouldn't do anything in her father's presence.

I started enjoying the scene knowing that now she was dead for sure; messing with the police was not cool. 'Indian police hits badly and makes the culprit's life next to hell, remember,' he said, raising his eyebrow. 'How dare you abuse the police? You will go to jail,' he said, and she started crying and apologised to him. I observed the scene, watching that rich loser getting punished.

I kept on appreciating him. 'You did a mistake, and, instead of apologising, you are abusing the police,' he said louder.

'If she had killed me, my father would have dragged her to court as it is not that easy to kill a rich brat,' I said confidently. 'The court case would have been in our favour as my granny would have bribed everyone including the judge.' He stared at me angrily as he seemed to be a true and loyal policeman. I apologised to him as I knew that he didn't like what I had just said.

'What do you want me to do? Put you inside the jail or get a female policeman to beat you like a culprit is supposed to be beaten?'
Pearl started crying louder, and I politely said into her ears, 'You did a mistake, and you will have to accept the punishment.' He called a lady constable and asked her to take Pearl and put her behind the bars. Pearl shouted, apologising. I was shocked as I wanted him to give her a few beatings.
I sat next to the policeman, praising him, 'I salute all the policemen like you.'

Pearl kept on crying, holding the bar from inside. I asked him why he didn't give her beatings. He continued doing his work. I went near the bar and murmured to Pearl, 'This is a small, dark, horrifying room that might have scorpions or crabs crawling. Go get your car and run it over them.' I laughed, teasing her, and said, 'Oops, this place isn't that big. You can run a toy car if you have any.'

'You come here,' said the policeman to me. I went back and told him that I was looking at the room properly as I had seen it only in movies before. He asked me if he should keep me also behind the bars so that I could look at it more clearly. I apologised, and he asked me to sign on a paper. I looked at it, and he reminded to sign it. I told him that I was reading what was written. He smiled at me and said, 'This isn't a property document.'

'I don't own any property. I am a student,' I said politely, sounding studious.

Pearl kept on crying, making strange whistles from her nose for God knows how long. I couldn't trust her crocodile tears, so I ignored her and suggested the same to the policeman, who laughed for the first time.

I usually kept my heart at home when I went for such things as my heart was very kind, and my mind didn't appreciate its kindness every time. By that time, Granny and Pearl's father were called inside the cabin. Her father was asked to sign a few documents and pay some amount for her bail as she didn't have a driving licence.

Granny was also asked to sign a paper. Another policeman came; he knew Granny well as my granny was into social work. Pearl was called out, and she apologised to that policeman again. 'I think she should do a few sit-ups, holding her ears,' I suggested to the policeman.

'It's my job to decide what she is supposed to do,' he replied, irritated.

Pearl's father got up and wished Granny. 'How are you, Jugga?' she asked.

'Another friend,' I said to myself and ignored the rest. He hugged his daughter, telling her that we should be friends and not enemies. She looked at me, giving a fake smile, but I didn't bother and asked Granny to leave for home.

Granny smiled at her father and asked me to shake hands with Pearl like a kid is taught to do. I could see Pearl stare at me with hatred. 'I wouldn't get into fights,' I had told myself, and also I thought of giving no importance to a loser like her because rich losers were so fake and untrue when they apologised, and I believed in the truth. 'Don't apologise. It's OK, but if you do, do it truly.'

SIXTEEN

On the eleventh day, before I was about to leave for school, Granny came to me and made me drink holy water. I respected her sentiments, and she once again reminded me that I was supposed to be the way I was before—true to her always. She kissed me goodbye and asked me to inform her if things went wrong in school as I was going after ten days after the restriction letter I was given by Madam Shanta. Also, she asked me to either talk about this to the principal myself or let her do that. I chose the first option, told her, and left for school. Granny dropped me till the auto.

On my way to school, I thought of my past, the unwanted brawls outside, and the school issues, including those rich losers. I reminded myself what Granny said to me 'Be the way you were before'. I found the meaning of this, which not only included talking the truth to Granny but also throwing away things I never wanted and would like to have in my amazing life. I had loose tongue and didn't know how to talk false diplomatically, and also I didn't appreciate it.

It was not that I had never come across some stupid people before, but I enjoyed them. It was fun having them around. For some reason, what had happened around at this age had broken my patience and irritated me, leaving me very angry, so I flushed them all in the sewer already, and also I stopped giving consideration to them in my life. 'I wouldn't take such stupidities seriously,' I said to myself. But I wanted to talk to my parents and get things sorted out but how, I didn't know.

I had reached school, and while walking towards the school gate, I looked at the sky which was beautiful and looked golden due to the beautiful sunrays that asked me to rise, and I said, 'What is the difference between me and those rich losers if I behave the same, listen to their humbug, and respond in their way? It is supposed to be "my way, highway".' I was not born to stand their stupid attitude because I didn't lack in universal quickness and dedication.

'I know that I need to alter my life by altering my way. I have already started doing it, and it has left me all sorted. The change is on the go after realising the importance of it in my life for always. People won't change for me. I will have to change the way I deal with things. Parents matter to me, no matter what I say to them angrily. I love them; they are mine.

'I will do things that I like doing, thanks to Karan for reminding me this. I am an independent creature, free to choose whatever keeps me happy.'

I was done with my true speech to myself, and I started walking towards the gate to get inside. I felt as if someone was hugging me tight in overexcitement in a harsh way. I looked behind and saw that it was Amaar.

I was glad enough to see him. We exchanged hellos when suddenly he told me that he had planned the best revenge against Madam Shanta. I laughed at the way he said so but refused to join in and told him that I didn't even want him to get into it after all that had happened. 'You just watch it,' Amaar suggested. I asked him not to do anything of that sort. He didn't appreciate it.

I thought that I would not be aggressive, but neither would I sit and listen to nonsense. The difference was that I used to reply to them in the way they wanted me to, like hitting them, getting angry with them, and so on. But now I would answer them in the way I should, that is, by being calm and patient. Like when Pearl wanted me to hit her hard after what she had done to me, I chose the better option of informing the police about it. That was a smart way indeed.

I knew too well what I wanted, and all I knew was either do or don't, but it shouldn't bother you once it was done. It is good to experience such things in life as it makes you learn many things, you become a better person, and you learn to deal with them in a better way every time you come across things like these. I had experienced them and might come across such stuff in future also, but I knew how to deal with them.

I got inside the school campus when the incharge of the office told me that there was a call for me. I went inside the office and answered the call.

'Baby,' said she, cheering me.
'Granny?'
'I wanted to know if you have reached school.'
'No, I am on my way. Of course I have,' I replied, laughing.
'Baby, I called you to see if you have reached safely.'
'What do you mean?'
'The auto man looked like a goon and was also staring at you.'
'Whatever, I don't give a fuck.'
'Did he misbehave with you?'
'Yes, he said that he wanted me to date him.'
'What did you say?' she asked, laughing.
'I said that I was in love with Karan and couldn't leave him and got off.'
'Good girl! Granny loves you.'

'Bye,' I said and disconnected the call.

As I got inside the class, my peers had a smile for me as if they were all bored to death in my absence. I waved to them and confidently took my seat. The prayer was done already, and I was late to school again, but nobody stopped me outside as they were glad to see students not miss the revision classes.

I looked at my class teacher, who was watching me with a mother's eyes that wanted to cry expressively and hug me with kindness. I looked here and there to avoid his gaze as it seemed unusual to me, though our class teacher was a jolly man.

After a five-minute silence, he suddenly stood up and said, 'I care,' in a loud voice as if he were endorsing some product and 'I care' was the tag line. The way he jumped in excitement in front of us seemed like a girl had jumped into the pool, wearing a bikini, flaunting her skin, and endorsing a sunscreen lotion brand.

He looked at the class, smiled at us, cheered us, and continued, 'You are my responsibility.' He was sounding extra cooperative. I thought of warning him not to take our responsibility as we might end up getting him thrown out of the school. He was a cheerful man at heart, though he had his own special way of cracking silly jokes. We liked the way he talked; even if he was serious, students burst into laughter.

Without wasting much time, I walked up to him and asked him if he could allow me to meet Father Edward. He knew what happened the other day and said that before meeting Father Edward, he would like to talk to me once. I agreed.

'What did you do that day, Mahi?'
I kept quiet and looked at the floor innocently.

'Tell me, Mahi, I care about my class. You have a right to inform me whatever you do as I am your guardian in school.'

I wasn't so stupid to tell him that we spat on Madam Shanta, knowing that we didn't do it deliberately. I politely replied, 'I am sorry to bunk the class that day. Apologies.'

He looked at me seriously and continued, 'What did Madam Shanta say to you?'

After five seconds, I replied confidently yet politely, sounding smart and innocent as I so wanted Madam Shanta to get punished for beating me hard. 'She blamed me for getting drunk and leaving some kind of garbage outside her house. I don't know what she meant by *garbage*, but I was definitely not drunk.'

'I am sure you weren't,' said he. He believed in me, and I could see that he cared for me and wanted to help me in this matter. I started liking him more.

'Also, she said that she wouldn't let me sit in the final exams by not giving me the admit card.'

He looked at me and put his hand on my head as if consoling that nobody could snatch it from me—my admit card as it was my right.

I knew I was lying to him. It was a white lie as I didn't want not to be allowed to sit for the exams and get thrown out, so I thought of not being stupid by telling the truth. 'So what if she was a teacher; she couldn't just do whatever with students. We didn't come here to get beaten up, that too so badly. I wouldn't apologise to her,' I thought as she didn't deserve respect.

He asked the class to stay quiet and took me to the principal's room with him. Walking on the way, I saw Madam Shanta looking at me angrily, and I confidently ignored that loser. I was not a spiritual leader who had learnt to stay quiet and accept what the world gives you. I wanted to be at peace myself by doing things that were needed in my life. She was a teacher after all; unlike Latika, I couldn't pull her hair. I laughed to myself and got inside the principal's room.

'Good morning, Father.'

'Mahi Arora, how are you now?' I looked at my class teacher to enquire if Father Edward knew the matter, and he nodded. Of course, he had to know.

'I am well. Thank you. How are you, Father?'

'I am well if my school students are well,' he replied.

I smiled at his courtesy as he was the best principal we could ever have.

'What did you do?' he asked sympathetically.

'I accept my mistake of bunking the class that day,' I replied obediently, sounding true.

'And you left your watch?' he asked.

'Yes, mistakenly.'

He was expressionless and said, 'Are students supposed to bunk the class during revisions?'

'No,' I said.

'Not just you, Mahi, but the entire class was out that day,' he said to my class teacher.

'I will make sure that this doesn't happen again,' replied my class teacher to Father Edward.

'Please,' replied Father Edward. I stayed quiet, looking at him, waiting for him to get back to the point, and he did.

'I will talk to her about this,' said he.

I told him that she hit me hard on my face first, leaving my eye swollen, and then with a wooden stick she hit on my legs and knuckles. I know I was being childish by telling him about the beatings, but whatever he thought, I had to.

He listened to me and comforted me, but said nothing. He pressed the calling bell in his room, which was used to call the ones he wanted to talk to. 'It could be teachers, helpers, office incharge, or parents,' I told myself, when I saw Granny coming inside the principal's room.

'Please take a seat, Mrs Arora,' said my class teacher to her.

I looked at her, not liking her presence. When I had told her that I would talk to Father, what did she come for?

And suddenly Father Edward told me that he had called Granny as he wanted to assure her that an action would be taken against Madam Shanta. 'Would you like to say something, Mrs Arora?' he asked.

I knew that Granny was a car with a failed brake and wouldn't stop unless she bumped into something.

She began, 'I would like to apologise on behalf of my child for the unwanted behaviour.'

Before she could vomit the truth, I interrupted her by saying, 'I have accepted that I bunked the class.' I sounded true to the men present and clarified my position to Granny.

Father Edward and my teacher nodded when I said so, but she was smart enough to understand what I meant. She continued, and I stayed quiet.

'School is a child's second family. We send our children to school to learn things we miss on teaching.'

You are right you never taught me how to bunk classes,' I laughed inside.

'I am glad that my granddaughter is part of the Bartha family.'

'Of course. I love my friends who constitute the Bartha family.'

'Students get the best from school.'

'No, Karan is the best, and he is not from this school,' I laughed inside.

'Instruction gets them many things, but motivation gets them everything.'

'True that is. Karan does both amazingly,' I said inside.

'Bartha family does both really well,' she said, and they agreed.

'Really?' I murmured to Granny, and she laughed while Father Edward and my teacher got into a small discussion.

They appreciated her, and she continued, 'Children are bound to get attracted to things like getting drunk, bunking classes, and smoking on the school ground. I don't say that they are right, but it's the age. A teacher is someone who gets joy in a student's life and motivates him towards obedience, not by beating or being harsh, but by being tolerant and kind.' She explained to them well, and I had never seen such a serious side of Granny.

She was done with her speech, and the men appreciated her.

'Mrs Arora, I am sorry on behalf of the school staff for what happened,' said Father Edward. 'Be rest assured, an action will be taken. Mahi, I appreciate that you thought of talking to us about this,' said Father Edward. I nodded, smiling. I was glad that our principal cared much about the students unlike other principals who watched children getting beaten up by cruel teachers and then said, 'We want discipline.'

We stood up and came out of the room. We could see Madam Shanta get inside the cabin, and I told Granny that this was her. She looked surprised and said, 'She looks horrible. Do you want me to break her bones?' She laughed.

'No, thanks, go away now,' I laughed.

She replied mockingly, 'What if I was Karan? You wouldn't let me go.'

I said goodbye and went to my classroom with my class teacher after seeing Granny go out through the gate.

I went inside the class, and Rasheen couldn't control herself from asking me what had happened. Suddenly Amaar said laughingly that Madam Shanta had hugged me tight and kissed me on my lips.

'Yuck,' I said, imagining her red lipstick on my lips. I looked at him and said, 'It's better to be unloved than being hugged harshly by giants.' I told Rasheen that Granny had also come.

'It would have been a lot of fun,' she said.

'A lot of serious fun really,' I replied and added, 'Like what you say, our parents send us to school for discipline.'

And Amaar laughed louder this time, and the entire class looked at him after getting scared by his voice.

At midday after revision, our class teacher came with a bundle of papers. 'Our admit cards,' yelled Newspaper. All of us quickly took our seats and waited for our class teacher to distribute them. He called us one by one. We signed the register with our name in the receipt column and looked at each other's photograph on the admit card. Rasheen looked funny; her eyes were half shut like a drunkard and her face was like that of a drug addict. Amaar had a fly sitting on his nose in the picture with his hair messed up as if somebody had pulled them hard. Soni looked good in the picture, luckily. I looked pathetic too; I had the biggest face and the serious look as if I had never laughed for ages.

'You make fun of Madam Shanta's big face. God gave you this punishment,' said Amaar, and we laughed.

Newspaper came and informed us that she had heard teachers talk in the staffroom that Madam Shanta was restricted from school until the next session. She was given the warning letter by the principal. Soni jumped on me in excitement and asked, 'What did you do, Mahi?'

'Got her fucked,' replied Rasheen.

'Did you use protection?' asked Amaar mockingly.

'Amaar, I said I *got* her fucked. How I would know?' We all laughed louder this time.

During the second-last period that day, Amaar told me that Rishabh had brought a bottle of vodka for us as none of us would meet after today in school. We had our exams the next week. I was shocked to see Rishabh get so brave to drink after all that had happened. Rasheen had started collecting food from the canteen. It was a Friday. I agreed but told Amaar that we would not drink on the terrace but somewhere else.

I could see Latika look at me wickedly. I looked away after concentrating on her forehead. 'What are you looking at, Mahi?' she asked, gnashing her teeth in anger. I didn't reply to her.

'I think you should finally tell her what it reads,' said Newspaper, making fun of her, and told me that Sagar and Latika had broken up.

'They were never together. They only kissed each other wildly, fulfilling their needs,' I said, and she looked at me with her eyes wide open and then looked at the ground as if she was making a note of this in her mind and could spread this in the entire school. I didn't care as it was fun having Newspaper around.

Amaar walked up to me and asked if I was ready to get drunk, and I agreed. They needed some time to make arrangements, and I was standing near the canteen when Latika interrupted us and shouted, 'What does my forehead read?' I didn't reply anything as I didn't want to talk to her. Patience had already taken birth inside of me. I was enjoying getting her curious for a reply which I didn't give.

'You know what, Mahi? You are a bitch. Yes, a bitch. I am way better than you. That is why Sagar dumped you for me.'

'And touched your breast,' replied Newspaper and added, 'The school knows that you are a wild girl. Boys should beware of you. Who knows, you might rape them any time.' I didn't expect newspaper to talk like this, not that I wanted her to be sweet as it was her choice to do whatsoever, but it sounded strange and funny to me.

'Mahi got laid off in school, not me,' she said. She wanted my response, but I didn't feel like responding to whatever nonsense she spoke.

Why should I respond when I didn't do anything of that sort? I enjoyed getting her pissed by not getting any response. She was irritated to the core. 'She was talking about some girl who got laid off. I definitely wasn't,' I said to myself.

Sagar came in and pushed Latika away in anger. She looked at him, crying, and Newspaper said, 'See, Sagar has respect for Mahi, not you, because he loved Mahi, not you. He just wanted to kiss you, use you, and throw you away.' I asked Newspaper to stay quiet and not to link me with Sagar, and she agreed.

I stood there, looking at Latika when suddenly she yelled, 'What does my forehead read?' She was curious to know.

I looked at her from head to toe twice, teasing her that I wouldn't respond, when Rasheen jumped in and said, 'Your forehead reads, "slut", "rich loser", "bitch of the highest order", "a frustrated wild animal", "circumstances fucked", and "Mahima's sister".' The last one was the biggest abuse ever. I went away, laughing and holding Rasheen's hand.

Sagar came running behind me and asked me to stop. I didn't wait; suddenly he stood opposite me and asked me to talk to him. I waited to confront him properly and speak my heart out, and he said, 'I still love you, Mahi.' I looked at him, and he asked me to talk to him at least now. 'I really love you, Mahi,' he said.

'Don't say that. I might find you having sex with her outside school like the other day,' I said boldly yet calmly.

'Get away, Sagar.'

'Mahi, you will always be my true love,' he said loudly.

I didn't respond anything.

'Talk to me, please, Mahi. I want you back into my life. I promise I would keep you happy and give you all that you deserve.'

'I already have what I deserve, the best thing,' I said calmly, referring to Karan.

'I know I didn't do good to you. I shouldn't have hurt you. I am sorry for everything. I want to love you all my life, Mahi. Nobody can ever have the place you had in my life. I know you love me too. I want to hear the truth. Talk to me just once.'

'Why are you being attractive on the outside when you are so ugly on the inside? I don't want to be a faker myself by putting our life back together. You wanted me to talk, right? So listen, Sagar, I am done with the entire nuisance. I don't want it really. I wish no other girl ever gets a faker like you, never. You are a loser. You lost me. I still remain a winner because I have the best thing in my life. Why would I want this any more? Excuse me,' I said and went to my friends.

Amaar looked at me and started shouting, 'We were looking for you, idiot. Stop wasting time and tell us where you are taking us all.'

'Does time matter to you?' asked Rasheen politely. He laughed and left to look for a place where the five of us could drink; Abhi was absent. We went with our bags to the burial ground and sat under the tree near the other exit gate. We cleaned the place, removed the stones, sat on the ground in that jungle-like place, made a circle, and started drinking.

Opposite the place where we were sitting was a girl's hostel. A girl stood there, smiling at Amaar, a middle-aged housekeeper. Amaar ignored her and concentrated on food. I noticed her smiling at Amaar many times. Soni started laughing at the situation and the way Amaar made horrible faces at that girl. Amaar warned Soni that if she made fun of him again, he would bury her alive in the ground. 'Don't look at me, Aunty. I am of your son's age,' he shouted while drinking.

'Amaar, compare your body with hers. You look like her daddy,' I said, and we all laughed.

'Mahi, do you want me to snatch your glass and drink your share of vodka?' he asked.

'You giant, why don't you party alone if you want to have everything alone?' said Rasheen. Rishabh laughed very weirdly in a girly voice, and we laughed at the way he laughed.

'Look at that.' Amaar pointed at something. We looked, and he quickly showed his middle finger to the lady who was smiling at him. He was irritated with her. We asked him what he was showing us. He laughed, saying 'Nothing, just for fun.'

Rasheen snatched the plate of chicken nuggets from me after seeing me emptying all of it alone and said, 'You shouldn't be close friends with

Amaar. You get it?' I laughed at the joke, and Amaar pulled her pony in a different direction.

'I try too hard to get my pony in the middle of my head. You got it on the left, you bastard.'

'It was already on the left, you Atul's girlfriend,' laughed Amaar.

'Don't abuse me,' shouted Rasheen.

'Atul's girlfriend?' said Rishabh, whom we called a zero-watt bulb, meaning 'very dim'.

Rasheen looked at me, requesting me to ask Amaar not to talk about Atul here as she was embarrassed to have chosen the stupidest creature as her boyfriend.

'Rasheen, you have always been unique amongst us and so was your love story. I appreciated the way he pampered his penis while staring at you from behind the mirror, and I know you appreciated it too.'

I couldn't control laughing and lay, holding my stomach; the way he said it was so funny.

'Mahi,' Rasheen shouted.

'Yes,' I said.

'Who matters to you? Me or this silly giant?' she asked angrily.

'None,' Amaar said and added, 'Only Karan matters to her.' I looked at him with a raised eyebrow; he started apologising to Rasheen by saying, 'You forgive me, or I will eat your bread roll.' She didn't respond.

Amaar took a bread roll from her plate and put it above his mouth to show her that he was about to eat it when suddenly Rasheen shouted, 'Forgiven. Give my bread roll back.'

It was Amaar's favourite warning: agree with him, or he would eat all your food and, if needed, you too.

We got up after the party and started walking with our bags towards the other side of the gate when suddenly Amaar shouted at us, 'Look at that!' We saw him; he was standing, holding that empty vodka bottle. He pointed towards Madam Shanta's house and started laughing loudly. We asked him to reduce his volume. He laughed and whistled, and we saw that Madam Shanta was selling that empty vodka bottle to a man who bought scrap. The man was collecting the vodka bottle with the other scrap and paying her—the same bottle we had kept outside her house, Looks like she had become really poor! We laughed.

'A rich loser,' said Rasheen. We all laughed loudly after seeing her sell those bottles for money to the man who bought scrap. 'No, it's a poor loser,' said Amaar.

'She wouldn't have no money to carry her basic needs as she is restricted from the school,' said Soni.

And Rasheen added, 'She should thank us. We have helped her during need.' They all laughed when I interrupted, reminding them that we should leave for home before she caught hold of our collars.

Suddenly Amaar asked me how much did Madam Shanta hit me the other day, and Rasheen answered, 'Two slaps while giving the watch, hurting Mahi's eye with her nail and slaps. Hit with sticks on Mahi's legs. A tight slap in the principal's room. Hit her on her knuckles while Mahi was rubbing her eyes.'

I looked at Rasheen, who was counting on her fingers, looking at the ground, and then she looked at me to confirm, and I nodded, embarrassed. Later, she told us that the boy who cleaned the terrace the other day gave her these details as he was also standing and observing the scene outside the principal's room.

We saw Madam Shanta going in the other direction for some reason. She didn't lock her house and just closed the door, which meant that she wasn't going too far and would come back after a few minutes. I decided that we should get up and leave. We saw that the gate was locked with chains and a big lock. Amaar went inside her house with the vodka bottle and a packet and came back empty-handed.

Rishabh cried, 'He will get us into trouble.' I asked them to step off the wall quickly and get out of there. Amaar didn't seem to be listening to me. I didn't want him to get into trouble, though we were all out of the building. Soni helped Rishabh by snatching his hand and helped him get off the wall, and Rasheen jumped on me to save herself and hurt my shoulder. She said that she was scared of the height. It was nearly six feet from the ground. We took help of the tree and also some stones.

I stood outside the wall with scratches on my legs, and my skirt was all untidy. My body was in the air, and my hands gripped the wall tightly; I wondered what the hell Amaar was up to.

I called his name and requested him to come back. He looked at me and continued concentrating on his work. I requested him again, but he ignored me. I was scared for Amaar because if he was caught, he would not be able to give final exams and his entire year would go waste and his father would kill him.

Amaar was looking for something inside his bag. He wrote, 'The planet can't bear you any more. You need to die. Your big butt needs rest and so does your long tongue covering your mouth.' He wanted to write more when suddenly I saw Madam Shanta coming back towards her house. I shouted at Amaar. He quickly went towards the entry of her house and, in bold letters, wrote, 'Have a blast.' I realised it was coal he was looking for inside his bag, not a stone.

He came running and jumped off the wall. I hugged him, thanking him for coming back all well and without getting caught when he muttered, 'Start counting till thirty.' He looked at the watch. After some thirty seconds, we heard bombs bursting. The sound was very loud and continued for a minute until all the bombs of chain of red bombs had burst.

I was on top of Amaar, looking from a side of the gate, where there was space, when Madam Shanta ran here and there, putting water on her house. She was overreacting because they were just bombs, not fire inside her house. We could see her surprised look, as though she was wondering what had happened in a few minutes. A part of me enjoyed the scene very much, though I didn't want to take revenge.

But the question was when Amaar didn't light those bombs, how did they burst? He then told me that he had wrapped a thread around a mosquito smoke coil and as the thread kept on burning, it lit the chain of bombs and gave birth to the blast. I laughed after recalling what Amaar had mentioned on her front wall—'Have a blast.' She indeed had a 'blast', leaving her sick. We couldn't fight with her, but this wasn't bad either.

Suddenly I felt that someone was lifting me up by my waist from behind. 'Who is the bastard?' I asked.

'Karan sir, pleasure to meet you,' said Amaar. I looked behind, and it was Karan. I hugged him tight and kissed his cheek like always. I got overexcited after seeing him come back from Mumbai. I introduced him to Amaar and Soni. He knew Rishabh already and of course Rasheen too.

'What happened?' he asked.

'Nothing. We were just having some fun,' I replied.

'I hope you didn't leave any of your stuff there.'

I looked at Amaar, and he assured us that he didn't. 'We played very smart today,' said Amaar.

'Yet childish,' said Rasheen, pretending to be grown up.

'There is a kid inside each one of us. We should never kill it,' said Soni, sounding smart yet true.

'I think we should leave now,' said Karan, ignoring them.

'Of course, she is all yours', said Amaar to Karan, pointing at me. Karan shook hands with him, laughing. I hugged Amaar and thanked him for this. I hadn't wanted him to do this, but I was by his side for whatever reason.

They all went in their respective directions. Amaar looked at me, smiling, as he had taken the revenge that he wanted to on Madam Shanta on behalf of the school. We wouldn't tell anyone about this, but if students came to know, they would love Amaar more than before.

I bid goodbye to Amaar and hugged him again. 'Do you want to take him home, bub?' laughed Karan. Amaar laughed louder like he always did, gave a high five to Karan, and left. His high 'five' was equal to a 'fifty'; he had big and thick hands like that of a gorilla. Karan was strong enough to take that; I was proud of him. I looked at Karan and hugged him again, jumping on the road. 'Bub, are you done with your formalities?' said Karan and added, 'May we leave, please?'

'Of course,' said I and got inside his car.

'Bub, look at your skirt, so untidy. Don't you dirty my car seat cover,' said Karan.

'Does this car matter to you more than me?' I asked, emotionally teasing him to break into laughter.

'Of course, she is my first love. You are just a silly friend, by the way,' he laughed.

'Shut up! Madrid is your first love, and I am second, which means that your car comes after me.'

'What about my shoes?' he said innocently.

'They are our kids, and their daddy loves me, I know.'

'Bloody overconfident creature! What makes you say that I love you?'

'Fuck you.'

'Please I would love to,' he replied in the same way when he had called me up as Lallan Baabu earlier.

'Dog!'

'Bitch!'

'Sit properly. Look at your miniskirt that is becoming shorter day by day. I have strict rules for girls. Girls like you,' he said seriously.

'It's not a miniskirt. I just pulled it up while jumping off the wall,' I said.

'What wall? Are you a thief or something, or have you run away from your house when your granny wanted to marry you off to some asshole fool?'

'Granny wants me to get married to the asshole fool I am sitting with,' I said, laughing. He looked at me, surprised.

'Really, the truth it is. She likes you,' I said.

'Mummy,' he cried.

'Granny,' I shouted.

'How are things, bub?'

'Very well. Thanks, Karan.'

'For? Letting you hug me again and again today? It's OK I'll take a shower when I get back home.'

'I am more hygienic than you. I wash my face always when I get back home after meeting you.'

'You mean you wash it only when you meet me, otherwise not?' he laughed.

I didn't reply.

'Bub,' he shouted. 'I so want to . . . start avoiding you,' he laughed.

'Please.'

'So we should not meet more than every day. We shouldn't talk more than the entire night on the phone daily. We shouldn't hug each other more than always. We shouldn't spend more time together than eternity. You-need-to-avoid-me,' he said.

I looked at him for some time.

'Oh, thanks for appreciating my million-dollar face, bub.'

I kissed his cheek and said, 'Long live your beautiful beard.'

'Eh!'

By that time, my house had come. I looked at him and smiled, and he said, 'What? Fuck off now.' I got off the car, and, pretending that I was angry at him, I closed the door hard. He came running behind me, held me up, and made me sit on his car.

I shouted, 'Karaaaan, I will fall. Please let me get down.' He took off my school shoes and kept them in his car. He then took a bag out, kept it next to where he had made me sit, took out red-coloured ankle-length shoes, and made me wear them.

I kept on smiling as he had bought them as a gift to me. He said, 'Bub, this is what describes your individuality, your quality. You stand unique and distinguished from the others. Your unique character is what I appreciate, the true you. I have always liked that Mahi who is bold and talks the truth, no matter how bitter it is. If that is what makes you spoilt, get spoilt more. You have been someone who never bothered for what you like to do as per what the situation needs. Throw away the bad interruptions, the unwanted. You are indeed a smart victor unlike those rich losers who are all the same, dull characters.'

He got me down and drove away. I kept on looking at my new shoes, which reminded me of what Karan had said to me. 'I don't say that I accept my mistakes. I don't call them "mistakes". I just do things that I think I should do. Telling white lies to have fun and spend some time the way I think I should is not a lie.

'I argue with my parents, hate them, and love them. I told a lie to Madam Shanta to save myself. That is what being smart is. Nobody likes to get into trouble. My mom hit me, I cried, and things were normal. I can't have a perfect life, though I hate them when that happens. I accept it now, and this doesn't include the fights I had with those rich losers. I don't want them.'

SEVENTEEN

It was the first weekend of March, just before our exams. I got a call on my mobile phone, and I answered it.

'Hello, people.'

'Hello, Mahi.' The voice echoed as the four of us were in a conference call—Nayan with Rishabh, Karan with Adhiraaj, and Rasheen and I this side.

'Bub, are you ready?' asked Adhiraaj, copying Karan and teasing him.

I laughed while Rasheen replied, 'Yes, I am,' thinking Adhiraaj had asked her, and Karan laughed, making fun of Adhiraaj.

There was a two-minute silence.

'So, people, are you ready for combined study?' asked Karan.

'Of course,' Nayan and Rishabh shouted.

'Come out of your house in the next ten minutes,' said Adhiraaj to them.

'You pick me up from Mahi's place,' said Rasheen.

On listening to Rasheen, Karan didn't reply, teasing her.

'All right, come soon, sweets,' I said to Rasheen.

'I am crossing the main road now. See you soon,' she said and disconnected the phone before I could tell her to get a set of clothes for the next day.

'Where the hell are you people? I am standing outside your house,' said Karan to Nayan and Rishabh.

'We are coming,' said Rishabh hurriedly and disconnected the phone as if he was about to miss his train.

I could hear Adhiraaj laugh as Karan told a lie as they were still about to leave Adhiraaj's house.

'Bastard, continue talking to her. I will drive your car.'

Karan wanted to talk to me alone, and he murmured politely, 'Bub, get proper clothes all right?'

'Don't worry, I ain't wearing a bikini.'

'Of course not, in front of all,' he laughed.

'Pig!'

'Combined study, holding hands, Karan and Mahi,' said Adhiraaj, teasing us.

'Learning chapters, holding each other, Adhiraaj and Rasheen,' said Karan.

'Bastard!' said Adhiraaj.

I laughed when Karan interrupted, 'Bub, I am coming to see you.'

'Eh!' I disconnected the call.

I went to my room while Granny had kept my backpack ready with a few books and clothes as we were all going to the farmhouse to get drunk just before the final exams. We had planned this day so that we could utilise the competition day that we couldn't spend and also because our parents wouldn't allow us to party just four days before exams. So we told them that we were going for combined study and they agreed. Granny knew the truth, and she agreed after knowing that I was prepared for my exams. She had faith in me, and also I knew that I had to score well to get admission in a good school for the next two years.

In the evening, we all left home to party at the farmhouse. Karan had come to pick us up; the same faces that went together on scooters were in a car. Adhiraaj sat next to the driver's seat, and the four of us, including Rasheen, Nayan, Rishabh, and I sat behind. We also bought drinks and ordered snacks on our way and thought of ordering food at night for dinner if needed as we had already ordered a lot of snacks.

I had also borrowed the key to Granny's room, which was near the swimming pool. We reached the place around 10 p.m. I had asked Granny to call the caretaker and ask him not to tell Dad anything about the party.

I took them to Granny's room and showed them the swimming pool through the window. They were all excited, and we decided that we would get into the pool before getting drunk. It was a bit cold as the area was open, and the first week of March was also not hot. We all had brought clothes, for we were to stay here all night and would leave tomorrow evening.

I brought the food and kept it with the drinks on a table near the pool. And each of us got into the pool, wearing shorts and T-shirts. Rasheen stood next to Adhiraaj, looking at him and admiring him as he looked great after getting wet. Rishabh was shivering due to the cold water and sat outside the pool, bending his shoulders and wearing just his shorts and nothing else. His ribs could be seen clearly, but he sat confidently, flaunting them, thinking those were his abs.

Karan was nowhere to be seen. I asked Adhiraaj, but he didn't have a clue. I went back to the room and saw Karan admiring his legs in the mirror, wearing shorts. 'It's all good, your assets,' I said and brought him out. He stood near the pool, looking at me from head to toe, pretending he didn't like what I was wearing. I was wearing a black cut-sleeves tee with orange shorts. I knew he liked both. He looked at me and asked if the water was too cold. I laughed as we were both very scared of cold water.

'It's not that cold, prep,' I said and pushed him into the pool before he could reply whatsoever.

He made strange noises and got out of the pool. 'What a loser!' I said to him. 'Look at Adhiraaj,' I said to Karan, praising Adhi for peacefully enjoying in the pool. Adhiraaj looked at Karan and smiled wickedly.

'Mahi, jump in my arms,' he said, teasing Karan.

'Fuck off,' I said and got inside as I was shivering due to cold water and the fresh air. I went towards Karan, gave him my hand, and said, 'Come on, prep, you are the bravest of all. Once you get in, you wouldn't feel cold. Trust me.'

Karan was someone who knew well how to overcome his fears himself without anybody's help. He went towards the opposite side, came back, and jumped into the pool. I knew it. He pulled me towards him and started throwing water on me with his hands, and everybody started doing it. We all shouted at each other. I could see Rishabh getting irritated at Nayan and Rasheen, for he was targeted by them. Karan was throwing water on me, and Adhiraaj was enjoying it. How could he be left out for making fun of us? I threw water on him, and he joined Karan, and they both targeted me. This continued for the next few minutes. I went towards the opposite side to take a breather.

'Amongst all of us, Karan looks the most handsome,' said Nayan, praising his physique. He was healthy, not thin or fat, but strong. He was fair, and I loved his hair. They were short and smooth like that of a newborn. He held me and took me inside the pool for some seconds. I asked him to pull me up. I wasn't so good at controlling my breath.

After some thirty minutes in the pool, we had started drinking and having food, sitting on the air mattress in the swimming pool. I sat, looking at Karan. He looked so adorable that for a minute I thought if I was his girlfriend, I would have fallen in love with him again. We talked and discussed about our lives. Adhiraaj thought of discussing our ex-girlfriends or boyfriends, not because we were missing them but just for fun, mentioning silly things about them and then bursting into laughter.

Rasheen didn't say anything about Atul as she really loved Adhiraaj, nor did I say anything about Sagar, for I didn't want him to be a part of this precious time I was spending with my mates.

Adhiraaj told us about a girl from his old school who was his girlfriend and wanted to have kids. He laughed at her, explaining the story. 'I was eleven years old when she said that she wanted to have kids. I was a child myself. How could I have children?' He laughed.

'Brother, you could have if you had tried,' said Karan, and we laughed.

Nayan had no one in her life, and Rishabh told us that he had fallen for a girl in our school, and it was Latika. Karan looked at me and asked if she was the same girl, and I confirmed it. I was shocked at Rishabh for liking a girl who was much beyond his expectations. Rasheen explained to him about the bus where Latika and Sagar kissed and did many other things.

Adhiraaj and Karan enjoyed the way Rasheen explained it, like a grandmother telling a story to her grandchildren. I couldn't control my laughter and nor could Nayan. Only Rishabh seemed to be listening seriously, for it was the same girl he had liked.

After it was all over, Nayan said that these school love affairs were nothing but just a mere attraction. Karan was surprised to see Nayan talk like this. 'This doesn't last long,' she added and told us that she had recently heard that on everybody's right thumb, the initial of their life partner's name was mentioned. Karan told me that this was the real Nayan, who believed in such stupid things, not the one who had just said that school love affairs were just attraction and not real love.

We were half drunk by then and started the game for some fun. Nayan was the first person, and we discovered that the letter *I* was written on her thumb. We guessed names.

'Ishant,' I said.

'Ishika,' said Adhiraaj and continued, 'Sorry, I just forgot you are a girl, so we need to guess a boy name, for she is like a tomboy.'

'Indraprasad,' said Karan as expected, coming up with a weird name of ancient times that somebody's great-grandfather's grandfather could have been known by.

It was Adhiraaj's turn now, and we found a *T* written on his thumb. 'Tina,' guessed Nayan.

'Isn't it *P* for Pearl?' confirmed Rishabh.

Rasheen, who had never liked Pearl, said, 'Pearl is a moody girl who doesn't love Adhiraaj truly like I do.' We could see Adhiraaj ignore her, and we laughed.

'*T* for Tuntoo,' said Karan, who called Adhiraaj by this name.

Rishabh quickly showed his thumb to Nayan, and she couldn't find any letter written on it. He was worried, wondering if he would ever get a girl.

'You might never get a girl,' said Adhiraaj, teasing him.

Rasheen found an *S* written and guessed *S* for Sonya.

Rishabh managed a smile before Karan interrupted him and said, '*S* for Shakuntla.' What timing! Our maid Shakuntla entered the minute Karan said it. She came with some plates and also to ask if we needed anything else.

Rasheen was superexcited for her turn but was interrupted when Karan asked her to pour some more drinks in glasses and keep snacks on the plates. Adhiraaj took whisky with ice and so did Rasheen, for she loved him. Nayan took vodka, and Karan wished her good luck as it was the first time she was trying it. Rishabh mixed whisky with beer. We were confident for Adhiraaj but not for Rasheen as she had never tried whisky before. Rishabh was half dead after two glasses of vodka. 'Whom was impressing by mixing whisky and beer?' I wondered.

Karan had a beer and I had a cold drink. We started having snacks with drinks, and Rasheen told us that it was her turn next, thinking that we might find an *A* for Adhiraaj written on her thumb. We ignored her deliberately and continued drinking.

Karan had ordered eight pieces of 'drums of heaven', out of which four were mine and four were his. We had also ordered honey chilly potato, kebabs, and chilly chicken. Rishabh and Rasheen asked for a piece to try drums of heaven. I gave them two pieces, and Karan said that I wouldn't get any from his share, for he was very fond of it and didn't want to share. I was happy to have the remaining two pieces, so I told Karan that I didn't need his share.

I looked at the table near the pool and was surprised to see one bottle of whisky and a set of beer cans with a bottle of vodka. 'Who would drink all this?' I asked Karan.

'We,' he replied, and I looked here and there at my mates who were already dead with eyes half shut.

On continuing the game after Rasheen made weird expressions at us, Nayan started looking for the letter on Rasheen's hand and found an *A* written. '*A* for Adhiraaj for now and always,' said Karan, teasing Adhiraaj.

Rasheen had a billion-dollar smile on her face, and Adhiraaj couldn't find a place to hide his face.

Pretending that he didn't hear anything related to Rasheen and himself, he said loudly, 'The place is awesome, and, Mahi, you look sexy.'

'And so does Rasheen,' added Karan.

'Bastard,' murmured Adhiraaj and threw a beer can at Karan, getting irritated. 'I don't like her. He knows that,' said Adhiraaj to me politely. I hugged him, asking him to stay calm as we were not getting him to marry her.

Nayan asked me to show my thumb and discovered a *Z* written on it. It was in slanting position. 'Either a *Z* or an *N*,' said Rishabh.

'Zebra crossing,' shouted Nayan, and Rasheen and she started laughing in their own special, stupid way.

'She will marry a boy named Zoolooloo from China,' said Karan.

'I will marry a king named Zorawar Singh,' I said and took a sip like a sad lover does to express his pain in love.

Karan refused to let them see what was written on his thumb and said, 'What's the use when I don't want to get married?'

'So clever he is,' I said to Adhiraaj, and by that time, they were all drunk.

We were in the pool when we decided to play another game after this silly one. We decided that any three amongst us would race, holding one person on his shoulder, and whoever won would decide what to do next.

Adhiraaj quickly called Nayan and asked her to sit on his shoulder before Rasheen could jump on him. Rishabh was unable to carry Rasheen, not because of her weight but for some reason. Rasheen gave a punch on his face and asked him to sit on her shoulder, and he did. I sat behind Karan, and he started running towards the end of the pool from the start. We won!

Much later, while we were in the pool together, Karan suggested that we contribute Rs. 200 each, and whoever won the next game would get the prize, which was Rs. 1,200 cash, for we were six people. The game was who would drink maximum beer, and we were all in. We all went with the beer cans upstairs to a room and decided to drink and throw the cans out of the window on the ground behind the villa.

They were all already drunk but were aware and continued drinking. I wasn't playing but was observing them. They all took a can, emptied it, and threw it out of the window. One each was done. Rishabh kept on drinking whisky with this, and after thirty seconds, he fell on the floor like a body does after getting shot in its chest. We laughed at him as he was out of the game and continued. Nayan had the second can and started vomiting outside the window instead of throwing the can after emptying it. She went to the washroom, came back, and lay, holding her stomach, on the bed.

The three of them kept on emptying the beer cans and stopped after the fourth can. Rasheen refused to continue, and Adhiraaj was already badly drunk, for he had whisky. He was badly drunk, so instead of throwing an empty can, he threw a filled can out of the window, for he had lost his consciousness and had forgotten what the game was; he copied Karan without noticing that Karan threw an empty can, not a filled can. He was out of the game too.

I was proud to see my capacity for holding my drink increase so much and went to visit the washroom. I came back, bumping into walls and furniture and also Adhiraaj, who was lying on the floor without his T-shirt. Karan gave me a can to drink, and I had half of it and started throwing it out through a closed window, and cracking stupid jokes like asking Karan why this was not falling on the ground as it was coming to me again and again, and my T-shirt was wet with beer. Karan snatched the beer can from me, emptied it, and threw it out through the window that was open.

I was very sleepy and tired and could see the others behave weirdly. Karan was the final winner, who emptied many cans of beer. He could have had more if needed—a tanker indeed.

He kept the money in his pocket and said that he would buy me a swimsuit so that I could wear it and get into the pool with him next time when we partied. He held me in his arms and took me near the couch to make me lie down, but he made me lie on the carpet, and he lay on the couch, too clever. But he was kind enough to get me a pillow and covered me with a sheet.

Karan was still conscious after drinking so much, and so was I because I wasn't drunk just over excited, but with eyes forcefully open, he showed me something surprising. Rasheen and Adhiraaj were kissing each other, and we heard Adhiraaj say, 'Kiss me' and 'I love you' again and again. Karan kept on laughing into my ears, and after some time, Adhiraaj pushed Rasheen away. Maybe he realised she wasn't Pearl and lay on the floor far from her and fell asleep; he was tired from all that had happened, and she kept on moving towards him.

Nayan was crying, lying on the bed and holding her stomach, for this was the first time she was drunk. She cried, 'Mommy,' again and again and moved here and there on the bed, unable to do anything. I could see them behave in a strange and funny manner but was expressionless, and Karan kept on showing their weird acts to me. I didn't laugh when Karan kept on making fun of them. I was with no expressions and was blank.

Rishabh was under the table, looking for his slippers for some minutes and rubbing his hand on the floor. Karan clicked pictures of everyone, and I started laughing unnecessarily with him. I kept on laughing loudly and then made strange poses like holding Rasheen's pony, biting my foot nails, and putting a side of my T-shirt in my mouth. I knew what I was doing, but I liked doing it. I behaved more like a mentally upset creature dancing stupidly

Karan was done clicking my stupid pictures when I jumped on his arm like a wrestler. He slapped me tight and pushed me away, laughing. I lay down on the carpet, looking at him, like an innocent dog looks at his owner after getting beaten up, and then I felt my head ache. I rubbed my eyes, for I was really tired and wanted to resign to the comfort. I knew what was happening around me, but I couldn't control anything but just observed.

The next day

What woke me up was Nayan shouting and jumping on the trolley where the music system's speakers were kept. She had put on the music louder to wake us up. I opened my eyes, saw Nayan jumping, and slept again. She then threw her slipper at me to wake me up.

'What the hell is wrong with you, idiot?' I asked her, and she told me that my dog Jwala had come and slept next to her on the bed and that had scared her.

Jwala was quietly enjoying observing Nayan dance as if she had put her finger inside an electrical socket and got a shock. I got up from the carpet where I was sleeping, hugging Karan's leg. We hadn't closed the door, so he had come inside the room. I pushed Jwala out of the room and closed the door.

'Thank you,' said Nayan to me, and I told her that she had scared me to death by crying like people did at somebody's funeral. She sat on the floor, and I saw the time was 4 p.m. and opened my eyes wider, and I shouted, asking everyone to get up.

Rasheen lay on the floor, hugging her pillow tightly as if she were hugging Adhiraaj. I woke Rasheen by kicking on her butt. Karan was sleeping on the couch with half of his body on the floor. Adhiraaj and Rishabh were nowhere in the room. Nayan came running to me and told me that Jwala was playing with Rishabh's shorts and maybe he had killed Rishabh. I asked her not to talk rubbish for my dog was very kind and generous to the ones I was friends with. I looked out of the window and saw Jwala tearing Rishabh's shorts, but not Rishabh.

I quickly woke Karan up and told him that Adhiraaj and Rishabh were missing. He told me that Adhiraaj might be sleeping in a different room, for Rasheen kept on kissing and hugging him last night.

Rasheen and Nayan went to look for him in the other rooms of the villa and came back, telling us he wasn't anywhere there. Karan got up finally and told us that Adhiraaj was smart enough and wouldn't go anywhere.

Shakuntla came to our room with some coffee and some snacks for us, and we asked her if she had seen our friends, for we were unable to find them. She said that she had got the swimming pool area clean and the entire villa clean, but she didn't find anyone.

Rasheen was worried, and, in nervousness, she started pulling out the ring from her finger and wearing it again. She did it again and again, and her ring fell on the floor, rolled, and went below the trolley. She bent to find her ring and shouted, 'Dead body.'

I came running to her with Karan, and we pulled the trolley and found Rishabh sleeping like a dead duck behind it. Karan pulled him out, and he was wearing his T-shirt with his underwear as his shorts were with Jwala for some reason. 'He is alive,' said Nayan to Rasheen, making a weird expression as if she wanted him to die. Karan gave a few slaps on his face and woke him up.

Adhiraaj was still missing, and Karan asked everyone to have coffee and sandwiches. Rasheen refused to have anything till Adhiraaj was found. Nobody forced her to eat, and she started crying loudly saying 'Adhiraaj, please come back. Please, Adhiraaj,' and kept on crying louder.

She cried louder, and the voice echoed in the room. She was shouting so much. After some five minutes, she started talking about Pearl. 'I will kill the person who doesn't let you live peacefully. I will kill her,' she shouted louder.

'Go kill yourself!' We heard Adhiraaj shout, but where was he? I laughed with Karan, Rasheen pushed me in anger, and we saw Adhiraaj coming out from under the bed without his T-shirt.

'What the hell were you doing under the bed?' I asked.

'I was sleeping peacefully till this moron started crying,' he said, addressing Rasheen.

And Karan interrupted mockingly, 'How can poor Adhiraaj sleep when his lover weeps?'

Rasheen told Adhiraaj that she was worried, for he was nowhere to be found. He ignored her and went to the washroom. I took Nayan and Rasheen with me downstairs for a shower and asked Karan to get ready as we had to leave for home.

After getting ready for home, we went out and kept our stuff back into the car. Six beer cans were unopened, and some whisky was left in the bottle; everything else was completely finished. Adhiraaj was asked to drive, and I sat next to Adhiraaj, sharing the seat with Karan. He took out his mobile and showed me the stupid pictures that included me behaving like a mentally sick person. I asked Karan not to tell anyone what we had done, for even I was sleeping, holding his leg, and he laughed at it. He showed everyone the money that he had won in the game, teasing them that he would buy me a gift. I knew what it was as he had told me that he would buy me a swimsuit when they were all drunk.

We dropped Nayan and Rishabh first, telling them to be careful at home, for they were still in that state of drunkenness, but aware. We all needed a long sleep and rest. 'The competition was good, and Karan deserved to win,' said Adhiraaj, making fun of us, and we laughed.

'I also clicked a photo with Yuvraj Singh,' I said.

'I think he knew you were coming, so he asked them to cancel the competition,' said Adhiraaj, kidding. And by that time, we had reached home. Rasheen bid goodbye to Adhiraaj, and he didn't reply. I gave him a tough look, and he laughed and said goodbye. Karan winked and said he would call me sometime soon, and they left.

As I got inside my house, my mom looked at me as if I was coming home after murdering someone. 'Hi, Mom,' I said politely.

'Where are you coming from? You are supposed to study as you have exams after three days.'

'I know, Mom, that is why we had gone to a friend's place for combined study,' I replied.

'What do you think of me? I am not a fool. Why didn't you take your books with you when you had gone for combined study?'

I was confident enough to reply, and I said, 'My dear Mom, my friends had notes which we used to study. Therefore, these books weren't needed.' She looked at me with no expression and went away. 'You are supposed to smile, Mom,' I yelled. She looked behind and smiled. I went to my room, praising my confidence, and Rasheen fell asleep the minute she lay on the bed.

Later that night, I resigned to the comfort of my bed, telling Granny all that happened last night and in the morning. She was amused when I told her how I had behaved, making silly faces and asking Karan to click my pictures and also how I jumped on his arm, laughing like an idiot. She enjoyed every bit of the conversation, and after seeing me yawning n times, she asked me to sleep and kissed me goodnight. She said that she had thought of inviting Karan for dinner sometime after our exams, and I agreed.

The exams had already started. I had kept all the things not related to studies aside until the end of my exams: I avoided drinking that I rarely did and talking over the phone with my friends for long hours. I did speak to Karan on daily basis for some five minutes, and also we discussed our problems related to studies with each other.

My family was so involved in my life and wanted me to study all the time. If I had listened to them completely, I would have neither eaten food nor taken a bath but would have sat rigidly at the study table and learnt the endless syllabus that they thought existed.

Granny was so awesome; she knew how to keep things balanced in my life. I got food on time with almonds that were meant to sharpen one's mind, and when she found that I was studying till late night, she ordered me to get good sleep, and I followed her advice.

My grandfather behaved like a spy. He came to my room daily early in the morning to see whether or not I was awake and went back to his room and slept. My mom caught me every time I was on the phone with Karan and never praised me when I studied. She wanted me to revise the chapters again and again when I interrupted her by telling her that I had never thought to be a topper of the state, so I would do things my way. I complained about them to Granny, and after the second exam, they didn't come to my room to keep an eye on me; rather they waited for me to step out of the house to take their blessings.

During high school exams, our school had a centre in a different school. It was to this school that we went to give our exams. This was a big school where mostly every convent had a centre. Karan, Adhiraaj, Nayan, Rasheen, Rishabh, and I had the same school for exams and, apart from us, also Mahima and her friends.

The first day when we went to give our first exam, our class teacher, Mr Pant, had come to wish us good luck. It was good to see him, and also he promised to keep in touch. He asked if any one of us had chits. Everybody said no except Amaar. He didn't say anything as he had stopped telling lies.

The bell rang, and we got inside with our respective school group like a needle lost in a haystack. The school was new for us, so we had to see our names with roll numbers in the list and get into the respective rooms as mentioned.

Amaar was, unfortunately, assigned to a different room as the roll numbers were arranged alphabetically. Rasheen, Rishabh, Soni, and I were in the same room, though far from each other.

I was made to sit in the front row on the second bench, and another school's students sat next to my row. The arrangement was such that students of the same school were made to sit in alternate rows. As we wouldn't know the students of a different school, we wouldn't cheat. We all sat in our places; I saw Mahima coming to the second row on the second bench, which was next to me, though not close to me. What a pathetic coincidence! Latika sat before me, and Mahima next to me.

I looked at the last row, where Rasheen sat before Rishabh. After looking at Mahima sitting next to me, Rasheen murmured, 'Best friends.' I moved my lips to say, 'Fuck off.' We were not allowed to make noise, and it was silent in the classroom.

I wrote my first exam well and could see Mahima look here and there. The teacher said to her rudely, 'Didn't you study anything? Look into your paper and write your exam instead of staring at the class like an owl.' She made faces and concentrated on her question paper.

A team had come for checking to see if students had chits for cheating and if things were fine. They looked horrible with big eyes and looked like goons searching for their enemy amongst the public. The entire class was clean. I was so happy to have completed my exam on time, and also I wrote it very well.

After the exam was done, we went out of the school and discussed the question paper with our social science teacher, who was waiting eagerly for us to give her the good news; then we left for home.

During the science exam, I maintained a good speed as I was a bit too slow in writing. I completed the biology part first and then the rest of it. I concentrated on my answer sheet when suddenly I heard Mahima crying as she didn't want to flunk in the exam as she hadn't studied anything.

The teacher didn't give her sympathy. This time, Mahima was crying truly. Her classmates ignored her, and it seemed like due to her rude behaviour with people, she didn't have any friend in her school. She looked at me thrice for sympathy, but I didn't pay attention to her.

Twenty minutes before the exam was about to end, Mahima called my name. I looked at her, and she said to me that if she flunked, her parents would marry her off. She looked at me like drunken humans who beg at the traffic signals in our country. I wondered about the unlucky boy Mahima would end up marrying. I couldn't let this happen, no way. I knew well what she needed from me. I tilted my answer sheet while our teacher was busy working on a register. Mahima started copying answers from my sheet hurriedly. She wrote three answers in just twenty minutes—good speed, unlike me, who wrote a half answer in twenty minutes. I helped her but didn't utter a word to her.

The bell rang, and the teacher collected our answer sheets, counted them, and asked us to leave. Mahima looked at me as she wanted to say something. I went out without paying attention and saw Amaar come running towards me, telling me that he had used his chits really well, though I had warned him not to get chits as he might be restricted from sitting for high school exams for five years.

'I know how to play smart, Mahi,' he said, adding that he had kept the chits in his underwear's pocket. Karan was the first person to laugh after listening to Amaar. He shared high fives with Adhiraaj also today.

'Dude, what do you eat?' asked Adhiraaj after seeing his power.

'He eats everybody's food,' said Rasheen rudely.

'Rasheen, you are not supposed to forget your school friend in your love's presence,' said Amaar politely.

Adhiraaj looked at Karan and me as if he wanted to bang his head on the wall and asked, irritated, 'Who else knows about it?'

'Just him,' I murmured, and Karan laughed.

Later, we all went back home after Rasheen told Karan how the teacher spoke to Mahima and how Mahima had responded the other day. Karan burst into laughter with Adhiraaj on seeing the way Rasheen made strange faces.

The last exam was maths. Mr Rana was the first person to come outside the school to wish us good luck and give suggestions like 'The question that has the weightage of maximum marks should be solved first and then, in this way, the rest of the question paper'. He was eagerly waiting for us to get him the best result. By that time, the students had started getting inside the school after rechecking their roll numbers on the list.

We got inside our class, took our seats, and smiled at each other as it was the last exam. I was very excited about my plans that included dinner with Karan and also a day alone with him—so much fun. Mahima was looking at me with true eyes today. I saw her and ignored her as I was supposed to concentrate on my exam. The sheets were distributed with question papers. I started solving the questions that were of eight marks each, as suggested by Mr Rana.

I could see Mahima stare at my answer sheet from the corner of her eye. I didn't have time to give attention as I had to complete my exam on time first and later think of social service like helping others. Suddenly, five tall men entered our class. They scared us with their horrendous entry. They looked at us with big eyes and checked our desks to see if we had things hidden inside; we didn't. One among them pulled my answer sheets in a rough, strict way, making my sheet fall on the floor. 'What an asshole!' I muttered. I was hoping that Amaar didn't have any chit with him; if yes, he shouldn't be caught.

Latika suddenly fainted after they were gone. Rasheen couldn't control her laughter. I kept on concentrating on my exam as they brought her water. The students had started cheating after seeing the teachers concentrate on Latika. The exam was about to finish. I knew that Mahima was copying from my answer sheet. I then revised my sheets to check if I had completed the exam, and the bell rang. We went out after submitting the answer sheets.

Amaar started shouting to Rasheen that his chit had worked again as he threw it under somebody else's table after he was done. The teacher had asked whose chit it was, as if somebody would say it was his. The teacher scolded a boy from the other school and warned him, while Amaar silently observed the scene. 'You said that you wouldn't tell a lie,' said Rasheen.

'But I didn't say I would tell the truth,' replied Amaar.

A girl from some other school came behind me and informed me that the teacher had called me to the room. I gave my stuff to Rasheen and went, telling them that I would see them outside school. Soni and Rishabh went with them.

I got inside the class when that teacher asked if Latika was from my school, and I nodded. She told me that Latika was suffering from fever and needed help. Latika looked weak and stared at me, embarrassed. I held her hand and took her to the medical room in the school. I made her sit and brought a glass of water for her. I didn't say anything but did what I thought I should; she was from my school.

I waited for her in the medical room for some time. Nobody was present, and I went out and got the nurse from the other medical room. She came in with an injection. Latika started crying, telling me that she was very scared of injections. I asked the nurse if she could get her a medicine. She went to another room while Latika looked at me with a smile. I looked out for nurse to come back. She gave her a syrup with water and informed me that she would recover from the weakness.

Latika got up. I took her out; our class teacher came, walking towards us, asking me what happened. I told him that she had fainted, and he asked me to make her sit in the school bus. I did and quickly came back to my friends. Latika seemed to have realised her mistake of talking nonsense about me in school. I wasn't waiting for realisation or apologies. I did what I thought I should.

Amaar saw me and shouted my name in such a loud voice that everybody started looking at me. I went to him. He was standing with my group. 'I will miss you, Mahi,' said Amaar and hugged me.

'If you hug me, squeezing life out of me, and kill me, my family will miss me too,' I said.

Karan laughed and added, 'Mahi, you will be remembered.'

'Why don't you die?' said Rasheen rudely to Karan.

'Do you want me to call the police because you have killed my brother, Adhiraaj, with your sentiments?' shouted Karan.

'Can't you just leave me single for some time?' said Adhiraaj to Karan. 'And stop behaving stupidly, Rasheen. It damages my reputation,' said Adhiraaj seriously and burst into laughter later. Adhiraaj shook hands with Rasheen and hugged her, and we went in our respective directions.

EIGHTEEN

Like a bald man who, without shelter, gets scared of small pellets of ice falling on his head during rain, we were also scared of our final exams. The bald man would run here and there to save himself. We too flipped through the pages of our notes to save ourselves from getting flunked during examination. And just like he would want the ice pellets to stop, we also wanted to get rid of our exams soon.

Our final exams had passed, leaving us happier than before. We all had done well. We knew what the results could be, so we didn't have anything to worry about.

I became lazier than before. My schedule changed completely, and I became more of a drunkard in Granny's company. I knew my limits, though. I celebrated every day, telling the family that I was done with those rich losers and also my final exams as if I might never have to study in the future. Rasheen had gone to her hometown in Shillong. I was happy alone. I had a lot of good things to do like writing letters to Karan, sometimes drinking beer with Granny, and enjoying football with Daddy.

I slept late daily after watching porn and reading about sex and would get up in the afternoon. It had been many days now that I didn't get a chance to see the morning. After having food in the afternoon, I would go to have a shower and complete other formalities. Also, sometimes I felt so lazy that I brushed my teeth after having food—that too only if I was in a mood to. My tummy had come out a little and also my butt. I had started looking like a chubby girl. My capacity had also increased with my speed. All I had in the evening was some beer and chicken.

'My life was very busy,' said my friends who came to my house to see me and went after waiting for a long time for me to wake up. I managed to call my friends when I was awake, that is, at midnight. I spoke to Adhiraaj and Amaar thrice a week. Rasheen sent me a text daily, and I replied to all of them during the weekend. And I also sent texts to my other friends. I didn't understand why I was considering Saturday and Sunday as weekends when the entire week seemed like a weekend to me. I was at home every day.

My dad had already started planning for the next two years of my studies. He asked me to select physics, chemistry, biology, and maths. I was fifteen, and still my dad couldn't understand what I wanted from life. I definitely didn't want Madam Shanta's subjects. I laughed to myself, though I liked reading biology. I listened carefully to my dad's lectures daily but never made points of everything he said.

I didn't want to become fat, so I told Granny that I would go for a jog daily to cut down the fat I had started putting on. Though the fat wasn't much, I believed in 'Prevention is better than cure'. Before it could increase much, leaving me look fat, I should take good care of myself. Otherwise Karan would get rid of me. I had two choices: either lose Karan or lose fat. I chose the second option.

I set the alarm daily for 6 a.m., but I never woke up. My hands had become clever; they shut the button without letting me know. I become sicker day by day. I did stupid, silly things like keeping my mobile phone in the fridge after I went to get a water bottle and then I would search for my mobile in the entire house. I did this when I wasn't drunk. 'What would I have done if I was drunk?' I laughed.

I wrote messages to Karan daily. He never replied as he was the first person to accept that I had become mentally sick after getting drunk daily though I didn't drink too much. I got emotional about his things. I wanted him to give me his blue T-shirt, his sipper, and a pair of his shoes. I wanted all the things that he loved. I would call him and tell him to give me all his shoes or else I would cry loudly outside his house, bringing everybody out of their houses. He refused strictly.

The next evening, at around 9 p.m., Granny came in while I was in bed, sleeping. She kissed my cheek and tried to wake me up; I didn't. She caressed my hair; I didn't. She pulled my cheek; I didn't. She tried to pinch me on my waist; I didn't. Finally, she kicked me, and I fell on the floor and bumped into an attaché case. I opened my eyes and yelled, 'Whose stuff is it in my room?' I kicked the attaché case, and it fell open.

'What the hell? These are my clothes. Who the hell was stealing my stuff while I was sleeping, Granny?' I shouted.
'Tell me,' she replied rudely.
'Who is taking my stuff?' I said, pointing out at the attaché case.
'I have packed your bag.'
'For what?'
'I have invited Karan for dinner tonight.' This was the surprise, I realised, and she added, 'You are going with him with your bag.'
'Where?' I asked.
'How would I know?'
'You packed my bag. You told me that I am going with Karan. Then you are supposed to know where.'
'You are grown-ups. Decide on your own and enjoy your vacations.'

'Wherever we go, we are definitely not going for a lifetime. Then why so many clothes?'

'Because I am fed up of you wearing these orange Bermuda shorts for the last ten days.'

'Because they are still neat and tidy.' She looked at me as if I had abused her.

'Shut up! And get ready and wear something good. I love you. That doesn't mean you will argue with me.'

'I am talking to you, not arguing. The dictionary is on my study table. You can see the difference.'

She went back to her room, banging the door hard. I put my stuff back in the bag and locked it. 'Even if I go somewhere, I am not taking this sixteenth-century attaché case with me. The attaché case is heavier than the stuff. Who the fuck invented this brand?' I wondered.

I checked the time on my mobile and found there were five missed calls from Karan. I dialled his number, and he answered, 'Little bitch, you fool, bloody idiot, rich loser.'

'Prep, my boy,' I said cheerfully.

'Where the hell are you? I am waiting to get inside your house for the last ten minutes.'

I went downstairs and opened the gate.

'Throw away your phone if you can't make use of it.'

'Shut up! Why were you behaving weirdly standing like a stupid lover and not using the bell?'

'I didn't want to distract other members. Your dad might be busy, romancing with your mother,' he laughed.

'What a stupid answer! Anyways he wouldn't stop if the bell rings. Beggar,' I said.

'Fuck you, bitch.'

'Where are the flowers? Don't you know that you should get a gift or anything of that sort when you come for dinner to somebody's house?'

'Of course,' he said and gave me a rose.

'Karan, you are not supposed to pluck flowers in the evening. Didn't anybody teach you to love nature?'

'Bitch.'

'Bastard,' I laughed, not acknowledging anything he said.

I took him inside, and while going from the veranda to the first floor, we smelt the beautiful aroma of the food Granny had prepared for dinner.

'Yum-yum, it's definitely chicken,' I said.

'Hungry beggar,' he replied.

'You are a beggar because you gift people their own things.'

'What do you mean?'

'If Granny comes to know that you plucked this rose from our lawn, she will slap you tight.'

He laughed as he was caught and said, 'She likes me more than you, so she won't, I am sure.'

'Pig.'

'Mahima.'

'Don't you dare abuse me ever by calling me Mahima,' I said, and he laughed.

'Latika.'

'Fuck you, Karan.'

'It's not the right time, bub. It's just 9.15 p.m.,' he laughed. 'You are Latika.'

'And you are Sagar,' I said and made weird faces.

'Then let's kiss', 'Sorry, it's not the right time.'

'There is no time for it. Is there?'

'Wild cat.'

I came back from my room after getting dressed up, all neat and tidy. I wore blue shorts and a sky blue T-shirt. Granny came up to me, giving strange expressions, and said, 'Are you going to play hide-and-seek with your friends in the colony?'

'I am much comfortable like this,' I said.

'Where is your black dress?' she shouted. I came back after wearing it. Karan was sitting on the terrace, holding his mobile phone, playing some game.

He looked at me twice from head to toe, and I asked, 'What happened, prep?'

'Game over,' he said, looking at me and then into his mobile phone.

'Shut this, or I will throw this out,' I said, pointing at his mobile that looked more like a video game remote.

'You look different,' he said.

'Granny asked me to wear this. I was wearing my shorts initially.'

'Yeah, shorts are good too,' he said and added, 'I think my mom made me wear shorts from the day I was born instead of a diaper.'

I looked at him, deliberately not appreciating what he had said.

'Jealous, I know you are because when my mom made me wear shorts, you wore pink skirts with flowers and butterflies drawn on them.'

'I wish I was wearing boots,' I said to hint that that I wanted to kick him.

'Boots in this month? You don't have a fashion sense, bub. I think you should spend some more time with me.'

I pushed him on the floor and started dragging him by his leg when Granny shouted, 'Is this the way to behave with guests?'

'Mahi, you should respect the guests who come to your house,' he said louder.

'Baby,' said Granny and looked at me with an angry expression. 'Behave!'

'Guest?' I quizzed. 'Karan is a thief who steals flowers'

'The dinner is for you and Karan only,' she said and went after keeping all the food.

'I can't tolerate two women together,' he said.

'But many women together,' I added, reminding of his Casanova image.

'I think we should concentrate on the food instead of the shit you talk.'

'You talk cream? Bastard.'

'Mahi, you look hot.'

I smiled and started serving the food.

'Sick village girl!'

'Beggar.'

'I am a developed country, unlike you,' he replied.

We started having food when he told me that he had come to take me with him. 'Where?' He didn't say anything. I kept eating, and after thirty minutes, we both ended up emptying almost everything. I looked at Karan, properly admiring him from head to toe. His shoes were amazing. I kept on looking at them, completely lost, like a lover when Karan's burp interrupted my thoughts.

I looked at him, and he said, 'Amazing night. You look beautiful. I never saw you this way before. The food was amazing too. Even if you looked like a beggar, as you usually do, I wouldn't have called you "bad",' he said and added, 'Loser.' I went on listening to him, entertaining myself.

'What a moron!' I said.

'I love you too, Mahi.'

'I think we should leave now,' he said. By that time, Granny had come with a small packet for Karan. It had a gift for Karan to thank him. 'Karan should have thanked Granny for the amazing food he rarely gets to have,' I thought. If, in a party, Karan was lost, the best and the exact place we would see him would be near any of the food stalls or drink stalls. I knew this well. I wondered if his mother knew that. Granny hugged Karan, and we went to bid goodbye at the gate.

He held my hand and said, 'You are coming too, bub.'

'What?'

'What what? I just told you that I have come to take you with me.'

Granny seemed so happy as if she were watching some romantic movie.

'But where?'

'Somewhere,' he said.

'Go get your bag and leave,' said Granny, overexcited.

'No, nothing else is needed. Just get inside the car without wasting time.'

Before I could say anything, Granny pushed me inside the car.

He got in himself, and we left.

He drove to a very strange place; I'd not seen it before. I didn't even know there were places of this kind in the city I lived in. It was an uncommon place, but people did live here. There were stalls of drinks and food on the roadside. I could see people have food with their families and also a few who had come with their dogs for maybe a walk. I confirmed from Karan if this was the same city we lived in, and he nodded. I could also see people fight with each other. Drunkards, I guessed.

We took a right turn and saw a lot of crowd on the road; Karan took me from behind the area through a residential area. It wasn't a bad place. It was all neat and tidy, though not constructed so well. 'Where are we going?' I asked Karan.

And he replied, 'Somewhere.' He told me later that he hadn't decided where to go, so we were just driving on the roads and looking at the surrounding. It wasn't a silent place. It was a part of the city that was usually unnoticed. It seemed like an exciting activity to me. And also I appreciated his presence.

I kept on looking outside the window, staring at the ice cream stalls while Karan admired the wine and beer shops. He stopped the car near a stall and asked me if I would like to have some shake. I refused, telling him that I was full, and so was he. He brought two mugs of chocolate shake. We shared a muted laugh. Both of us were hungry beggars and behaved like someone who rarely got food to eat. Even if we had emptied all the bowls, we would still eat something as our eyes were always hungry.

We got inside the car when suddenly his phone rang. It was Adhiraaj. He answered the phone and told Adhiraaj the place we were in.

'What?' I asked, and Karan told me that Adhiraaj wanted to join us, so he asked him to come.

I looked at him when he interrupted, 'I will ask him to get lost after sometime so that we can have some time alone.'

I smiled and replied, 'I am absolutely all right with Adhiraaj because I like him.'

'I am not all right with him, though. You better not like him, bub.'

I laughed and said, 'I won't dump you and date him, so chill.'

'I don't look upset. Do I?'

As we moved towards a lane that looked scary—like the one shown in movies where the heroine is kidnapped or killed—I asked Karan to get out of there as I was getting scared. He told me that nobody would dare to touch me when I was with him. Suddenly a man who looked as if he hadn't taken bath for many years came and knocked on the window. I got scared and looked at Karan, who waved his hand at that man, and he went away.

'Who the hell was he? Since when have you started being friends with beggars?' I said to Karan.

And he told me that he was a car mechanic who took care of his car. He had come to say hello to Karan. He asked me not to panic, and I told him that if I come across such scary people in these dark places with broken buildings around, I wouldn't get excited and shout wow.

By that time, Adhiraaj had come. He sat in the back seat, and Karan drove the car. We kept on laughing and discussing various topics; Karan stopped the car outside a building. 'It is a hotel,' said Adhiraaj, and we were supposed to go along with Karan, and we did.

It was a hotel with bar and dancers. I looked at Adhiraaj after I saw a transparent room with yellow lights and dancers dancing to some song.

It wasn't a movie song, probably a song they had made themselves. There was a man standing with a mike, wearing funny clothes with threads on sleeves and belt. He was dancing funnily but confidently, thinking he was no less than a choreographer. He was also wearing black shades for some reason.

Karan asked Adhiraaj to take care of me while he had some important work at the reception. We waited for five minutes, and Karan didn't come. We lost all the patience, so the minute I looked at Adhiraaj and smiled, he nodded, and we went towards that room. We got inside and saw men getting drunk and dancing with dancers. They were all more than forty years old; a few were also kissing and touching the girls here and there.

I was curiously observing them, holding Adhiraaj's hand and looking at them through the glass. Drunken men were dancing as if they were injected with some drugs. They all seemed mentally sick to me; The worst part was when they started removing their clothes while dancing. The girls had started dancing without wearing anything on their upper body. We stood there, concentrating on what they were about to do next when suddenly Karan came from behind, pulled us, and abused us.

'What are you both doing here? Mahi, do you even know what it is? Get inside the car, both you bastards,' he shouted, getting irritated. Adhiraaj kept on laughing, and I tried to control my laughter as I had never shared things like these with Karan ever.

Changing the topic, I asked, 'What did you go in for?'

'I had to give some money to a friend who was in need,' he replied. 'You are not supposed to do what you were doing, bub. He is an idiot. Are you the same?' he asked.

'You can have all, and we can't even see it,' said Adhiraaj, laughing when Karan asked him to shut his trap.

'Have you been here, Karan?' I asked, surprised.

'Yes bub, but never for sex' he replied.

Karan drove the car and stopped outside Adhiraaj's house. 'I am not going home,' Adhiraaj cried.

'It's already late, and I am supposed to drop Mahi back home. Get lost. I have less time to waste,' said Karan. Adhiraaj got out, taunting him by asking me if I really enjoyed the dancers and people there. I laughed, and Karan started the car, and we went away.

I looked at Karan who seemed to be happier. He looked at me and smiled, telling me that he wanted the time to stop as he wanted to live this moment more than eternity. 'Can we have a laugh together, bub?' he asked, and we started laughing for no reason, making strange noises and then laughing at it.

He said, 'Bub, you remember this strange place we just visited? Life is like this, known, unknown, unfamiliar, and familiar. *Change* means learning to react in a better way. Give time to yourself, talk to yourself, and ask yourself. Go where you are celebrated. I will admit that I do value the real you—what you are now, what you have always been—not what you were forced to become by situations. Well, that is good too. For a change, you should pull their hair.' He laughed.

'Don't settle until you get answers from yourself. Keep searching. You were always in a hurry to respond to unwanted situations. Though what you did wasn't wrong or bad, you can do much better than this. Stay calm and aggressive. There is a storm behind patience too. One thing is for sure that we both hate senseless things passionately. Twins!'

It was late already, and we were now outside my house in his car, saying nothing, just looking at each other and feeling the silence.

'I think I should leave now.' I was feeling strange and didn't want him to go away.

'I think you should, bub,' he said politely.

I opened the door and looked at him. He had nothing to say, nor did he smile. I could see him looking at me. Before I could go towards his side, he drove and went away.

I went home, feeling that something was missing. I always hugged him before he left, but for the last few days, he had been acting strangely; he would not wait for anything and would go away immediately. It had happened four times now after exams, though I didn't think much about it. Later, I consoled myself by saying that I would hug him next time when we met. I wanted him with me; it was what I thought should happen, though I wasn't scared of the opposite happening.

I went inside my house and got back to my room. I lay on the bed, thinking about my life, which included my parents too. After some time, I went back to thinking about my family; after fighting, arguing with my parents, and crying for *n* times, I had become more patient as feeling bad didn't leave me in peace. My parents said many things to me, and I listened to them. I didn't take things too seriously like when my mom still praised my family friends. She wanted me to listen to her, and I did to keep her happy.

My father was the same; he gave me many lectures and told me things that he thought I should do. I listened to him patiently and confidently explained my views too, though he rarely acknowledged them. I no longer hate them. I knew I shouldn't. How could I? They were my parents, after all. If they didn't talk about me to me, who else would?

I also stopped getting too emotional and irritated, not completely though. I wasn't perfect; nobody is. I was just learning about life and circumstances and how to deal with them after thinking about what was needed and how I should respond. When my parents scolded me, I used to say that I didn't want to live with them. But of course I did. I realised that when my parents scold me, they are normal after a few hours or the next day. 'Then why was I taking things too seriously by saying that I wouldn't talk to them ever and wouldn't live with them?' I wondered.

They don't seem to understand me too well even now, but I understand what they say and why they say it. I am sure they would understand me, too, some day. 'I have to be more expressive,' I thought. I did feel bad about arguing with them on some issues, but I didn't get too involved and thought much about it. Time will change things, I know.

My parents are still after me all the time about what I said earlier, but now I have realised that they care a lot for me and, therefore, are very possessive. I don't like it though, but it's OK as they are doing what they want to do, and I am supposed to respond in a better way by acknowledging them; if I don't like doing something they want me to do, I talk to them patiently.

There are still many things my parents don't acknowledge about me, but I don't hate them for it. They are free to choose what they like and what they don't. My granny is my true mate and my real mother. She understands everything about me, maybe because she has spent her life with me in her room. She encourages me.

I have become a better child by listening to my parents and understanding them as something had to be done to avoid arguments and hatred. I can't be a perfect child; nobody can, but I have learnt to compromise and deal with situations in a better, effective way, keeping in mind that I don't hurt them and things are normal. Also I have learnt that patience and persistence make life unbeatable, no matter what the motive is.

I realised that I had not changed my clothes since the time I had come after meeting Karan, so I went to the bathroom and came back after freshening up. My parents came into my room. I smiled at them, and they said that they wanted to talk to me about something serious. I acknowledged them and sat next to them, patiently listening to them. My mom looked at my father and vice versa to ask who should start first.

I was confident and waited patiently to listen to anything they had come up with, and Mom began, 'Mahi, we have both decided something important for your life.'

'What?' I asked.

'It's not that we don't love you and that is why we are sending you far from us, but because we want you to have a better future.' I started feeling sad about what they were about to say, but I was patient enough to listen to them.

My father looked at me with a smile which had love for me. I asked Mom to continue, and she told me that they had decided to send me to a school in New Delhi for the next two years for better result and environment. I told them that I loved this city and my friends meant a lot to me. I said it while thinking about Karan. Dad said that they were not asking me to leave my friends, but they wanted me to get the best environment. 'What environment were they talking about?' I wondered. I loved the environment I lived in.

My mom said that friends kept changing with age and as I grew up, I would come across many people and could make them friends too. I knew that. 'But how will I live without Karan and my other friends as Delhi is not near? It's a six-hour train journey.' I sat patiently, trying to understand what they meant; they seemed to be waiting for my answer.

I spoke to Dad and told him that there were good schools in this city too, so why were they planning to send me to a different city? He replied that he wanted me to have a better future and that he wanted to make my life great and added that once I studied well and became 'something', I would have a respectful life. This was a good school in the city, and he had already decided to give a big donation and get me an admission. All they were waiting for was my answer.

I sat rigidly, looking at the floor of my room while Dad kept on praising the school staff. Mom looked at me, wanting an answer, and after thinking about what all this could lead to, I patiently yet confidently stood up and agreed by saying, 'Yes, I agree,' as they were doing this for me.

My father looked at my mother, smiling and feeling happy like he did when Real Madrid won a match, and thanked me. I looked at them and smiled as they were going out of my room. I heard Mom say to Dad, 'I knew that my child would keep my word and wouldn't refuse, for she is the best child a mother can ever have, and I love her very much.'

I didn't like getting emotional, but for some reason, I had tears in my eyes, and I quickly wiped them off and got back to my bed, trying to sleep. I recalled again and again what Mom said about me to Dad and liked being appreciated.

I was in my room the next night after having a lot of cold drink with Granny. She said that she wanted to say something to me. What was it? I wasn't bothered as Karan was never far from my thoughts. I always daydreamed about him. This was definitely nothing romantic; let me be clear. I asked Granny not to sit next to me and hug me or caress my hair. I asked her to leave me alone, and she gave me a punch, irritated, went to her room, came back, and shouted that she loved me more than everything in this world, and went back.

Around 3 a.m., I dreamt that a thief had come into my house and was stealing all my special stuff. I opened my eyes and realised that it was a dream, and later, I thought of actually getting up from the bed and checking my attic that had my special stuff. I got up from the bed, rubbed my eyes, and went towards the door, banging my knee in the walls of the room. I couldn't find the switch, so I went to the attic, making way for myself.

The place was very dark, though not far from my room. I could feel all the fear I felt while watching horror movies. A part of me inside, which I named Karan, was saying that there could be hands coming out of the walls, ghosts making noises into my ears, and witches pulling my hair and scratching my face. I put both my hands on my cheeks, thinking I would not allow anyone spoil my million-dollar face. I got inside the attic, walking slowly without making a noise so that if there was any thief, he shouldn't know that I was coming inside. I made my way towards the old *almirah* which was owned by my great-grandmother. I kept all my stuff in it.

As I walked towards it, something struck my foot, and I fell on a box. What I felt was so scary that I woke up instantly and took note of my surroundings. I felt rough hair on my arms, a snake-like thing on my face, and a scratch on my cheek. 'What the fuck? Who the hell dared to spoil my face? I've got to meet Karan in the next two days,' I thought. I managed to find the switchboard. I quickly switched on the light. I looked here and there behind the door, behind the *almirah*, under the sofa, and in the big box. There was absolutely nothing. No ghost, I realised, and when I went to close the door, I saw a cat staring at me as if I had illegally occupied her property.

'You bloody bitch, you scratched my face,' I yelled. I wondered later why I had called the cat a 'bitch'. 'Your rough dirty hair needs smoothening, and your tail is like a snake. I will cut it into pieces,' I shouted at her. She looked at me with her shiny eyes as if I was dating her boyfriend. I threw my slipper at her and shouted, 'I have already dumped Sagar. Get away from here. He might be waiting for you on his bed, you bloody wild Latika.' She stared at me the same way that Latika did.

I got inside the attic and closed the door. I opened the *almirah* and started viewing my stuff, which was something I loved doing as it kept me in touch with memories that made my life interesting. I was seeing my stuff almost after a year now. The last rack had a lot of mud and dirt.

I could see a book. I took it out, and it read *Malgudi Days*. My childhood friend Chia had given me this when we were in class IV. We studied in the same school till class IV, and after that, her uncle took her to The United States, and we never met again after that.

I opened the first page. Chia had written, '1999—to my bestest friend Mahi with hair like Goldilocks. I love you more than everything. From your best friend Chia with the voice like hummingbird.' She called me 'Goldilocks' as I had very long hair. Later, Granny got them cut as she thought my body was weak comparatively. I called her 'hummingbird' because she had a very sweet voice. I really liked the way she shouted, 'Behave yourselves,' to our class boys, and they laughed as she had a very thin voice.

I took the book and flipped through the pages. I smelled the pages, kissed the book, and kept it back. I looked at the other stuff. I saw a plastic egg, yellow-coloured. I took it out, smiled, and opened it. It had a cushion that read, 'My pretty friend.' This was from another junior school friend named Samar, who wanted to get married to me and vice versa as he said that I looked like a beautiful Indian mother with long hair. I liked it when he said that to me, and now I hated it. I laughed after I saw it.

I heard someone walk on the stairs; it distracted me. I looked out and saw no one. I got inside the attic and got back to my work. I started looking here and there for other things and saw a card given to me by a friend named Naval from my junior school with the worst drawing ever. It was a handmade card given on a Friendship Day to me. The card didn't have anything funny written apart from the name Naval. He was a friend like Amaar, but not fat. He was very poor in studies and used to tell our class teacher, when asked about his aim, that he wanted to be a daddy when he grew up. I had always liked keeping such things safe. They constituted memories so treasured.

The sound of footsteps became louder and faded after seconds. It was very scary to face someone while enjoying favourite things alone in an attic-like scary place at three in the night and that too in a dreamy state. I felt my heartbeat quicken as I heard the footsteps louder now. I looked out through the hole of the door, and I thought there was a witch in a white dress standing at a distance. I kept looking at it and opened the door and later realised that it was nothing but a curtain hanging. I closed the door and got back to my work.

I admired the gifts my friends had given me with so much love. I missed my junior school and remembered my friends whom I never met after that. I sat on the floor and remembered that Chia and I once hit a boy who always bullied her in school, calling her a mouse. During recess, we had hit him badly on his head with our lunch boxes. He was said to be the cruellest boy in our school, but we made him cry.

Chia and I were the best of friends. We had a lot of unity too. She cried when she was leaving the school. I was expressionless and was left remembering the wonderful friendship we shared. She was always by my side when I fought with my classmates for things like rubbing the blackboard. I was short but still liked rubbing it, jumping and doing it, and also, as my hand didn't reach the top of the blackboard to delete the subject name, Chia used to keep chairs for me to stand on and rub it clean.

I missed those golden days of my childhood. I had also helped Chia in things like checking the notebooks as I was the best at copying our teachers' signatures. Once when I signed her Hindi notebook, our teacher caught her and hit both of us as she had taken my name for signing it. I didn't hate her. She wasn't so brave to take the beating alone, so Imla Madam hit us badly. Her original name was Vimla, but because she was very fond of giving dictations, which are called *imla* in our national language, we called her Imla instead of Vimla.

Chia was scared of horror stories but loved listening to them, and Samar was the one who told us scary stories. He told us that our principal's, Father John's, dead body was buried in our school ground after he died as he wanted to take revenge on students, that was us, who made fun of the frock that he wore and also irritated him with mischiefs.

Later, I thought of getting up and walking back to my room, making sure that I kept nail clippers under my pillow because Granny once told me that keeping anything made of iron like a pair of scissors or nail clippers would keep bad dreams away. She used to do it when I used to watch horror movies and get scared.

As I got out of the room after rechecking all my stuff, I started looking for the slipper I had thrown at the cat, but I couldn't find it anywhere. So I walked back to my room, wearing just one of the slippers on my left foot.

I heard the sound of someone walking and coming towards me. I could see a figure clearly. It was definitely not my imagination but a human being. There was someone walking towards me, wearing a big shawl kind of thing. I couldn't see the face clearly. All I could recognise was his amazing shoes.

'Oh my God! Karan, what are you doing at this time?'
'I knew too well you would recognise me,' he replied in a drunken state.
'Did you see the time?' I asked and closed the door.
'Yes, it's 4 a.m., and I am your 4 a.m. friend. Ain't I?'
'What the hell?'
'I was about to ask you. What the hell was wrong with you? Why were you abusing the cat calling her 'Latika'?'
'It's bad manners to listen to private conversations,' I said.
'But why?'
'I felt that it was Latika, the shit queen!'

'No, bub, no way. We ain't talking about rich losers. We have flushed them in a gutter already,' he explained.

'The gutter also had crabs. Did it not?'

'I have never been inside, bub, so I don't know. Sorry,' he said, making an innocent face.

'Rich losers! They have always thought shit about me, something I never was. I am me—often nice and always awesome.'

'I am glad. You are not meant to get violent when you have the strongest asset, which is your tongue. You can remove anybody's clothes by proper utilisation of your tongue,' he said.

I looked at him and said, 'I think things are all there in the right places.'

'True.'

'I am very happy with my life. I don't cry now.'

'You always cry, bub. You just said that I was not supposed to come here at this time,' he laughed.

'Shut up! I am back with all my characteristics.'

'I love you the way you are. I wouldn't change a damn thing. Nor should you, bub.'

'A tease. Cheese!'

'Mahi, you are my life. Don't you ever go anywhere, leaving me. Does it sound convincing?'

'Not really,' I said, raising my eyebrow.

'Never mind. I know you love me more than I love you.'

'Fake expectations. Fuck hard.'

'You look good in these orange Bermuda shorts.'

'You are not bad either.'

He took the comb from my dressing table and started doing my hair.

'What are you doing, Karan?'

'Something that's needed.'

'What?'

'You look horrible, worse than your teacher Madam Shanta with hair messed up.'

'Bastard!'

I sat on my bed while he did what he wanted to do. I admired his shoes.

'Karan, what if I tell you that I messed up my hair deliberately?'

'I wouldn't do it and leave you looking worse.'

'Fuck you.'

'Please.'

I saw him looking at my tummy when he was done. I quickly pulled up my shorts and covered the little fat.

'Bub, you look perfect to me.'

I smiled, looking at the floor, having nothing to say.

'I want you desperately in my life, now and always. Do you know why?'

'You want me, Karan. How would I know why?'

'We have become too close to be separated. You add days to my life.'

'Karan, you are drunk,' I said nonchalantly.

'Not me. We are drunk.'

He made me stand exactly opposite him and said, 'You are a teddy whom I hug when I miss my girlfriend. You are like a can of chilled beer when I am dying to have water. You are a blanket that I wear when I feel cold. You are like paint that makes my life colourful. You will never know how amazing you are. I do. I love you.'

'I don't want to miss you, Karan.'

'I would always make you see me. You wouldn't miss me. We are brothers for life!' There was a two-minute silence.

'Go away, Mahi,' he said softly.

'This is my house. You are supposed to go, Karan.'

'Yeah?'

'Yeah!'

Somebody knocked on the door. We both looked at each other when suddenly he said, 'Is that Rasheen? We might never get time alone. Tell her Adhiraaj hasn't come along.'

'Get out, Karan. What if Granny sees you with me now?'

'I will tell her that I have come to take you far away, and I will,' he said confidently, drunk.

'A piece of shit you are.'

'A bag of shit is you. I am just a part of you, Mahi.'

That somebody started banging the door hard, and I had to open it. There was Granny wearing her nightgown, holding the slipper I had lost near the attic.

'Just for you,' she said.

'Of course!'

She stood opposite me; her body was not still. She was finding it difficult to stand straight as she was drunk. I then took her to her room, telling her that I loved her the most, and she confirmed if I loved her more than Karan. I nodded, and she slept, smiling.

I opened my rack to put on the red shoes he had bought for me. I wore them and looked into the mirror, admiring them and my traits and came back to surprise Karan. He was not there.

I looked through my window, searching for Karan. I couldn't find him anywhere. 'He might have already left for his house,' I thought and came back to my room. 'How dare he go back without biding goodbye?' I thought. 'Karan has rarely done things completely,' I consoled myself.

I lay on my bed, appreciating my choice of choosing Karan over the others and making him a part of my life. I was trying to sleep. I was unable to sleep, though. I kept looking at the ceiling and thinking of all the precious moments spent with him. I knew it was silly, but I didn't like it. He should have gone after hugging me tight.

'What a stupid idiot I chose!' I said to myself. 'He comes at his own time, does all that he likes to do, and goes back home in his own way and is free to choose whatever.' I realised it was fine. 'It's Karan. He has a licence to do anything he wants as long as he is happy. I will appreciate it. We both hate boundaries and instructions. Anyways, we both have no owners, so it's all right to do things our own way,' I explained to myself.

I tried to get some sleep, but I couldn't, so I continued to think about Karan. When he was with me talking, I didn't much appreciate him. And now that he had gone, I wanted to be with him just wanted to be with him. Silly me, clever him! I got off from my bed and went outside and looked at the sky. It was beautiful. It was five o'clock by then, and the darkness had started disappearing.

I brought my mobile phone and dialled Karan's number. He didn't pick up the call. I dialled again, looking at the sky, feeling the lovely wind on my face, throwing my hair back. I looked in the lawn and saw Karan sitting near a flowerpot, looking at me like a beggar with the strangest look. I was amazed. I quickly went downstairs to him and hugged him tight, laughing inside and loving him in my own special way. This time he was in my arms.

'I thought you were gone.'
'I thought the same, bub.'
'Shut up! Why didn't you go?'
'You didn't kiss me goodnight.'
'It's morning, Karan.'
'For you. For me, it's night, and I am supposed to sleep.'
'You are supposed to go home and sleep, not here, prep.'
'Bub, you look cute with pink cheeks.'
'Get up, Karan. You look your opposite.'

'People talk weirdly when they are drunk,' he laughed.

'You look like a beggar.'

'Fuck you, Mahi,' he said and got up. I hugged him.

'You look like a king otherwise,' I said, changing the topic.

'I think you should get back to your room before your father comes with his pistol to kill me.'

'My daddy doesn't have a pistol.' I laughed and added, 'He has a rifle.'

'Be a good girl. You are not supposed to stay with a boy at this time, holding him in your arms.'

'What is the boy supposed to do? Come to my room in the dark, wearing a shawl, looking like a villain of some village, and scare me to death?' I said and felt something hit on my head. No, Karan hadn't hit me. It was something else. I looked here and there and saw a bundle of a newspaper and a magazine. The newspaper man had thrown it inside the house, and it hit me.

I stood up, rubbing my head, and Karan continued to laugh. I looked at him seriously, and he said, 'I've waited for these brown eyes to gaze into mine. These eyes are so similar to what I have always desired to look into. So true and genuine. They talk so much to me. They are exactly like my own thoughts, something I always wanted. I will never get tired of you, bub, because you are so much like me. Laughter for life! But remember, we aren't dating,' he said.

'I know that already, Karan,' I laughed.

'We aren't in love either, bub, though we both love each other,' he said, and I kissed him on his beard, so soft and smooth, and he started climbing the wall, just as he had done to get inside. It was not that I couldn't open the gate, but I so wanted him to fall down so that I could get another laugh with him; unfortunately, he didn't fall. I went upstairs and was inside my room when I heard the honk of his car, indicating that he had left for his home. I lay on my bed, smiling at myself; I looked into the mirror, remembering all that Karan had said to me when I realised that I felt I was looking at him in the mirror, as I was concentrating on his face when he said that he liked my eyes.

After a while, Karan sent me a text message on my mobile phone that read, 'Bub, did I tell you that I came for you?'

I replied, 'Of course! Granny has a boyfriend in Shillong.'

'Little bitch,' he wrote.

'Baby bastard,' I replied, and we both slept.

I thought that no matter what happens and what situations occur in my life, I will be patient and confident at the same time. I still get confused in my life, but when I wait, I get the best answer. Endurance is bitter, and I love the truth—which is bitter too. They both make me pay attention. I can't let my preconceived notions or my fears ruin my present and bother me by interrupting my laughter. I am trying, and it's going well. I had promised my parents that I would study in the school they wanted me to.

My present life has been good, living with family and friends, and my life has become better as I have learnt to deal with the surroundings in an better way. I have decided to accept things that destiny brings to me and then decide what I really want and how I am supposed to deal with things that I don't want. I will face it all boldly and smartly as going far or not meeting up on regular basis doesn't end life or relationships. We get hurt, we perk up, we grow up, we fall, we change, and life keeps going.

And as far as mental peace is concerned, it's true that nothing can bring you peace but yourself. I am so cheerful that a chilly breeze can drive away the heat from my body. My beautiful positive thoughts will live and travel with me all my life. I know well how to keep myself happy by doing things I love doing in my life like reading books, writing, chatting, and writing letters to someone like Karan, and, above all, reacting to life in the best way I find. I also draw funny pictures these days. I have drawn one of Madam Shanta wearing a bikini. I have given one to Karan, which has him wearing just his shorts and his shoes. I made him look great.

I have started to stay calm and keep living. No matter what right and wrong I do, I will put on my new shoes and keep moving. If my reputation gets spoilt, I may become more daring. In the past, I had become insecure, things went out of control, and I had started feeling weak.

I have a control over my life and the consequences that my acts can bring. Fighting and getting violent is as demoralising as smoking cigarettes and is a waste of life. I can't bear this expense, and, therefore, I have resumed laughing, which is free.

My actions do speak louder than my words. They describe the way I respond to situations on my own, keeping in mind I am not forced to do anything. Accept things only if you agree with them, and not to make someone happy. If you do so, you are spoiling your own laughter; avoid selfishness.

I know well that I need to react sensibly by behaving in a way the 'smart me' wants to. Also, I was never addicted to this lifestyle; then why fuck my system, my life? I might fight or argue with people in future, but I will definitely do it more thoughtfully, keeping in mind not to get upset.

Like those rich losers who made me upset, I fought, argued, and hit them. I didn't lose anything. I learnt and became a better person with many qualities. I know that I don't want shit like this, but there is no guarantee that it wouldn't come back ever. If it does, I know how to throw it away and scratch when it itches.

I am not a perfect human being who will make a list of all things that one is not supposed to do. I have never followed schedules. My life doesn't end here. I am just fifteen; there is a long way to go, and I still have bits of stubbornness, arrogance, laziness, curiosity, white lies yet true heart, a loose tongue, and a crazy life with friends for life. It's not a movie that shows happy ending in just three hours; it's my life. I am still learning and will keep learning because these bits add interest to my life. I don't need a boring life with nothing happening. And if you call me spoilt, then I boldly accept it, because life will go on and so will I.

I will do things as needed but will try to do them more generously and self-assuredly than before as I am still in the learning phase of my life. I won't just sit and listen to things people say to me but rather will also respond in a straightforward way. I am living freely and independently without any hesitation like I used to. I am trying to be more understanding towards the right things.

I am bravely and smartly open to everything that comes next because I am a 'smart victor' and not a 'rich loser'. Appreciate my red shoes that Karan brought me.